THE STRICT BRITISH BARRISTER
Book 1 & Book 2

Maggie Carpenter
Copyright © 2019 Dark Secrets Press

Published by Dark Secrets Press LLC.
http://www.MaggieCarpenter.com
Maggie Carpenter's Books
https://www.Amazon.com/author/maggiecarpenter

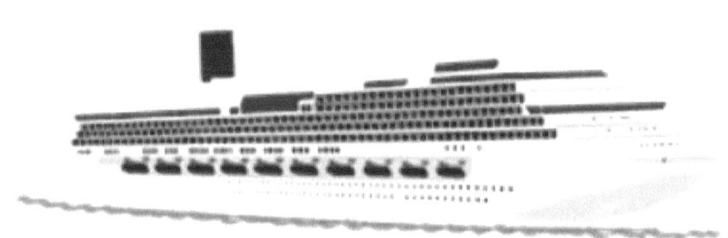

PROLOGUE

AS SHE WATCHED THE handsome, dark-haired man board the ship, Brittany Carter's heart skipped. She needed a fling. A no strings wild romance. Wearing khaki slacks with a spotless white shirt that couldn't begin to hide his well-muscled arms, the dashing stranger towered over the porter. She was a first class passenger, and she prayed Mr. Gorgeous Man would be as well.

"Duncan Rhys-Davies," he declared, approaching the steward.

She caught her breath. Mr. Gorgeous Man had a distinctly British accent. It was too good to be true! She adored British men.

"Welcome aboard, Sir. My name is Joe Gardner. Ah, Miss Carter," the steward said, catching sight of her as she casually moved closer. "Your staterooms are quite close to one another. If you're ready we can go there together."

"Yes, yes, I'm quite ready," she replied, feeling Mr. Gorgeous Man's eyes on her.

As they started off, Duncan Rhys-Davies ushered her forward, and offering him a soft smile she fell into step slightly behind the steward. The expense of a first-class ticket had given her pause, but now the extra money was worth every penny. Entering the elevator, the subtle scent of the sexy man's cologne teased her nostrils. Lifting her eyes she risked a sideways glance. He was looking directly at her, a half-smile curling the edges of his thick, luscious, insanely kissable lips. Her stomach burst into a somersault. She'd only experienced a somersault once before. In her first year at college the sexy quarterback had cornered her at a party, pinned her arms above her head, and kissed her. Deeply kissed her.

Lifting her gaze, she caught Mr. Gorgeous Man's eyes.

Blue with astonishing brown flecks, and long dark lashes framing their inviting stare.

A covert glance at his left hand revealed no ring or suntan mark.

"Miss Carter?" The steward's voice snatched her attention. "After you," he offered. "Turn to your left."

Grateful she was wearing the provocative white and lemon silk dress with a halter top, she stepped into the hall. The cut accentuated her figure, and she was glad of the lift from the high-heeled sandals. She guessed Mr. Gorgeous Man was at least 6'2", and standing at 5'6" she needed the extra height.

"Mr. Rhys-Davies, this is your stateroom," the steward announced, stopping at the third door and sliding a card key into the lock. "Your luggage will be arriving shortly. If you'll excuse me for just a moment I'll show Miss Carter to hers, then I'll be back to answer any questions you may have."

"Nice to meet you, Miss Carter," Duncan said, his devilish grin sending a warm flush across her cheeks. "I'm sure we'll run into each other again."

"Yes, I'm sure we will."

He turned and walked into his cabin, but as the steward continued down the hall, she couldn't pull her eyes from the handsome Brit. His dark hair fell in a soft wave at the back of his neck, and his shoulders were wonderfully wide.

"Miss Carter?"

Embarrassed, she jerked her head around. The steward stood waiting a few doors down, and she hurried off to join him.

"I'm one of three attendants who will be taking care of you during the cruise," he said as they entered the luxurious cabin. "Both the bedroom and living room open to a private deck shielded from your neighbors."

Stepping outside she was disappointed to discover he was right. There'd be no opportunity to lean over the railing and wave to her handsome shipmate.

"Feel free to call for service at any time," Joe continued, guiding her to the bedroom. "We're at your disposal twenty-four hours a day. Do you have any questions?"

"No, thank you, Joe."

"Then please excuse me."

With a smile and a nod he left, and returning to the living room, she kicked off her shoes and dropped onto the couch.

"Duncan Rhys-Davies," she said dreamily. "That's one heck of a name. Could he be my crazy fling? I hope so."

Closing her eyes she pictured his panther-like walk, the sensuous twinkle in his hypnotic blue eyes, and his wicked grin with those kiss-me-now lips.

He was all sex.

He reeked of it, and she idly wondered if he was a man who enjoyed his women packaged in something slinky and sensuous, or a decadent outfit like garter belt and stockings. She carried salacious fantasies, but had yet to meet a man to make them a reality. Her pondering sent a need firing between her legs, and stretching out on the sofa, she slipped her hand under the waistband of her lacy lemon panties. In her mind's eye Mr. Gorgeous stood over her admiring the view laid out before him. Shuddering with the tantalizing imagery, her well-practiced fingers expertly circled her sensitive nub. She could see him naked, his member standing at attention, oozing drops of his need. The vision took hold, and as she let her mind wander, she pictured herself on all fours as he kneeled behind her and slowly peeled back her panties to spank her naked backside with gusto. Crying out as the eruption sent shock waves through her body, the spasms caused her back to arch and her legs to tighten, until finally sinking into the residual tingles, she let out a happy, satisfied sigh. Grabbing a throw cushion and cuddling it against her, she made herself a promise.

"I'm going to make this happen with him! I don't know how, but I will."

CHAPTER ONE

BRITTANY WATCHED AND waited, but two days had passed and Duncan Rhys-Davies remained mysteriously missing. Though other men had approached her, she remained consumed by thoughts of the intriguing Brit. Each time she walked past his cabin, she prayed, by some miracle, it would open and he would appear. On the third morning, after indulging in a buffet breakfast served on the deck and returning to her room with no sign of him, her disappointment began turning into anger.

"Why is it so damn difficult to bump into you?" she muttered as she changed into her bikini. "What's the point in taking a cruise if you're going to stay locked away in your stateroom day and night? I have to summon the courage and knock on your door."

Ambling on to her private deck, she stretched out on the deeply cushioned lounge chair. The sun was mild, the sea twinkling, and the cool ocean breeze tickled her skin, but she found it impossible to relax. Moving to the railing she stared down at the foamy wake created by the immense ship as it powered through the water, then leaning forward she turned her head. The decks were designed for maximum privacy, and though she could peek around at the patio next to hers, the others remained hidden from view.

"What do you do all day, and who are you? What I wouldn't give to have a poke around your cabin."

She'd done some crazy things in her life, and for a moment the notion tickled her, but dismissing it as completely ridiculous she returned to her lounge chair and sank into the soft, enveloping foam pad. Picking up one of several fashion magazines she began to flip through the pages, but after five minutes she threw it back down. Bored and frustrated she returned to her bedroom, changed into shorts and a T-shirt, and headed off to the ship's jogging track. An avid runner, she pounded out the kilometers, but try as she might she couldn't exorcise the sexy man from her thoughts. Returning to her cabin, she took a long, hot shower, then donning her robe, she strolled into the lounge and dropped into the sofa. As she picked up the folder outlining the ship's activities and services, her eyes fell upon the advertisement for their massage therapies. Perhaps the hypnotic effect of kneading, practiced hands would erase Duncan Rhys-Davies from her thoughts, at least for a short time.

BRITTANY LIKED THE spa the moment she stepped into the lobby. The subtle aroma of lavender filled the air, and the smiling receptionist offered her a glass of chamomile tea. It was only a moment later the attractive massage therapist appeared, introduced herself as Martha, and led Brittany into a warm, dimly lit room.

"I'm sure you know the drill," Martha said. "I'll be back in a minute, and I hope I'll be able to erase that crinkle on your forehead."

"I didn't realize I had one."

"My eyes are trained," Martha replied with a wink. "Make yourself comfortable. I'll be right back."

Removing her clothes and covering herself with the thin sheet, Brittany nestled her face in the cushioned headrest.

"Are you ready for me?" the therapist asked, tapping on the door.

"So ready. I need this like you wouldn't believe."

"This is a cruise," Martha said as she entered. "It's supposed to be relaxing."

"Yeah, well, I've run into some stormy weather."

"Let me guess. Is this a man problem?"

"How did you know?"

"It usually is. I'm like a priest or a doctor. If you want to talk about it, I won't tell a soul. Sometimes talking helps more than the massage."

"Maybe you're right. It's not a big deal, not really. I met this guy when I first boarded and I can't stop thinking about him. He's British, which totally turns me on, and he's so good-looking he could be James Bond. He's driving me crazy."

"That would drive me crazy too. Do you know his cabin number?"

"That's what makes this so frustrating. He's only three doors down from me, but I haven't seen him. Not even a glimpse. Not once!"

"Wow, your muscles just tightened. Take a deep breath. If you're so close by, maybe you should stake out his door, and when he leaves pretend to bump into him. He can't stay in his stateroom forever. Maybe he likes to be out when most people are sleeping. I knew a musician like that. He was a total night-owl."

"A night owl," Brittany repeated. "Interesting. Huh. You might be right. I wonder if he's a celebrity and leaves his cabin late so no-one will bother him. He's handsome enough to be famous, that's for sure. Thanks, Martha. I love your suggestion. I'm going to do that. I'm so glad I came here."

"You're welcome. Now you can chill and let me get these knots out."

Martha's theory made sense, and surrendering to the deft fingers rubbing her back, Brittany let herself drift away to fantasies of meeting the elusive Mr. Rhys-Davies under the brilliant ocean stars.

But fate stepped in with an unexpected surprise.

Meandering down the corridor back to her room, she found the maid's trolley parked outside his door, and she paused to catch a quick glance. Her heart skipped. He was standing in the middle of the room with his back to the door! Dressed in navy shorts and a cream, loose fitting shirt, her eyes devoured his muscled arms, wide shoulders, and tanned, toned legs, but to her shock, as if sensing her gaze, he began to turn. Panicking, she ducked away and hurried to her cabin.

"Oh, no! Why didn't I wave?" she muttered, leaning against the door. "Damn. I'm such an idiot."

But a moment later she realized she was glad she hadn't. Wearing no makeup and disheveled from the massage, she was a mess. Moving into her bathroom, she stepped into the shower, and as the hot water splashed across her body she realized just how tired she was. The long jog, the deep tissue massage, and her ongoing obsession with the handsome Englishman had worn her out. Toweling off, she dressed in a white sundress and white sandals, then opening her door she peered down the hallway.

Her heart leapt a second time.

Duncan was outside his cabin, his hands on his hips and a frown on his face. Grabbing a chair, she sat down to resume her surveillance, and though the maid's trolley was still in place, the elusive Mr. Rhys-Davies had slipped away. Her shoulders slumped in dismay.

"Damn, I need a nap," she muttered, surrendering to a heavy yawn. "I'll have a quick snooze then start watching in earnest."

But just as she rose to her feet, Duncan Rhys-Davies reappeared in a dark blue track suit and running shoes. Her imagination suddenly ran rampant. *He could be related to the royals, maybe a spy, or even a glamorous international jewel thief.* Giggling at her wild thoughts, her cheeriness quickly faded as he marched down the hallway and disappeared around a corner.

Her eyes fell on the maid's trolley outside his cabin.

Her crazy notion to have a quick snoop around his cabin suddenly popped into her head.

She stepped into the passage.

She knew the idea was completely foolish, but when she reached his open door the temptation overwhelmed her.

She could hear the maid vacuuming in the bedroom.

Though every bit of common sense she possessed told her to turn around and leave, she crept inside.

CHAPTER TWO

SECONDS AFTER HER FIRST furtive steps she heard the maid turn off the vacuum. Afraid she couldn't zip back into the hall without being seen, she made a panicked dash to wriggle behind the armoire positioned in the corner of the lounge. Finding refuge just as the maid entered, heart thumping and holding her breath, Brittany waited until she heard the cabin door click closed.

The room fell eerily quiet.

Letting out a relieved sigh, she moved from her hiding place and into the center of the lushly appointed cabin. Burgundy, chocolate brown and cream gave the space a far more masculine feel. By comparison, her stateroom bloomed like spring with an array of pastels, but the thrill of being in his cabin suddenly took hold. Taking a deep breath to steady her nerves, and telling herself she'd be quick, she scanned the room seeking out clues that might tell her more about the sexy Brit. A paperback on the side table next to the sofa caught her eye. Swiftly moving across the room, she picked up the book and studied the cover. The blood drained from her face. Fur covered handcuffs rested on the cream satin bedspread of a four poster bed. The scrawled title floating across the bottom of the page read, *A Man's Discipline. A Woman's Secret Desires.* Pulse racing, she opened the naughty novel to the bookmarked page.

The hot sting burned Susan's naked backside, the feather tickling between her pussy lips had her dripping with desire, and she longed to plead for her release, but he had instructed her not to make a sound.

Brittany's thighs tensed as the words swirled around her head. For years she'd secretly ached for a dominant, and endless nights she'd pleasured herself to thoughts of being tied up, blindfolded, and teased into oblivion.

A loud click snapped her head around.

The door handle moved.

She'd never understood the term, frozen stiff, but she found herself unable to move as Duncan Rhys-Davies, tall, striking, and bigger than life, stepped inside. All she could do was watch the puzzled frown cross his brow.

"What do you think you're doing?"

She tried to utter something—anything—but she couldn't find her voice.

"Nothing to say? I believe security can take care of this," he declared, striding purposefully past her to the phone on the coffee table.

"I'm t-terribly s-sorry," she stammered, his unexpected threat breaking the spell.

"I'm sure you are. Everyone's sorry when they've been caught."

"I wasn't here to steal, honestly, I just wanted to, uh..."

"To what?"

"This is s-so embarrassing."

"Embarrassing or not, I suggest you continue."

"I'm really sorry. I, uh, I wanted to know more about you."

"So you broke into my cabin?"

"I thought you were interesting when we met boarding the ship, but I haven't seen you anywhere. Not in the dining room, on deck, anywhere."

"Why didn't you just knock on my door?"

"I, uh, don't exactly know," she answered sheepishly, feeling like a foolish teenager as her face flushed deep red. "Would you please just let me leave? This is painful, literally painful."

"Painful? I'm not sure you know the meaning of the word," he remarked, taking a step towards her. "I see you're interested in that book."

Realizing the steamy novel was still in her hands, she hastily dropped it back on the side table.

"Sorry."

"Pick it back up."

"Excuse me?"

"I said, pick it back up."

A rush of tantalizing tension gushed through her body.

"No? Then I will."

As she watched in scarlet-faced horror, he strode past her, lifted the scandalous paperback and opened it to the bookmarked page.

"The hot sting burned Susan's naked backside, the feather tickling between her pussy lips had her dripping with desire, and she longed to plead for her release, but he had instructed her not to make a sound."

Brittany prayed desperately for the floor to split apart and swallow her in one, large, purposeful gulp.

"Tell me, Brittany, why do you suppose Susan had a hot, stinging backside?"

She wanted to answer him, but once again her voice failed her. Not only had her heart become a jackhammer, her nipples betrayed her, pressing against the thin cotton of her dress. In a vain attempt at self-protection she crossed her arms.

"I asked you a question," he said impatiently. "Why do you suppose Susan had a hot, stinging backside?"

"I, uh, I, uh…"

"Brittany, if you're not willing to answer I can always call security."

"No, please don't."

"For the last time. Why do you suppose Susan had a hot, stinging backside?"

"Because, uh, she'd done something wrong?"

"Do you think breaking into my stateroom could be described as doing something wrong?"

"Yes," she squeaked, trying to control her rising panic.

"Wouldn't you agree you deserve a hot, stinging behind?"

His unwavering stare compelled her to answer

"Uh, yes."

"Yes, what exactly?"

"I, uh, deserve a spanking."

Stepping forward he grabbed her hand, and moving swiftly to the couch, he sat down and yanked her across his lap.

"Stop! What the hell? Let me go, let me go!"

"Do you really want to leave?"

"Of course!"

"Then you can," he said brusquely, though still holding her firmly. "I won't call security and that will be the end of it. Is that what you want, or do you want to be punished for your disgraceful behavior? Do you want a hot, stinging backside like Susan?"

Brittany let out a plaintive cry. She wanted to be spanked by him more than she'd wanted anything in her whole life.

"Do you want me to spank you, Brittany," he pressed, his hand caressing her upturned bottom, "or do you want me to let you go?"

"S-spank me."

"You're sure?"

"Uh, yes," she replied, hating how thin her voice had sounded.

"Then you must ask."

"Ask?"

"I'm waiting."

"Please will you spank me?"

"Please will you spank me, Sir."

"Please will you spank me, Sir," she repeated, her butterflies bursting to life, then softly whimpering, she added, "Oh, God! Is this really happening?"

"It most certainly is," he replied, slowly lifting her dress and peeling down her knickers.

"Please don't spank me hard."

"You're in no position to be making demands."

Though simultaneously horrified and excited, as his soft caress continued she began to breathe a little easier, but when his palm abruptly landed a flurry of peppery smacks she squirmed in protest.

"Ow! Stop! Please! That really hurts!"

"It's supposed to," he growled, not missing a beat. "Behave! Stop that yowling."

But the rebel in her took hold, and continuing to wriggle and wail she almost toppled off his legs.

"If you keep making such a fuss I'll be forced to gag you," he warned, pulling her back into position, "and I'll add twenty hard smacks for my trouble. Do I make myself clear?"

"Twenty? No, please. I'll be good."

"Your backside will suffer if you're not."

As he continued the relentless chastisement, she clenched her teeth to keep from crying out, but just as she was about to beg for mercy the spanking miraculously stopped.

"Thank me for your punishment."

Though her butt burned and she was filled with swirling emotions, she let out a deep breath and sank into his lap.

"Thank you for punishing me, Sir."

"Good, girl."

Quiet seconds ticked by as he rubbed her scorched skin, then to her delight and surprise his fingertips whispered across her sex. Unable to stop herself, she wriggled, chasing his touch.

"My goodness, Brittany, are you asking for more?"

"Yes, please, Sir."

As he pushed his finger into her slick depths, and pressed his thumb against her engorged clit, she surrendered to the erotic massage. It was only moments later her soft moans filled the room, and she could feel the approach of her orgasm.

"Please, don't stop. Please, Sir, please let me come."

"Why should you have such pleasure after sneaking into my cabin?" he replied, withdrawing his hand to tickle her inner thighs. "It seems to me you should be thinking of a way to make that up to me, not asking for your own satisfaction."

"What do you want me to do, Sir?"

"Kneel in front of me. Perhaps something might come to mind."

Crawling awkwardly off his lap and on to her knees, she looked up at him expectantly.

"Unfasten your dress and let it fall to the floor."

Slowly pushing the straps of the sundress down her arms, she slid down the side zipper, catching her breath as the loose fabric dropped away, exposing her braless breasts.

"Aren't you lovely?" he crooned softly, lightly touching a nipple. "Close your eyes."

The tantalizing play lasted several scintillating minutes, until his hand withdrew and she heard rustling. Suddenly the tip of his cock was at her mouth. Wrapping her fingers around him, she parted her lips, but he grabbed her hair and pulled her back.

"Beg me."

"Please Sir, please may I suck you? I'm not just saying that because you told me to," she added fervently. "I really want to."

"Since you asked so nicely, you may."

Lowering her head, she gently slid her lips over his shaft. His girth filled her mouth, but as she began sucking with gusto, he clutched her hair and slowed her down. The minutes ticked by, his soft groans growing louder. His grip suddenly tightened, and holding her still he began to pump. His cock swelled, tiny drops of pre-come touched her tongue, and she was sure he was about to burst down her throat, but he stopped and slowly withdrew.

"Open your eyes, stand up, step away from your dress and take your knickers off."

Unsteadily rising to her feet and pulling her panties from around her knees, she kicked them off, feeling an awkward embarrassment as she stood naked before him. She wanted to shift her weight, scratch her arm, or lower her hand to cover her full, fuzzy bush, but smiling a wicked smile he abruptly stood up, swept her into his arms, and carried her into the bedroom. As he laid her down and sank his lips on hers, she drifted under his lingering kiss...

A sharp sound jolted her.

Her eyes flew open.

She was sitting in the chair.

As her door had closed the lock had clicked—waking her up.

CHAPTER THREE

BRITTANY BROKE INTO a mischievous grin. Her decision to take the cruise had been based on a fanciful thought: she'd meet a handsome stranger and have a wild shipboard romance. The salacious dream left her more determined than ever to bring the fantasy to life. Ambling to the bathroom, she splashed her face with cold water and stared at her reflection.

"Maybe I should do what I just imagined. Maybe I should keep my eyes open for that trolley and sneak into his cabin. If I'm lucky I might get caught."

Giggling at the thought she patted her face dry, applied fresh makeup, and changed into white jeans, an aqua T-shirt, and high-heeled sandals. As she left her cabin and passed Duncan's door, she paused, smiled a naughty smile, then continued on to the elevator, taking it to the lounge offering an all day buffet. Surprised to find the elegant eatery virtually empty, she chose a spicy vegetable dish, poured herself some coffee, and moved to a table against the window. As she settled in and gazed at the ocean, a flash of white caught the corner of her eye. Darting her eyes to the door, she spied Duncan Rhys-Davies dressed in white shorts and shirt, and carrying a leather satchel.

Her butterflies exploded.

He was sauntering to a nearby table.

Telling herself to stay calm, she took a breath and gazed back at the sparkling blue sea, but she couldn't resist a covert glance. The sexy James Bond look-a-like was even more attractive than she remembered. As he placed his bag on a chair and strolled to the buffet to plate a salad, she couldn't take her eyes off him. Suddenly, to her surprise and delight, he turned, smiled, and walked slowly towards her.

"Care for some company?"

"Sure," she managed, trying to ignore the butterflies fluttering their frenzied dance.

Placing his dish on the table, he retrieved his satchel and sat across from her.

"Did we officially meet?" he asked. "I'm not sure we did. The name's Duncan Rhys-Davies."

"We did, sort of. Brittany Carter."

"That looks and smells far more appetizing than my salad."

"You're welcome to have some."

"That's very kind of you. I might take you up on that. Are you enjoying the cruise?"

"It's been very relaxing," she replied, wishing it were true. "I feel so far away from everything out here."

"That's the whole point for me, getting away. I'm an author. Out here I can focus."

"An author!" she repeated, her decadent dream and the spicy novel flashing through her head. "What sort of books do you write?"

Titling his head to the side, a devilish grin crossed his face.

"Naughty novels. I hope that doesn't make you uncomfortable."

"No, no," she said hastily. "I wonder if I've read any of your books."

She wanted to kick herself. Why had she just confessed to reading erotica?

"So you enjoy steamy romance novels."

"Doesn't everyone?" she quipped, hoping the remark would disguise her embarrassment.

"I'm impressed. Most women get flustered when I tell them, or they look at me as if I should be shot."

"Not me," she lied, thinking she'd never felt so flustered in her life. "I think it's great."

"I carry a few copies," he said, opening his satchel. "I'm happy to give you one."

She stared, mesmerized, as he withdrew a novel and placed it in front of her. Wondering if her dream had been a psychic vision and the book would be the one she'd imagined, she studied the cover. A young woman dressed in a low cut dress looked over her shoulder at a man's fingers wrapped around a riding crop. Brittany grinned.

"It meets with your approval?"

"The cover is very provocative," she replied, hoping her voice didn't betray her excited nervousness. "Emily's Education. A. S. Cane. Your alias I assume."

"Does it ring a bell?"

"I think so, a vague one."

Lifting her gaze, she studied his warm brown eyes. A shiver rattled down her spine. The man was more than just a sexy hunk. She liked him. She *really* liked him.

DUNCAN FOUND THE BEAUTIFUL young woman confident, witty, and very bright. But he wasn't surprised. He'd been caught off-guard when they'd initially met. Though all she'd said was, *thank you*, as they'd left the elevator, the soft southern lilt in her voice had captured his imagination, and she'd continued to wander through the corridors of his mind ever since. Being a disciplined soul he'd been able to stay focused on his work and rarely left his cabin, but the few times he'd taken a short break he'd hoped to bump into her. When he'd entered the buffet and spied her at a table by the window, he'd been elated.

"Thanks for keeping me company," she said, rising to her feet.

"The pleasure was all mine," he said with a smile, pushing back his chair to stand with her. "I'm sure we'll see each other again soon."

As she walked away, his eyes fell on her curvaceous backside. Her tight white jeans left little to the imagination. Sitting back down, he took a few minutes to finish his coffee, mostly to give his manhood time to settle, then headed back to his stateroom.

Though he'd told Brittany he was an author, he hadn't mentioned he was also a barrister, lived in London, but kept his wicked novels private, pursuing his dark desires at a private club. It was his professional success that offered him the luxury of long ocean cruises, where he'd hibernate in his stateroom to write his saucy stories. Though he often indulged in a shipboard dalliance, he'd never met a real life Scarlet Ohara with a maple syrup voice, and reaching his door, he glanced down the hall. He could easily picture her reading his prurient prose.

His hand slapped her inner thigh—hard. She winced, then uttered an exclamation of pain. The shackles holding her wrists to the wrought iron headboard clinked as her arms jerked.

"Sir, please, Sir."

"Please, what?"

"It stings."

"It may sting, but if it didn't you'd be disappointed. A hard slap is far more satisfying than one too soft."

"True," she whispered, "but it's a love-hate thing."

"I know it's a love thing, but it's not really a hate thing, is it?"

"No, not really hate," she admitted. "None of it."

The image of Brittany spread on his bed, her wrists and ankles firmly secured, danced through Duncan's head. She'd been red-faced when she'd studied the cover of his book. Could he interpret that to mean she shared his love of kink? Might she be open to a wild shipboard fling?

LYING ON HER BED, BRITTANY'S fingers lingered between her legs. Educating Emily captivated her. Duncan's heroine carried the facade of a proper young woman, but harbored dark thoughts of sexual slavery. As Brittany read his wicked words, her fingers urgently massaged her clit.

Emily's eyes grew large. Her Master had warned her, but still she had disobeyed him, and the fearsome riding crop carried a frightful sting.

"Turn around and place your elbows on my desk."

Whimpering her regret she pivoted and bent forward. Dressed in a corset and stockings her bottom was already bare, and she cringed as the riding crop slid menacingly across her cheeks.

The image of the naughty young woman in the perilous situation sent Brittany to the edge of her orgasm, but eager to read more, with great effort she pulled her fingers away.

Emily knew the crop would bite, but when the first stroke landed she wasn't prepared for its fiery kiss.

"Ow. Ow. Please, Sir! No more!"

"I warned you. Perhaps next time you will listen."

"I will. I swear."

Abruptly throwing the book aside, Brittany rubbed herself into a glorious finish. The climax rattled down her spine and sent sparks though her limbs, then breathlessly sinking into the tingling after-glow, wishing she was curled against Duncan's muscled body, she drifted into a soft doze.

When she finally stirred, she decided to read one more chapter before heading out for a drink, but she found herself once again engrossed in the salacious lives of Emily and Master Jonas. Hours later, bleary eyed and yawning, Brittany finished the last page and dropped the book on the nightstand. She'd read many spanking ro-mance novels, but none had engaged her as completely as Duncan's account of the proper young lady finding the courage to live out her licentious longings. As she turned off the bedside lamp and closed her eyes, the final chapter lingered.

Master Jonas had spanked Emily with his slipper, then tying her over an ottoman, he'd idly toyed between her legs while watching television. When his show finally ended, he kneeled behind her, thrust his turgid member home, and pumped her into a powerful orgasm.

Swept up by a heavy yawn, Brittany wondered if Duncan had patterned Master Jonas after himself. Was he strict like his hero? Did he discipline immediately? Did he carry a small paddle in his pocket? With the questions burning through her brain, she drifted off to sleep.

CHAPTER FOUR

DUNCAN'S CHANCE MEETING with Brittany had breathed new life in to the last chapters of his new novel, and working late into the night he typed the last line with a flourish. When he woke the following morning he ordered a celebratory breakfast.

"That's enough food for a party," Duncan remarked with a grin as Joe rolled in the cart and laid the dining table.

"I thought you might be expecting company. I asked the kitchen to include an extra place setting just in case."

"Not a bad idea," Duncan mumbled under his breath.

"Will there be anything else, sir?"

"No, thank you, Joe."

The steward left, and surprised by an unexpected flutter of anticipation, Duncan reached for the phone and called Brittany's cabin number.

"Hello?"

"Brittany, this Duncan Rhys-Davies," he announced, wishing he hadn't sounded so formal. "If you haven't already eaten breakfast I have quite a feast here. I finished my latest book last night and I'm celebrating. Would you care to join me?"

"Thank you, Duncan, that would be great. I'm on my way."

"Excellent, I'll see you shortly."

She'd sounded excited by his invitation, and wandering into his bathroom he ran a comb through his hair and splashed on some cologne.

"I wonder what else excites you," he said, grinning at his reflection. "I hope I have a chance to find out."

STILL TIRED AFTER HER marathon reading session, Duncan's unexpected invitation had sent a shiver of anticipation rippling through Brittany's body. Donning the sun dress she'd been wearing the day they'd first met, she quickly applied her makeup and headed out the door. Reaching his stateroom, she took a deep breath and lightly knocked.

"It's open."

Walking in she found the handsome Brit pouring champagne into a flute half-filled with orange juice.

"Hello, Brittany. Would you care for a Mimosa?"

"Yes, I would, thank you."

"Please, have a seat," he offered, nodding at the dining table by the window. "I thought about eating on the deck, but it might be a bit windy. Seems the weather is kicking up."

"I noticed that too. I poked my head out a few minutes ago and it was blustery."

"I hope we're not in for a storm," he remarked with a slight frown. "It's unlikely this time of year, but squalls are unpredictable. They can whip up almost any time."

"This is my first cruise," she said as she took her seat. "I'm not sure how I'd cope with that."

"The ship's doctor can give you something if you get queasy," he declared, placing the champagne glasses on the table and sitting opposite her. "Hopefully that won't be necessary, but you're here to help me celebrate. Drink up!"

"How exciting it must be to write a book, and congratulations," she beamed, lifting her glass. "Surely you didn't write the entire thing since you came on board."

"No, I'm not that fast," he said with a chuckle "but these last few days have been extremely productive."

"I'm so honored to be sharing this with you," she said happily, clinking his glass and sipping the fizzy drink. "I really am very complimented."

"I'm honored that you accepted, and I'm curious. Did you have an opportunity to read Educating Emily?"

Feeling a hot blush move across her face, Brittany lowered her eyes and spooned scrambled eggs on to her plate.

"Quite a few chapters," she replied, wishing she had the courage to tell him she couldn't put it down, and the story was the sexiest she'd ever read. "You're such a good writer. It was a real pager-turner."

"I'm glad you think so."

"Duncan, the book you just finished. Is it the same, uh, subject matter?"

"I don't write about anything else."

Lifting her gaze, she caught his intense, brown flecked, blue eyes across the table.

"I hope you don't mind me asking this, but are you like your hero?"

"Your courage is to be commended. I'm surprised."

"Why?"

"It's not a question I'm often asked. The answer is yes, I'm very much like Jonas. Now it's my turn. Why are you on this cruise by yourself?"

Brittany's heart skipped.

"I was bored. I wanted an adventure."

"Your honesty is so refreshing," he remarked, smiling at her. "You'd be amazed at how many times a simple question produces a flurry of white lies."

"I've been told my candor is unsettling, but I don't know how to be any other way."

"I'm sure it can be, but don't change," he said approvingly. "But on another matter, now my book is finished I have some time to enjoy myself. Would you care to have dinner with me this evening?"

"I would, very much."

"I prefer dining away from the thundering hordes. Would you mind eating here, perhaps on my deck if the weather permits?"

"I wouldn't mind a bit."

"Good, then it's settled. If you don't have other plans, would you like to take a walk when we finish breakfast? Though I suppose, considering the time, it's brunch."

"No, I don't have other plans and I'd love to hear what your new book is about. The story, I mean."

"If you're a good girl I might email you the manuscript."

"What does that mean? How can I be a good girl?"

"That's easy," he said, lowering his voice and fixing her with a steady gaze. "Just do as you're told. You've read the book. You know what happens to bad girls."

BOTH BRITTANY AND DUNCAN knew why they were strolling the length of the deck. He hadn't used the word, but his comment had made his thoughts abundantly clear. He wanted to spank her, and she wanted him to. Whether a one-time event, or the beginning of something more, her potential trip over his knee loomed like a huge, white fluffy cloud. The promise shone through their eyes when they shared a look, and tingled through his fingers as he gently wrapped his hand around hers. By the time they were back in the thickly carpeted corridor, the erotic energy crackled between them. Standing next to her as she fumbled with her key, he finally took it from her hand and slid it in the lock.

"When should I be ready for dinner?" she asked, wondering how she'd survive the day.

"Seven o'clock, but before you go..."

Placing his hands on her shoulders, he suddenly leaned in and kissed her. She was sure she would faint from the divine pleasure, but he slid his fingers into her hair, he tilted her head to the side, and moved his lips to her ear.

"I know you're a very cheeky girl underneath your polite exterior."

"Sometimes."

Heart hammering, the whispered word was all she could manage, and leaning against his chest, she closed her eyes and inhaled his spicy, masculine scent.

"We have things to talk about," he purred, encircling her with his arms. "I must get back. The book may be finished, but writing the darn thing is the easy part."

"I really am looking forward to hearing about it," she said softly, reluctantly stepping back.

"As I said, if you're a good girl."

He winked, then turned and strode down the hall.

Entering her cabin, she closed the door and leaned against it, seeking support for her quivering body. His kiss had sent a warm flood through her sex and made her weak at the knees.

"He's going to break my heart. I shouldn't see him tonight, but I have to, I absolutely have to."

INSIDE HIS STATEROOM Duncan smiled a Cheshire Cat grin. He'd tasted her hunger, her craving, her need to be over his knee with her bottom bared and his hand slapping with gusto. The thought of it had sent his cock to life, even more than the exquisite feel of her breasts pressed against his chest, and her soft yielding energy as she'd melted in his arms. Scanning his room, he considered where he might administer his discipline.

"Poor baby, you need to be spanked so badly. You possess a submissive soul, and you're aching to be set free."

Though the afternoon would be a long one, anticipation was half the fun and the hours would tick by much more slowly for Brittany. But the kiss had left him restless.

"A jog," he declared, moving into his bedroom. "That's what I need. A long run around the track."

THOUGH THRILLED BY the prospect of the evening ahead and the promise it held, a nagging doubt had crept into Brittany's head. Duncan could decide to simply have dinner and send her on her way. The spanking she so desperately craved might not come to pass, and her long-held fantasy might remain just that, a fantasy. The thought was almost too much to bear.

"I can't leave this to chance, I can't," she muttered as she paced. "I have to do something to make it happen. The maid will be here soon. I could slip into his cabin and—ooh, I could open his computer and sneak a peek at his book. When he catches me he'll wallop me for sure."

CHAPTER FIVE

GRABBING A CHAIR, BRITTANY cracked open her cabin door and settled in to watch. She'd been keeping vigil only a few minutes when the housekeeper appeared pushing the trolley down the hallway. Stopping outside Duncan's cabin, the maid knocked twice before unlocking his door and walking inside.

Brittany took a breath. It was time.

Ignoring her voice of reason she hurried down the corridor and peered into the room. There was no sign of the maid, but Brittany could hear her humming in the bedroom. Darting across to the armoire in the corner, to her horror she discovered she couldn't fit through the narrow space to hide. Fighting panic, afraid to move back past the bedroom and into the hall, she moved quickly out the sliding glass door and onto the deck. Taking a moment to calm her frazzled nerves, she peeked into the bedroom. Pulling the vacuum behind her, the maid was on her way into the lounge. Brittany pushed open the slider, crept inside, and searched for a place to hide.

The closet was her only option.

Pulse racing she hurried across the thick carpet, cringing as she opened the folding door, then closing it softly behind her, she hid behind a row of hanging trousers.

STROLLING DOWN THE hallway, still breathing heavily from his jog, Duncan saw the housekeeper rolling her trolley to the stateroom next to his. Entering his cabin he moved swiftly to the bathroom, stripped off, and stepped into the shower. As the water splashed over him and he roamed the soapy sponge across his body, he could feel the relaxing benefit of the long run. Quickly drying off, he wrapped a towel around his waist and ambled into the large walk-in closet. A cold nip lingered in the air, and he'd spied more than a few whitecaps during his trip around the track. Reaching down to retrieve a sweater from the built-in shelving, his eye caught an odd shape on the floor. Narrowing his eyes, he tried to discern what he was looking at.

Manicured red toes in high-heeled white sandals.

Hastily scooting the hangers aside, Brittany's wide eyes stared back at him. Rarely was Duncan speechless, but he had no words.

"I, uh, am terribly sorry about this," she stammered. "I can explain."

"Get out of there immediately," he retorted, grabbing her arm. "Go and wait for me in the other room. I'm not even dressed for heaven's sake."

Taking in his naked torso, she ruefully moved past him, but as she did a fierce sting burned across her backside. Squealing in shock she spun around to see a long, thin, polished wooden stick. It took her a moment to realize he was holding a shoe-horn.

"Duncan! Shit!"

"What did you expect? Get yourself into the living room immediately, and don't even think about disappearing."

Hands clutching her bottom, she raced into the lounge.

Though furious, as he quickly dressed his anger gave way to curiosity, but marching into the living room he maintained a stern expression. Perched on the edge of the sofa appearing appropriately ashamed, Brittany stared up at him. He wasn't sure he believed her sheepish expression.

"What do you have to say for yourself?"

"There's no excuse for what I've done. All I can do is apologize."

"Why the uninvited visit? I'll guess, shall I? You want me to spank you, but instead of allowing things to develop you decided to take matters into your own hands."

"I'm that obvious?"

"Completely transparent. I assume you slipped in while the maid cleaned the room."

"I'm sorry, Duncan, I really am."

"If we were back in London I'd take my cane to your backside. It would be the last time you'd pull such a stunt, I can assure you. Such childish behavior! I can't believe it!"

"Sometimes I do things like this. I can't seem to stop myself."

"Discipline. That's what you need."

"Maybe."

"There's no maybe about it. In a few days I'll be heading back to London and you'll be returning to South Carolina. Perhaps I should spend the next few days taking you in hand."

"Yes, absolutely, yes," she nodded, her butterflies fluttering wildly.

He hadn't meant it as a serious suggestion, and her enthusiastic response caught him by surprise, but the thought of it held great appeal.

"You may be familiar with the adage, be careful what you wish for," he said solemnly. "Yes, I will spank you for this ridiculous prank, but I suspect you'll get more than you anticipated. You must be disciplined, and that, Brittany, is a different matter, very different indeed."

WITH PRACTICED EASE Duncan prepared Brittany for punishment. Wrapping the satin sash from his black silk robe around her eyes, he guided her to the side of the couch, and slipping his hands under her dress, he pulled down her knickers, but left them around her thighs. A necktie secured her wrists at the small of her back, then clutching a fistful of hair, he bent her over the cushioned arm of the sofa.

"Duncan, I—"

"Sir!" he said sharply, pushing her skirt over her waist.

"Sir," she said hastily, her face flaming red from the lewd exposure. "I'm truly sorry. I know I—"

A hot slap suddenly landed on her naked backside.

"Ow!"

"No more talking, and if you must squeal, turn your head into the cushion."

"Yes, Sir. Please may I say one more thing?"

"You're testing my patience."

"Please don't be too hard. I've never been spanked."

"That is painfully obvious, and I'll spank you as I see fit. Are you ready?"

"Yes, Sir."

Holding her breath, she waited for him to begin, but to her horror he gripped one of her cheeks, pulled it aside, and touched her virgin rosebud.

"No, no! Oh, my God! What are you doing?"

His quick response was a shocking volley of stinging smacks.

"Discipline can take many forms," he said sternly. "You attempted to control me, but you will learn I have the control, and I will do with you as I see fit. You are suffering embarrassment and humiliation because of your arrogance. Be quiet and take the punishment you deserve, or you can leave. Which is it to be?"

"I'll stay, Sir," she whimpered. "Sorry."

"Who's in control?" he demanded, pulling her cheek to the side and positioning a butt plug.

"You are, Sir,"

"What happens if you misbehave?"

"I'll be punished, Sir."

"Correct," he said brusquely, pushing the plug forward. "There. Now I'm going to spank you. You will not beg me to stop, you will not lift your head to cry out, nor will you gyrate your hips to avoid my hand. You will show me your obedience and remorse by remaining still."

"Please can you take that thing out before you start?"

Duncan could not believe his ears.

Can you take that thing out?

He had to stifle a laugh. In all the years he'd been harpooning and spanking naughty bottoms, never had he been met with, *can you take that thing out?* Though momentarily stumped, the appropriate response came to him. Withdrawing the unwanted intruder, he waited until he heard the breath of relief, then thrust it back in, paying no heed to her wail of displeasure.

"Any other requests?" he asked, continuing to move the unwanted intruder in and out.

"No, no, Sir, no. I'm sorry."

"Since you delayed your spanking I'm adding ten additional swats with a leather soled slipper. You'll then kneel in the corner and think about this entire episode. Now I shall begin, and be prepared to have a very red, very sore bottom."

She had barely processed his scolding words when the spanking began. He dispatched his hard slaps in a methodical, measured pace, occasionally rubbing his palm over her blushing skin. When her bottom was sufficiently scarlet, he tapped the flange of the unwelcome invader, then slowly pulled it out.

"You can rest. I'll be back in a moment."

Brittany's backside burned, and never had she endured such embarrassment. Duncan's heroine in Emily's Education had suffered a similar fate, and salacious scenes from the book flashed through her head, but the sound of Duncan's return snapped her from the decadent thoughts.

"These swats will be quick," he warned, placing his hand on the small of her back, "and they will not be pleasant."

"None of this has been pleasant," she muttered, then hastily added. "I wasn't being sassy."

"I would call it cheeky, and you'd better learn to hold your tongue. I have no compunction about landing my slipper twenty times rather than ten."

The slipper swished down on her scalded behind, and though the punishment was over in seconds, she was bleating and twisting her hips when he finished.

Moving to the bar, Duncan poured himself a shot of cognac, lifting his glass in a private toast. She'd taken her spanking with fortitude, never once begging him to stop.

"You are unique," he mumbled under his breath. "This is going to be a very interesting few days."

CHAPTER SIX

UNTYING HER WRISTS and slipping her panties off her legs, Duncan placed Brittany in the corner with instructions to ponder her outrageous behavior. Though her foolish escapade should have consumed her thoughts, it was the erotic heat washing through her sex that held her attention. She ached to be naked with him, feel his lips on her breasts, and listen to his whispered promises.

"Do you have anything to say?"

She hadn't heard his approach, and snapped from her decadent daydream, it took her a moment to gather her wits.

"I'm waiting."

"Yes, Sir, I have many things to say, and something to ask."

"What's your question?"

"How much longer do I have to stay here?"

Her brazenness baffled him, but leaning forward he placed his lips at her ear.

"After everything you've just endured, surely you know the answer to that."

"As long as you want me to, Sir."

"And how do you think I feel about that question?"

"That it's inappropriate, Sir."

"I understand this is new so I'll give you some latitude, but not much. There must be consequences for that insolence, and they'll come at dinner, assuming you still wish to join me."

"I do, Sir."

"Spread your legs."

The instruction took her by surprise, and wriggling her knees apart she waited expectantly for his touch.

"I know what you want," he said softly. "You're praying my fingers will slide into your sex and pleasure you. They won't. I'm putting you in touch with your need."

"But Sir, I am in touch with it."

"Be that as it may, you must return to your cabin, strip naked, sit on your sore bottom and write me a letter. Tell me what you thought and felt during your discipline and while you've been kneeling in the corner. When you're finished you'll slip it under my door, then return to your bedroom to nap, but you're not to touch yourself. Any questions?"

"No, Sir."

"You can get up."

He helped her rise to her feet, and to her great joy he brought her into his arms.

"Poor Brittany, you have such a sore backside" he purred, slipping off the blindfold. "You've lacked discipline for a long time, but now you've finally met someone who can meet that need."

Swept up by an unexpected wave of emotion, she sank against his chest and tried to swallow the unexpected heat in her throat.

"If you're feeling the need to cry that's natural. I'm here, and I won't let you go until you're ready."

"How did you know?"

"It's my job to know."

"I'm not the crying type, but I do feel emotional," she admitted, burying her head in the crook of his shoulder.

Lifting her chin with his finger, he dropped his lips on hers. The potent kiss fired their passion, and as their mouths moved in unison, Duncan felt a stirring in his soul, a stirring he'd not experienced in many years, a stirring that told him Brittany would haunt him long after they left the ship and went their separate ways. As her arms clung to him, he sensed she was feeling it too.

The indefinable magic.

One of the most powerful forces on earth.

BRITTANY SPENT ALMOST an hour writing the letter, delivered it as he'd asked, then returning to her cabin she sank into bed. The nap was just what she needed, and when she stirred she felt surprisingly calm. Stepping into the bathroom she stood with her back to the mirror and stared over her shoulder at her blotchy red cheeks. Wanting a shower, but with her skin still tender, she made sure the shower was tepid, then stepping into the stall she began soaping herself with the pomegranate bath gel supplied by the ship. As she closed her eyes and breathed in the citrus fragrance, an unexpected thought flashed through her mind. Sneaking into Duncan's cabin had fast-paced their relationship. She caught herself.

"What am I saying? There is no relationship! This is a shipboard fling. That's it."

But even as the words left her lips, she knew leaving him would be painful. Very painful.

DUNCAN HAD A NANNY cam.

After being the victim of theft during a previous cruise, he carried the covert camera with him whenever he traveled, zipping through the footage every evening. As he watched her uninvited visit, he had to chuckle when she discovered she couldn't fit behind the armoire and made a panicked dash for the deck. Deciding to save it for posterity and share it with her at some point in the future, he downloaded the film to his computer.

Turning his attention to the evening ahead he moved across to the dining table. White roses sat in the center with two tapered candles either side. Dom Perignon chilled in an ice bucket, and crystal goblets waited to be filled. In his bedroom, a bouquet of white and yellow roses rested in an ornate vase. Duncan spared no expense when defending a client. His fees were high, but those who could afford him received the best representation money could buy. So it was in his personal life. He did not hold back or play games, and he thoroughly enjoyed pampering the women in his life. Brittany's gentle knock announced her arrival for their dinner date, and opening the door he found her dressed in a shimmering green cocktail dress. A string of pearls graced her neck, and she had parted her hair on the side, causing it to fall coquettishly across one eye.

"Exquisite," he smiled, taking her hand and kissing it softly.

"Thank you, and you could be James Bond."

Duncan had opted for a dark suit, a sharp white shirt, and a bow tie with a roguish streak of purple.

"Dom Perignon is chilling, and a very good year I might add."

"You're spoiling me."

"Are you complaining?"

"Not for a minute," she replied, and as he ushered her forward her eyes fell on the beautifully set table. "This is gorgeous. I don't know what to say. No-one has ever gone to so much trouble for me."

"I want you to know how special I think you are."

"I am?"

"Yes, you are. Please sit down and close your eyes. I have something for you."

As she took her seat and felt her tender backside, a soft smile crossed her lips. Not only was her fantasy coming true, it was beyond anything she'd dared to hope. She heard the rustle of his clothes as he walked away, but he quickly returned.

"For you, Brittany. Take a look."

Opening her eyes she discovered a stunning arrangement of roses in a multi-colored art glass vase.

"They're so beautiful, and the vase, it's lovely. What did I do to deserve all this?"

"There is no gift I can give, equal to that which you've given me. Your trust and submission."

"I don't know what to say."

"The white and yellow roses represent purity and friendship," he continued. "What you experienced today was pure. You surrendered, and that is a truly precious thing. We're bound by that and the friendship blossoming between us."

"This is so much. I'm sorry, I can't help thinking...never mind."

"Thinking what? Tell me."

"We'll be saying goodbye so soon."

"I know," he said with a sigh. "We must treasure the time we have, but if this is too overwhelming—if you've changed your mind—I'll understand."

"No! I haven't! Not for a minute!"

"Good. I'm glad. I'll call for our meal. I've ordered Cajun Chicken and Pepper Salmon. Which would you prefer?"

"The salmon, thank you."

As he stood up and expertly popped the cork on the champagne, Brittany felt a million miles away from her safe, boring life. She was dining with a dashing British Dominant, and would soon be the willing victim of his wicked ways.

"What's our toast?" she asked, as he filled their glasses.

"Living for the moment."

CHAPTER SEVEN

BRITTANY FOUND DUNCAN'S charm and humor captivating, and when they finished dinner, he selected a CD and pulled her into his arms to dance. Sinking against him, with the honeyed voice of Michael Buble singing a haunting rendition of *The Way You Look Tonight,* he slowly slid down the zipper at the back of her dress.

"Duncan, are you going to break my heart?"

"Maybe you'll be the one breaking *my* heart," he replied, sliding the spaghetti straps down her arms and letting the silky garment puddle around her feet. "There are two of us in this dance."

She was about to answer when he suddenly swept her up, carried her to his bedroom and laid her on the bed. Stretching out next to her, he deftly unsnapped her bra.

"Gorgeous," he sighed, gazing at her breasts.

Moving his mouth to nibble her nipples, she raised her chest, moaning softly as he devoured one, then the other.

"Close your eyes and raise your arms above your head."

As she followed his instruction, he withdrew the sash from the robe he'd left in the nightstand drawer and deftly tied her wrists.

"There, lovely and helpless. Now spread your legs."

"Duncan, I've wanted this for such a long time."

"I know," he crooned, pausing to whisper the words in her ear.

Moving to the foot of the bed, he secured her ankles with two of his belts, and enjoying the salacious sight of his bound Southern Belle, he casually removed his clothes, returning to tickle her sex through the gusset of her panties.

"I can't make love to you with your knickers on, and I have no intention of untying you."

"I don't understand."

"You will."

Teasing her until her groans became whines of aching need, he grabbed the sides of the lacy panties and ripped them apart. Though she gasped as he yanked them off, he dropped his head between her legs to twirl his tongue against her sensitive button, and she was quickly bleating her need.

"Are you ready for me?" he asked, kissing her inner thighs as he slid his finger inside her.

"Yes, yes, please, Sir."

"I believe you are," he said huskily, and kneeling between her legs, he positioned his cock, clutched her hips, and thrust forward.

"You're so big! Ooh, Duncan!"

"Relax and take it," he purred, slowly pumping. "That's right. Just like that."

Her breathing was heavy, her chest red, and as he accelerated she sucked in the air, then suddenly let out a wail.

"Did I hurt you?" he asked urgently, coming to a sudden stop.

"No, I'm just so close."

Slowing his strokes, he leaned down to nibble at her breasts, then thrust vigorously, bringing her to the brink before slowing again. Though she begged him to let her climax, he continued the torment until he could no longer contain himself, then stroked with renewed gusto. In seconds her climax took hold, sending a tsunami of sparkling sensations through her body, and as the spasms began to wane, she heard Duncan's euphoric groans. As the last convulsion swept over her and her body fell limp, he followed suit, and slipping from her depths, he collapsed beside her and brought her into his arms. Lost in the post-orgasmic bliss they rested together for several serene minutes. It was Brittany who spoke first.

"That was incredible. I knew it would be, but Duncan, what did you mean when you said I could break your heart?"

"Mmmm, incredible, yes," he mumbled with a sigh. "How can you break my heart? I'm offering you something unique."

"Are you suggesting I'm only interested in you because you're a Dom?"

"Are you?"

"No!" she exclaimed, sitting up. "How could you think that? The minute I saw you walking up the gangplank I wanted to meet you and I knew nothing about you."

"My goodness. I stand corrected."

"And you weren't exactly easy to meet. You were like the Invisible Man. You drove me nuts."

"If I didn't know better I'd think you were looking for another trip over my knee."

"That's impossible. I haven't had a trip over your knee, just an embarrassing bend across the arm of a couch."

"And there you are. The other side of Brittany Carter. A cheeky, feisty, femme fatale, but I won't let you be a brat, not for a minute."

"I'm not a brat, though there are times you've made me feel ten-years old."

"No, there are times you behaved like a ten-year old and I treated you accordingly. Now I think it's time for some sleep," he said, suddenly caught up in a yawn.

"I agree. I'm totally wiped out."

"Duncan?"

"Yes, Brittany?"

"We didn't talk about what I wrote."

"We may, or we may not, but it was exactly what I wanted. Goodnight, Brittany."

"Goodnight, Duncan.

EARLY THE FOLLOWING morning Duncan was roused from sleep by Brittany's hand wrapped around his semi-erect cock, and her breasts pressed against his back. Sinking into the pleasure, he indulged himself for a few minutes before rolling over her to devour her luscious nipples.

"Mmm, good morning, Mr. Bond. That feels so good."

"Good morning, Cheeky," he replied, raising his head. "Shift so your back is towards me."

"Aye, aye, Commander."

"I know someone who's going to have their pretty little behind smacked."

"Do you promise?"

"Oh, yes, young lady, that is definitely a promise," he purred, and sliding into her hot, wet depths, he began stroking with quick, strong thrusts.

"Duncan, ooh..."

But his battering ram offered no pause, and caught up in a white-wash of scintillating sensations, her simmering orgasm quickly began to build. Holding her breath she waited for the eruption.

He spied her fingers clawing the bedspread.

Her body arched.

He paused.

"No, Sir. Please."

"You can only come on my command."

"I'll try."

As he resumed his vigorous thrusting, his plunging penis taking her even higher, he watched for the signs, and when he sensed her climax approach he gave the order.

"Come for me. Come for me now!"

The glorious pins and needles flowed through her limbs, and as she wailed out her joy, he sank his teeth into her neck like a hungry vampire. Fresh waves seized her, and moments later she heard his deep groans, but their mutual spasms finally began to abate. Feeling him slip away, she rolled over so she could snuggle into his chest.

"If I was a kitten I'd be purring," she murmured. "What a wonderful way to wake up."

"And last night?"

"A rocket ship with several after burners, then shooting into space," then pausing, she asked, "Duncan, is it like this with all the women you date?"

"All the women? How many do you think I have?"

"Is it this intense?" she pressed. "It's okay, you can tell me."

"No. Not every woman wants my special brand of attention, and our chemistry is unique."

"Thank you for saying that. Not that it matters I suppose. We'll soon be going our separate ways and you'll return to your harem."

"Cheeky, cheeky," he muttered, pinching her bottom. "I'm sure you have many men knocking on your door."

"Not really. In fact, when I tried to provoke my last boyfriend into spanking me, he called me childish and walked out."

"Why didn't you just ask him?"

"I guess I was embarrassed, and looking back he would have been too."

"Poor Brittany, living in a world that doesn't understand her. Speaking of spanking, how's your bottom? Still a bit sore I trust?"

"Uh-huh."

"Good. Just as it deserves to be. Are you hungry? Ready for breakfast?"

"Absolutely. Will you shower with me?"

"You go ahead. I have to think about something."

Kissing him lightly, Brittany climbed from the bed and ambled into the bathroom, but before she could step into the shower the ship suddenly lurched. Quickly donning the robe hanging on the door, she hurried back and found Duncan at the sliding glass door.

"I thought you were taking a shower," he remarked as she joined him.

"That jolt scared me. What's happening?"

"We're heading into weather," he said, putting an arm around her, "but nothing to worry about. Just think of the waves as potholes in the ocean."

The ship suddenly rolled sideways, and panic-stricken she threw her arms around his waist.

"Try not to worry. I doubt these rough seas will last long, probably just a passing squall. I've ordered us breakfast, but if you'd prefer the main dining room we can—"

"No, I want to stay here," she interrupted. "Please can we stay here?"

"Of course, but if you're too unnerved to take a shower, you should at least go back to your cabin and change. I doubt you want to spend the morning in that green silk dress."

"Dammit, there it goes again," she exclaimed as the ship pitched. "I don't like this."

"Do you want me to come with you? I'll get the sash for the robe and you can stay in that. I don't think we'll run into anyone, and even if we did I doubt they'll care."

"Would you mind?"

"Not at all. Give me a second."

He fetched the sash, quickly dressed in one of his track suits, then they headed down the hall to her door, but as they entered the ship abruptly rolled again.

"I'm trying not to be freaked out," she declared, "but it's not easy."

"You have a Knight In Shining Armor. Go and get changed. I'm not going anywhere," he promised with a smile, but as the last four words left his lips, a soft shiver rippled down his spine.

CHAPTER EIGHT

RETURNING TO DUNCAN'S stateroom, though the storm was relatively mild Brittany found it truly frightening and clung to him as they walked down the hall. When they entered his cabin and settled on the couch to watch a movie, she curled into his lap and refused to budge.

"You might be scared but at least you're not seasick," he remarked. "Believe me, that's a good thing. The medication can knock you out."

"There's nothing good about this! Nothing," she exclaimed as the ship lurched and rolled. "How long will this last? I can't stand it."

"Perhaps there's a way I could take your mind off it."

"I can't imagine anything will do that. I don't even know what movie we're watching. This tub is rolling all over the place."

"When you read Emily's Education did any particular scene appeal to you? Something you'd like to experience?"

"You want the truth?"

"Of course I want the truth."

"Everything. Every single thing."

"That book contained segments featuring severe discipline. Are you sure?"

"I am, though it's possible once I went through it I might change my mind."

"Pick one thing, just one, and I'll bring it to life for you. That should distract you."

"Okay, here goes. I want to kneel between your legs, take you in my mouth, and have you train me with a cane."

"Ah, yes, I remember that scene. You'll have to be careful though. With the ship moving like it is we don't want any unfortunate accidents."

"Ha. That's funny. I'll do my best not to turn you into a eunuch, but there's something you should know. I've avoided oral sex, but when I read that passage I desperately wanted to experience it with you."

"That's not uncommon. Often a fantasy we wouldn't dream of doing with one person, we find ourselves craving to do with another. Unfortunately I don't have a cane with me, but I think there's something else I can use. Are you able to let go of me now? I'm going to lose circulation in my arm."

"Sorry, and I just realized for those few minutes I didn't imagine the ship sinking."

"Excellent. I'll be back in a minute, but when I return I expect to find you naked and kneeling in front of the couch with your hands locked behind your neck."

"Yes, Sir."

"Excellent. You're in the mindset already."

"I don't think it ever goes away," she said thoughtfully. "I'm always thinking about bondage and spanking."

"Excellent point."

Heading into his closet he sought out his long, thin shoe horn. She'd offered quite the reaction when he'd swished it against her bottom after he'd discovered her in his closet. Confident it would be more than adequate he strode back into the living room, smiling with approval as he entered. The naked young woman had her hair tucked behind her ears, her hands were locked at the back of her neck, and she looked appropriately demure.

"Isn't that what you hit me with when you found me hiding behind your trousers?"

"Indeed it is," he said, sitting in front of her. "You must understand it is a privilege to worship my cock. As my submissive you—"

"Am I your submissive?" she interrupted excitedly. "You consider me your submissive?"

His instinct more than desire flicked the rod smartly against her naked backside.

"Ow, ow, ow," she protested, dropping her hands to rub away the sharp pain. "Ooh, it hurts. Why?"

"Return your hands to your neck and stop that noise immediately. It's rude to interrupt, especially when I'm giving instructions."

"Sorry, Sir. I'll never interrupt you again," she promised, quickly assuming the position. "Not ever."

"As long as I'm training you, I consider you my submissive, now back to the lesson. To worship my cock is a privilege and you must ask permission."

"Please, Sir, may I worship your cock?"

"You may, but if you soil my clothing you'll be punished."

"Yes, Sir. Do I unzip you?"

"I will always instruct you, and because this is your first time I don't expect you to swallow—unless you want to. Do you?"

"I do, Sir, but I want to do it correctly."

"Correctly means you don't spill a drop. Are you sure this is what you want?"

"Yes, Sir."

Unzipping his fly and withdrawing his rigid manhood, he placed his hand behind her head and gripped her hair.

"Come closer. I'll use your hair to guide you. When the cane hits your bottom you're to go faster or show greater eagerness. If you don't the second strike will be harder. Any questions?"

"No, Sir."

She was going to ask if she could start, but thought it better to sit quietly and wait for his direction.

"Good. You didn't presume to begin. That's the first time you've understood your place. You'll be rewarded for that."

Feeling an unexpected sense of pride, she opened her mouth as he pushed her head down, keeping her attention at the tip, then slowly taking in more of his rigid manhood.

"Tighten your lips around me and suck."

His order was accompanied with a stinging tap of the rod. Wincing, she did as he directed, but his cock was large and the task proved difficult. The stick landed again. Determined to please him she responded eagerly, slurping her tongue around him each time she pulled back.

"That's good, very good," he said huskily. "Not quite enough though."

The make-shift cane struck again. She moved faster, sucking with renewed gusto. When it landed again, she tickled his balls with her free hand. Small drops of liquid dropped against her tongue.

Closing his eyes Duncan sank into the lewd attention. His cock had enjoyed many such visits, but in spite of her inexperience Brittany's unique knack of drawing him in and stimulating him with her tongue sent sparks though his loins. When her fingers began tickling his nut sack, it was all he could do to hold back his looming climax. Not wanting the lascivious lapping to end, he tightened his grip on her hair to slow her down, but after landing a few more stripes on her backside and enjoying her eager responses, his orgasm would not be denied.

"I'm going to climax now. I'll do my best to control the flow, but that doesn't mean you're allowed to be messy. I meant what I said. You're not to spill a single drop," he warned, then placing the rod on the couch next to him, he held her head in his hands and slowly fucked her mouth.

The change startled her, but in a flash she surrendered to the intense domination and readied herself for his gift. As his cock started to jerk and spit, she squeezed her eyes shut and concentrated, determined to accept all he offered. His cream was hot and tangy, but there wasn't as much as she'd feared, and as he groaned his last groan and fell flaccid against her tongue, she waited patiently until he withdrew.

"You are exceptionally good at that," he said with a heavy sigh. "Fetch me a damp hand towel."

Though the ship still rolled, she barely noticed as she rose to her feet and made her way to his bathroom. Pausing to rinse out her mouth, she dampened a clean wet cloth, returned to her kneeling position and offered it to him.

"Thank you," he said as he wiped himself. "Brittany, is there something you want from me? You may ask for anything."

"Please will you hold me?"

Pushing himself back into his trousers, he zipped up and placed the damp cloth on the side table, then touched between her legs. She was dripping.

"Come with me," he said, rising to his feet and helping her up. "We'll lie together on the bed."

"Duncan," she said abruptly, "I get the whole, you being dressed and me being naked thing now. It's hot."

"Hot?" he said with a chuckle as they moved into the bedroom. "Yes, it is."

"I don't know how else to explain it, but it's sexy as hell."

"There's a bit more to it than that," he remarked as they climbed on the bed and he wrapped her in his arms. "Is this what you want?"

"Mmm, yes, heavenly. Thank you. Can I ask you something?"

"Anything."

"This is crazy. I'm feeling like a teenager again. I can't help it."

"What's you're question?"

"Do you think I'm sexy?"

"Brittany, you're blindingly sexy, and I'm sorry to say you'll have to leave me soon. I need to get some work done."

"Will I see you later?"

"Absolutely. I'd like to have dinner at The Mermaid tonight."

The Mermaid was the ship's formal restaurant, and she brightened immediately.

"In that case, can I make a request?"

"What did you have in mind?"

"I want to experience what Emily did. Go to dinner wearing no bra. I don't know if you've noticed, but I don't always wear one."

"As long as you understand it's not just about a little exhibitionism. You'll be completely under my authority. You'll have to do whatever I ask."

"Of course. Just the thought is a total turn on, but if you don't want to..."

"On the contrary," he murmured, raising his eyebrows. "I'll make a reservation at The Mermaid. Five minutes, then you'd better leave, or I might decide to keep you here and ravage you all afternoon and I have work to do."

CHAPTER NINE

HER PENDING DINNER date with Duncan devoured Brittany's thoughts for the remainder of the day, but when the hour drew near she had a terrible time deciding what to wear. The thought of walking through a restaurant with her nipples thinly veiled had her pulse racing. Finally making what she hoped would be a good choice, she was on pins and needles when Duncan arrived to pick her up.

"Look at you," he murmured as he entered. "Stunning. Absolutely stunning."

Her nipples subtly apparent through a white silk shirt tucked into a black pleated skirt, and wearing black and white glossy stilettos, she oozed elegant sensuality.

"Are you ready?"

"I am," she grinned, grabbing her evening bag, but as they headed to the door she paused to touch his arm. "Why do I think there's something bothering you? Do you not want me to do this?"

"Of course I do. I can't wait to see how you handle it. This will be a very exciting and entertaining evening."

"I still think there's something on your mind."

"Move," he said, landing a quick swat. "You're stalling."

Her highly tuned senses surprised him. Even as he'd been working he couldn't stop thinking about her. It wasn't like him. It wasn't like him at all.

Once out of the elevator it was a short stroll to The Mermaid. The door was opened by a uniformed attendant, and the Maitre d', a middle-aged portly man, walked up to greet them.

"Mr. Rhys-Davies, how nice to see you. If you would follow me please," he said with a warm smile.

Duncan suppressed a wicked grin as he caught the man's eyes fall on Brittany's chest, staying there a moment too long. Reaching their table, she took her seat and glanced around. The dining room was beautifully appointed, boasting floral arrangements in large venetian vases. The dim lighting offered an intimate ambience, the pale pink tablecloths sported white napkins, and the dishes white porcelain trimmed in gold.

"This place is like a first-class restaurant in New York or London," she remarked. "I didn't know ships offered dining like this."

"Are you ready for your first instruction?"

"So soon?"

"Go into the ladies room," he began, ignoring the comment, "take off your knickers, and bring them back to me balled up in your hand."

"You're kidding?" She immediately bit her lip. "Sorry. I just was thinking out loud."

"Question me again and I might spank you in the middle of this room."

"You wouldn't," she breathed, the color draining from her face as her stomach did several backflips.

"Test me and find out."

Gritting her teeth, Brittany rose from her chair, scanning the room for a sign.

"Ask the maitre d'."

Leaning back in his chair to enjoy the scene, Duncan studied the face of the maitre d' as Brittany asked for directions. The man tried to hide his anxiety, but Duncan could see it in his flushed face and overly zealous gestures. Walking around the tables, she disappeared past the bar, but Duncan's attention shifted to a blonde man standing at the counter drinking a glass of red wine. Above-average looks and a golden tan, he reminded Duncan of a California beach boy. He had unabashedly leered at Brittany, and Duncan paid close attention as she reappeared. The man moved swiftly from the bar putting himself directly in her path, but Duncan caught her eye.

Her panties in her hand and feeling wonderfully wicked, Brittany had smiled across at him, but when Duncan stared back at her, his gaze inexplicably darted to his left. Pausing her step, a furtive glance revealed the blonde man walking straight towards her, and deftly skirting a couple of tables to effectively avoid him she made it safely back. But he had looked directly at Duncan, a sneer crossing his lips. Duncan had received the message: *she's fair game,* but Brittany had missed the covert interaction.

"That was interesting," she whispered settling into her seat. "Thanks for the warning."

"You handled that like a pro."

"I certainly didn't want to meet him, whoever he was."

"Regardless, you did exactly the right thing," he assured her. "Now to more important matters. Where's my gift?"

"Your gift? Oh, you mean these," she grinned, opening her fist.

Closing his fingers over hers, he took them from her, then stuffed them into his pocket.

"They're a gift because they're mine now, a treasured reminder of tonight. When you see them missing from your drawer, you'll be reminded too."

"Duncan," she whispered, "this is...you are..."

"I believe the waiter is coming," he said softly, but silently thinking, *Yes, this is special. We are special, but bloody hell, it doesn't feel like some meaningless fun.*

A few minutes later they placed their orders, but to Duncan's dismay the blonde man had returned to the bar and was blatantly staring at Brittany.

"He's still at the bar, isn't he?" Brittany asked quietly. "I can feel his eyes on me."

"Yes, he's still there, but he won't be for long. Just follow my lead."

"I'll do my best."

Sitting tall in his chair, Duncan signaled to the wine steward standing near the bar.

Patric Dupont, a French-born sommelier, knew how to spot a well-traveled and accomplished man. The gentleman who had just requested service was exactly that, and Patric moved quickly to his table.

"Good evening, Monsieur. My name is Patric Dupont. How may I be of service?" he asked with a slight bow.

"Good evening. We're both having the pheasant. I'm partial to the M. Cosentino 2001 M. Coz Meritage from Napa Valley, but I would like your recommendations."

As he suspected he would, Patric's eyes widened and he broke into a warm smile.

"Monsieur knows his wine. An excellent choice."

"But I see you also have the Corton-Charlemagne 2009 Louis Latour. With pheasant, the choice isn't always so easy."

"Oui, this is so," Patric nodded, even more impressed with his customer. "Perhaps mademoiselle has a preference."

Brittany had been raised by parents who often entertained, and though not an expert, she was familiar with the basics of pairing fine wine with gourmet dishes.

"The pheasant is served with plum sauce," she said thoughtfully, "so I believe the Meritage would best please the palate, but I'd be happy with either. White burgundy's are always an interesting alternative."

Brittany's erudite observation took Duncan by surprise, especially her knowledge that the Louie Latour was a white burgundy.

"Mademoiselle, you are familiar with these wines?" Patric asked, smiling a toothy smile.

"I am, and I'm finding myself partial to the Meritage."

"Then the Meritage we shall have," Duncan declared.

During the conversation he had unabashedly sent his eyes to the bar several times, and as Patric took the wine list from his hand, Duncan frowned and leaned slightly forward.

"Is there something wrong, Monsieur?"

"I don't want to make a fuss."

"Monsieur, we pride ourselves in making sure our guests are comfortable and satisfied. If there is something not to your liking please allow me to make it right."

"Rest assured it is not this lovely restaurant or the impeccable service. How remiss of me. My name is Duncan Rhys-Davies, and my companion is Miss Brittany Carter. Forgive me, Brittany, but perhaps Patric is right."

"Perhaps he is," Brittany said with a sigh, "but as you said, we don't want to make a fuss."

"Monsieur, please, tell me," Patric insisted. "How may I be of help?"

"Very well, and thank you. That fellow at the bar, the blonde man who looks like a surfer," Duncan said discreetly, knowing the description would give Patric the image of a man in thongs, loud trunks and a disheveled appearance. "He's been staring at Brittany since we arrived. It's most disconcerting."

"Please do not concern yourself further, Mr. Rhys-Davies. This will be handled," Patric promised, and with a pronounced strut to his step, he marched across to the maitre d'.

"Duncan, that was masterful," Brittany said softly.

"Thank you. I have something in mind, and it certainly couldn't happen with that joker staring at you."

"Can you give me a hint?"

"I'll do more than give you a hint. You're going to have an orgasm."

Brittany stared at him in disbelief, but didn't speak.

"You're learning. That's the first time you haven't shot back a question or a comment. Are you wearing the thigh-highs stockings I requested?"

"Of course," she replied, then let out a small gasp. "Duncan, look!"

Turning his head, Duncan saw two waiters and the maitre d' escorting the blonde man from the restaurant.

"Good. Now we can begin. Reach between your legs, and as you rub yourself tell me one of your fantasies. I want one of your own, not something from my book."

"I can't believe I'm going to do this," she mumbled, moving her hand under the table. "I've wondered about being flogged."

"Dressed how?" he asked, lowering his voice and leaning closer.

"A black garter belt and—wait—Patric is headed over here," she said hastily, spying the wine steward from the corner of her eye.

"Don't stop what you're doing unless I say blackberry, then you can take a short break."

"Your unwanted admirer has left," Patric announced, arriving at the table with their wine.

"We're very grateful," Duncan replied.

"Yes, very," Brittany managed, her fingers continuing to agitate her clit.

"I am only sorry for any inconvenience," Patric continued, pouring a splash of wine in Duncan's glass.

Duncan swirled the deep red liquid, inhaled, then took a sip.

"Such rich blackberry. Marvelous."

Discreetly sighing, Brittany brought her hand back to the table.

"Thank you, Sir, and for mademoiselle," he continued, pouring the Meritage into Brittany's glass.

"Smooth as velvet. Wonderful. Thank you."

With a sharp, quick bow, Patric placed the bottle in the center of the table.

"Bon appétit, and if I can be of further service, please don't hesitate to call on me."

"How did you know about the white burgundy?" Duncan asked.

"My father is a wine lover. He has quite a collection."

"And here you were pretending to be a simple Southern girl from a small town."

"I am a simple Southern girl from a small town. My father runs his business from home and he likes the country."

"Fingers back between your legs, please, We're not leaving until you climax. Tell me every time you reach the edge."

"Oh, my gosh," she muttered, returning her hand to her sex.

As the meal was served, Brittany found herself caught up in the salacious scene, and each time she told him she was nearing her moment, he instructed her to stop. By the time they had finished their main course her eyes were filled with carnal hunger. Ordering Baked Alaska for dessert, Duncan reached across the table and took hold of her free hand.

"When the waiter returns and flambes the meringue, that's when you'll climax. You'll pretend you're reacting to the flames."

"I'm not sure I can pull this off."

"You can, and I'll be right here holding your hand."

The famous dessert arrived, and as it ignited Brittany exclaimed her awe. With the flames taking center stage no-one paid her any attention, except Duncan. When the bluish glow around the meringue began to subside, so did her waves of orgasmic euphoria. The waiter served the slices, but Brittany was too overcome to do anything but sink into her chair and stare at her plate.

"You are fabulous," Duncan whispered. "I'm immensely proud of you."

"I wish I could curl up in your lap right now."

"Soon. Take a mouthful, you'll love it."

Her eyes glittering and her face flushed, she slowly picked up her fork and took a bite.

"Incredible, and this was the tastiest meal I've ever had," then pausing, she added, "Duncan, this is truly one of the best nights of my life."

CHAPTER TEN

WHEN DUNCAN AND BRITTANY returned to his stateroom and climbed into bed, they made warm, sensuous love, but while Brittany fell into a deep sleep, Duncan was restless, and the following morning he woke with a growing unease. This was not his first shipboard escapade, but it was his first shipboard romance, and he wanted to kick himself. The attraction had been intense from their first meeting and he should have walked away. In just a couple of days they'd be faced with a gut-wrenching goodbye.

"Duncan?"

Her sleepy voice drifted up to him, and rolling over he brought her into his arms.

"I love sleeping with you," she breathed as she nestled against him. "It's the best."

"Me too."

Duncan's head began to spin. Shrouded by a need to protect her and take her further into his dark, decadent world, he knew his feelings would only grow deeper as the days floated by, and he was feeling disingenuous. She saw him as an author and a mysterious romantic, but his life in London as a barrister was courtrooms and cocktail parties.

He suddenly wanted her, and rolling her on her back, his hands roamed across her body, fondling, pinching and teasing. Her moans filled the room, and moving on top of her, he pushed her legs apart with his and slid his cock forcefully forward. Devouring her mouth as he began to thrust, Brittany threw her arms around his neck, returning his kiss with zealous hunger. In just minutes her fervor sent him tumbling into a sudden climax, and letting out a startled cry as her orgasm abruptly exploded, she clutched him urgently, refusing to let him go even after their spasms had dissipated and he'd slipped from her depths.

"Something's wrong," she breathed, "I can feel it. You just made love to me like the ship was going down."

Dropping next to her and pulling her against him, he searched for the words.

"I'm not sure how to say this," he began, uncomfortable with the emotion surging through him. "We're speeding forward, and it's going to come to an abrupt end in only a couple of days."

"What are you saying?"

"I'm worried for you," he muttered, silently adding, *for both of us.* "If the feelings are this strong already, how much harder will it be when it's time to say goodbye? I think—"

"But you showered me with a fabulous dinner and those beautiful roses," she exclaimed, sitting up and glaring down at him. "You said we should enjoy the time we have. What the hell?"

"I'm simply voicing my concerns, Brittany. You need to calm down."

"No, I won't calm down," she railed, grabbing her pillow and hurling it at him.

"My God. You're actually throwing a tantrum."

"I am not! I'm reacting to a bastard who got what he wanted and now wants to dump me."

Deftly throwing her on her back and straddling her, he pinned her wrists on either side of her head.

"You truly are a spoiled little girl. Twenty-something going on ten, and I'll bet your wealthy father is wrapped around your finger. You need a man who will discipline you and make you behave."

"I don't know what you're talking about. Let me up."

"You're still in that small town of yours because you have everything you want at your fingertips."

Brittany suddenly stopped struggling. His words had hit home.

"You want to voice your feelings, don't you, Brittany? You want to share your dreams with me, and your fears. Am I not accorded the same right?"

"I, uh, didn't think about it that way."

"The fact is, I owe you an apology. It's been a long time since I've experienced such amazing chemistry and I got swept away. So did you, and that's why you reacted so badly when I said what I did. It was wrong of me to let this happen, and I'm sorry." Then pausing, he added. "In my defense, I didn't think our feelings would be turbocharged, but if things continue, how miserable are we going to be when we have to go our separate ways?"

"This isn't fair," she muttered, her lower lip trembling.

"No," he said grimly, releasing her wrists and moving off her body. "But that's the way life can be sometimes."

"Sorry I lost it, and you were right about my dad and why I don't want to leave."

"I should end this by putting you over my knee and spanking you for that tantrum."

"Would you?" she asked softly, sitting up and looking down at him.

"You know if I do I won't hold back."

"It's the one fantasy I've been craving forever. An over the knee spanking, but if you think we should part now..."

"I should at least give you that," he replied, feeling a sudden, unexpected lump in his throat, "but let's get one thing straight. It's not that I want to say goodbye, I just think—"

"It will be easier now than in two days."

"I'm going to spank you for that too. You interrupt. It's a bad habit."

"I'm so sad," she bleated, her tears beginning to fall.

Engulfing her in his arms, fighting his own swelling emotion, he tried to conjure up words of comfort.

"I'll spank you the night before we dock. The time apart will help us come to terms with things, and a spanking will be the perfect way to say goodbye."

"If you think that's best."

"You should take a shower. I'd ask you to stay for breakfast, but that would—"

"Be impossible. Sorry, I interrupted you again. I'd rather just head off, but could you take a shower? I can leave while you're in there."

"That's sounds right," he murmured, and giving her a tight hug, he padded into the bathroom.

Closing the door, he leaned against it for a moment, then moving to the counter, he stared at his reflection.

"At least I know I can feel again, and there's nothing to be done about this. I'm not interested in a long distance relationship. Besides, we barely know each other."

But as he moved to the shower stall and turned on the faucets, a shadow of doubt lurked around him.

When he returned to the bedroom and found her gone, he decided to take a jog. Dressing in his sweat suit he headed out, but when he reached the track and began to run, the blonde stranger from the night before floated into his mind. Recalling the man's purposeful attempt to intercept Brittany, and the determined look the man had sent from across the room, the more concerned Duncan became. As much as he wanted the jog to settle him, the lingering worry continued. The long run was offering no relief at all.

FIGHTING HER TEARS as she returned to her cabin, Brittany hurried to the bathroom and splashed her face with cold water. Duncan's reasoning made sense. If she was crazy about him after such a short time, there was no question she'd be in even deeper when the ship docked.

"So much for a wild shipboard fling. Why did I have to meet Mr. Perfect? Couldn't I have met someone less perfect, someone easier to say goodbye to? Did it have to be James Fucking Bond?"

Walking out to the deck and gazing at the infinite horizon, a frown crossed her brow. Wouldn't two more days have been better than no more days? Unable to settle she ambled back inside, turned on the television, and searched for something to take her mind off her aching heart.

Kate And William - The Untold Story.

The title flashed on the screen. Not knowing much about the fairytale royal couple she sat back to watch. With a clipped British accent, the narrator began with how the couple had met at St. Andrews University in Scotland. William was tall and dashing, and Kate was almost as tall and very attractive. The story continued, but it was halfway through the show that Brittany leaned forward and pricked her ears.

*"**Kate did not let the grass grow under her feet after the breakup, embarking on a social whirlwind of hi-profile parties and clubbing around London. Kate and her sister were constantly photographed enjoying London's nightlife, and Kate even dated several of William's friends. Apparently this brought William to his senses, and it was only weeks later they were back together.**"*

Brittany hit the pause button.

Strutting her stuff had won Kate Middleton the heir to the English throne!

STILL PANTING FROM his jog, Duncan turned down the hall towards his cabin, the cocky blonde man continuing to consume his thoughts. Reaching his door, desperate for a hot shower and a stiff drink, he reached into his pocket for his key, but he couldn't stop himself from glancing down at Brittany's door.

He caught his breath.

Her hair hanging loosely around her shoulders, and black mascara coating her eyes, Brittany was wearing an obscenely short maroon skirt, a low cut pink shirt, and glossy black stilettos. She was dressed to kill, and he barely recognized her.

"Brittany," he exclaimed, striding towards her. "Where are you off to?"

"The Seven Seas bar. I need cheering up."

"You look like you've already had a drink."

"Actually, I've had two," she said with a giggle.

"Are you sure this is wise? I mean, the way you're dressed is—"

"I'm wearing a bra. Oops, cut you off!"

"But if that blonde chap happens to be around, I'm not sure—"

"Don't worry about it. Go and take a shower. You need it."

As he watched her walk away, her bottom pushing against the tight skirt, he felt his blood pressure rise; helpless was not something he did well.

"Brittany, wait, I'll come with you."

She paused, and slowly turned.

"I thought we were going to avoid each other. Besides, you're all sweaty."

"Give me five minutes. You can wait—"

"No, it's okay," she replied, interrupting yet again. "You were right, it's better this way."

But rounding the corner, Brittany broke into a cheeky grin.

"That was easy. Thanks, Kate. I owe you one."

CHAPTER ELEVEN

DUNCAN'S HEAD WAS SPINNING. Brittany wanted men to fawn over her and make her feel better, but he couldn't understand why she felt the need to wear such outlandish clothes to get their attention. Taking a quick shower, he hurried out the door and down the hall, bypassing the elevator and running up the stairs two at a time, but as he reached the deck and moved towards the bar, he checked himself. Bursting in and making a scene wasn't his style. He managed to compose himself, but the thought of Brittany having a drunken roll between the sheets with a slobbering stranger made him shudder. Moving purposefully forward to the door and opening it just a hair, he spied her perched on a bar stool, her skirt so far up her thighs she could have been wearing shorts.

"What the blazes are you playing at," he muttered under his breath. "I know you're hurt, but why are you behaving so outrageously."

I was watching through a crack in my door, I guess you could say I was staking you out.

Her comment flashed through his head.

She'd done it again!

Wanting him to see her in the scandalous outfit she'd been waiting, peeking down the hall, then purposely stepped from her cabin when he'd returned. Turning away, he walked to the side of the deck and stared out at the infinite blackness. She'd manipulated him a second time, but the modern day Scarlet O'Hara was under his skin. He didn't want her to be, but she was, and he was worried about her. Leaning his elbows on the railing he pondered his choices.

BRITTANY WAS BECOMING increasingly agitated. She'd been sure her Knight In Shining Armor would appear shortly after she took her seat at the bar. He'd scold her for wearing such dreadful clothes, then whisk her back to his cabin for a sound spanking, but long minutes had passed and there'd been no sign of him.

"Hi, I'm Simon," a young man said, perching on the stool next to her. "Can I buy you a drink?"

"I'm waiting for someone, and when he shows up you don't want to be there. He can be very jealous."

"Okay, but if he doesn't arrive you're welcome to join me. I'm not so bad once you get to know me."

"I doubt that."

He sighed, then leaning closer, he fixed her with a steady gaze.

"You may be gorgeous, and you may be out of my league, but you don't have to be rude. Someone should spank some manners into you."

So shocked she couldn't find her tongue, she watched him slide off his barstool and start to walk away, but he paused, and turning back, he added,

"Whoever that someone is, he should also tell you not to dress like a tramp. You're beautiful, you don't need to do that."

"How dare you."

"He's right!"

Duncan's voice growled over her shoulder, and spinning around she stared into his puzzled eyes.

"I know I am," the young man declared, happy to have backup from such a debonaire stranger, "but thanks for saying so. Hi, I'm Simon, and I guess you're her date. I'll leave you two alone."

"Duncan Rhys-Davies," Duncan said quickly, "and no, I'm not her date, but I would like a private word with her."

"No problem I'll just...uh...go away."

"Duncan," Brittany said breathlessly as Simon ambled away. "Why are you so upset?"

"As I just told him, I'm not your date, I'm just someone you like to play games with."

"That's not true!"

"I wasn't sure what to do about your little act, Brittany, but I—"

"Act?"

"I have to admit," he continued, ignoring her interruption, "you have made me realize two very important things. If you want to hear about them you can come to my cabin."

"Please, you—!"

But he was already leaving.

"Cool. I love that guy," Simon remarked, strolling back to her.

"Please, just go away," she grunted, sliding off the bar stool to chase after Duncan.

Hurrying out into the cool night air, she looked around the empty deck, then walked briskly to the elevator, tapping her foot impatiently as she waited for it to arrive.

"Need some company?" She didn't recognize the voice, and turning around, she spied the blonde man from The Mermaid the night before strolling towards her. "You look dressed to break some hearts," he grinned, his green eyes twinkling down at her.

"Sorry, I'm in a hurry."

The ding of the elevator announced its arrival, and much to her dismay he followed her in. Locked together in the intimate space, she wished she was anywhere but there, and with anyone but him.

"Don't worry, I'm not an axe murderer," he said warmly, as if sensing her nervousness. "I honestly didn't mean any harm last night.

I just thought you looked beautiful and I couldn't take my eyes off you."

"You tried to run into me when I was walking back to my table!"

"Yes, I did, and I'd do the same thing again," he admitted. "I really wanted to meet you."

"Whatever," she sighed, relieved he appeared to be less threatening than she'd thought.

"I'm surprised to see you out by yourself. My name's Cooper, by the way, Cooper Cross. I'd be honored if you'd let me buy you a drink sometime, or just coffee if you want. I'm in Cabin 42C if you want to contact me."

The elevator came to a gentle stop, but before she stepped out she looked up at him.

"I won't, but thanks anyway."

"Wait. Can you at least tell me your name?"

"Brittany," she replied, moving into the hallway. "Brittany Carter."

The elevator doors closed, and walking quickly down the hall she reached Duncan's cabin.

"Expect the best, prepare for the worst. That's what dad always says," she muttered, tapping lightly on his door.

"It's open."

He sounded grim, and nervously walking inside, she found him standing in the middle of the room, hands in his pockets, looking as if he'd just lost his best friend.

"Duncan, before you say anything, let me explain."

"Please, don't. I told you I realized two things tonight, and I'm not going to tap dance around them. I know you tried to manipulate me again, just as you did when you decided to sneak into my room so I'd—"

"Yes, but I—"

"Be quiet," he barked. "Stop with these constant interruptions."

His anger was evident, but as she meekly apologized, she could see his hurt and disappointment.

"You wanted me to feel concerned and protective," he continued. "Well, Brittany, you succeeded. That's exactly what happened, and I discovered just how much you've come to mean to me. Your plan worked! It worked brilliantly."

"It did? You do?"

"Unfortunately there was a second realization, and I'm afraid it voids the first. Even if I was prepared to be with you for the rest of the cruise and see where things might go from there, how can I? As much as I've come to care for you, how can I be with someone so deceitful and conniving? How can I trust a woman like that? The simple answer is, I can't."

Brittany stared at him, a deer in headlights. There was no defense, but as his words jangled through her head, she had her own epiphany.

"How else could I make you see how much you care for me? I know what's in your heart, Duncan Rhys-Davies, I know you've fallen for me just like I've fallen for you! The difference is, I can admit it, and I'm not afraid of it like you are."

"Steady on!"

"No, you've been on the soapbox, now it's my turn. You're scared, and you're using my attempt to put you in touch with your feelings as an excuse to say you don't trust me and therefore can't be with me. You know what, that's fine. You don't want to be with a scheming, conniving woman? A woman who uses her wits, who's resourceful and tenacious, and won't give up on a man she's crazy about? Well, Mr. High and Mighty, I don't want to be with a coward and an idiot who can't see the forest for the trees. Have a nice life!"

Spinning around, she stormed from the room, slamming the door behind her.

Stunned, Duncan stood completely still for several long seconds, then moved to the bar and poured himself a shot of scotch, downing it in a single gulp.

"Bloody hell, is she right? Am I a coward? Am I using her behavior as an excuse? What the hell have I just done?"

FURIOUS, HURT, DISAPPOINTED and confused, Brittany marched into her cabin, flung herself on the bed and sobbed into a pillow.

"Fuck, fuck, fuck. He's the man of my dreams. He's handsome and tall and British, and he's strong and...and...dammit! What's wrong with me? Why did I pull that crap? He might have come to his senses all by himself. Why did this happen?"

Finally coming up for air, she moved into the bathroom and wiped away her streaked mascara.

"I can't stay locked up in here, I'll go crazy. I should go back up to The Seven Seas, or maybe..."

Slowly walking back to the bedroom, she hesitatingly picked up the phone and dialed cabin 42C.

"Hello?"

"Hi, this is Brittany Carter."

"Brittany! What a pleasant surprise. Your timing is perfect, I just popped back to my cabin for something."

"I'm going back up to The Seven Seas for a drink. I know this is a bit weird, but..."

"Are you asking me to join you?"

"Yes, if you're interested. Just a drink, mind you. Nothing else."

"I'll meet you there. You can cry on my shoulder or dance on the tabletop. Either is fine by me."

CHAPTER TWELVE

SEATED NEXT TO COOPER Cross in a booth near the dance floor, Brittany bobbed her head and drummed her fingers to the beat of the music.

"Thanks, Cooper, you've really helped," she said gratefully, "and you were right. This wine is really good."

"Uncle Cooper knows how to take care of you. I'll make sure you forget about that British jerk. What an asshole."

"Thanks for all this. It's nice to have someone to talk to."

"You're welcome. I'm happy to be here for you," he replied, emptying the bottle into her glass. "If you'd gone to all that trouble for me I would've been thrilled. He's crazy. Drink up."

"Do you want to dance?"

"I'd love to. Finish your wine and we'll tear up the floor."

Watching from a nearby table, Simon grimaced, then made a decision. When Brittany had reappeared he'd been delighted, but then he'd seen her join Cooper Cross. The man was bad news. Though she'd been rude, Simon didn't want her to fall victim to Cooper's lechery, but Simon was no match for the tall, athletic, powerfully built jock. There was only one person he could think of to call for help.

TRYING TO TAKE HIS mind off Brittany and the accusations she had leveled at him, Duncan was unsuccessfully trying to focus on the cover for his new book when the phone rang.

Startled, he stared at it.

Hoping she was calling him, simultaneously hoping she wasn't, he picked up the receiver.

"Hello?"

"Hi, is this Duncan?"

"Yes."

"Hi, Duncan, this is Simon. We met briefly at The Seven Seas bar."

"Hello, Simon. How can I help you?"

"I hope you don't mind me calling, but I'm a bit worried about your friend, Brittany."

Duncan hesitated.

"Did she put you up to this?"

"What? No, not at all. There's a guy on the ship called Cooper Cross. You might have seen him around. He's blonde, good-looking, kind of smooth. He takes these cruises all the time for uh, various reasons. Anyway, he keeps filling her wine glass and she's really out of it. I wouldn't have bothered you but I can't tackle Cooper. Perhaps I shouldn't have called. This is none of my business, but like I said, I'm worried. He's bad news."

"Simon, you did the right thing and I'm grateful," Duncan said solemnly, a chill creeping through him. "I'm on my way."

"Thanks, Duncan. I'm really glad you're coming. Like I said, he's bad news."

Duncan's logic kicked into gear. Mr. Smooth wouldn't give her up easily, and Duncan didn't want to cause a scene. He needed help, and decided to call the steward.

"Joe, this is Duncan Rhys-Davies. I apologize for the late hour."

"Good evening, sir. How may I be of assistance?"

"I need some assistance. Brittany Carter is at The Seven Seas in the company of a man by the name of Cooper Cross. Are you familiar with him?"

"He's not a first class passenger, but yes, I am familiar with Mr. Cooper," Joe replied diplomatically. "Is there a problem?"

"There might be. He was escorted from The Mermaid last night because he was leering at Miss Carter and making her uncomfortable. I've since come to learn he may not be the most reliable of men, and I fear Miss Carter may be in over her head. I'm heading up to The Seven Seas now, and I'd appreciate you calling the manager to alert him, and ask him to keep an eye on the situation until I get there."

"I have heard rumors about Mr. Cross, and you may be right," Joe said carefully. "We're not supposed to intervene in personal matters with passengers, but in this instance I believe it's appropriate. I'll call the manager right away. His name is Peter Abrams."

"Thank you. Please tell him I will be taking her out of there in a rather unceremonious way."

"Unceremonious?"

"Brittany can be a handful, and what I have in mind will get her out of there quickly, and with the least amount of difficulty."

"I'll call Peter, and I'll swing by myself in case you need me."

"Thank you, Joe, I appreciate that."

Though Duncan hurried from his cabin and raced up the stairs, when he walked into the bar he appeared calm and casual, but spying the cavorting couple he had to summon all his self-control. Cooper's hands were locked on Brittany's backside and he was grinding against her. Duncan's first instinct was to march across the room, punch Cooper in the nose, then grab Brittany and drag her away.

"They're quite a sight."

Turning around, he found Simon standing behind him.

"I'm really glad you're here," Simon continued. "Thanks for coming."

"And I'm really glad you called," Duncan replied. "Looks like I got here just in time."

"Good evening, sir," Joe said, abruptly appearing at Duncan's side. "Peter will be joining us. Ah, here he is now. Peter Abrams, this is Duncan Rhys-Davies."

"Nice to meet you," the manager said, extending his hand. "I was already concerned when Joe called. We want our guests to enjoy themselves, but the bartender informed me the young lady appeared to be drinking heavily."

"I'll take care of her," Duncan said, "but could you please keep Mr. Cross at bay?"

"Shouldn't be an issue," Peter assured him. "Mr. Cross and I are acquainted."

Duncan headed to the dance floor with Joe and Peter following closely behind. The moment Cooper saw them, he stopped dancing and raised his palms.

"Hey, I don't want any trouble! Take her back. She's all yours."

But with her eyes closed and continuing to gyrate to the music, Brittany remained blissfully unaware that Joe and Peter were escorting Cooper to a nearby table.

"Brittany!" Duncan said, his lips at her ear, trying to be heard over the band. "You're coming with me."

"Oh, it's you!" she grumbled, opening her eyes. "Why are you here? Cooper and I are having some fun. Huh, that's weird, where did he go? No matter, I'll find him, but you, Mr. High and Mighty, you can leave."

"Are you refusing to come with me?"

"Hell, yeah, I am refusing."

"Are you sure?"

"Of course I'm sure."

Taking a step back, Duncan bent down, effortlessly lifted her off her feet and threw her over his shoulder.

"Put me down," she squealed, squirming furiously. "Put me down now! Right now!"

"Stop that noise at once or I'll put you over my knee and spank you right here in this bar."

The threat worked, and Duncan walked quickly through the bar towards the door, pausing briefly as he passed Simon.

"Simon, I owe you. Tell Peter to put your drinks on my tab."

"Hey, thanks. Glad to help, I won't forget this moment for a long time, if ever."

"Trust me, neither will I," Duncan said ruefully.

Marching outside, abruptly hit with the cold night air, Brittany pushed herself up as best she could, and gazed around the dark, empty deck.

"Please, Duncan, please put me down. I'm freezing."

"This should warm you up," he declared, landing a hard swat. "Sobering up yet?"

"Definitely, and I didn't plan this," she exclaimed as they entered the elevator. "Please, you have to believe me."

"Do you honestly think I would have come to your rescue if I thought you had?"

"Can't you please put me down?"

"Stop asking and I might think about it," he said brusquely. "Honestly, Brittany, you really are a very bad girl."

As the elevator gently stopped, he marched to his cabin, and taking her directly into his bedroom, he dumped her on the bed and ripped off her clothes.

"These are going in the trash," he declared, disappearing into the bathroom.

Shivering with the cold and beginning to feel nauseous, she was about to slide under the bedcovers when he reappeared and pulled her to her feet.

"Oh, no, you're not going to bed."

"But—"

Grabbing her wrist, he pulled her to her feet, bustling her into the bathroom and under the shower.

"Get that makeup off your face, and wash away the stink of cigarettes. There'll be a toothbrush waiting when you come out."

As he closed the stall door, and as the hot water splashed over her, she didn't know if her sudden tears were of shame, or joy that he'd come to her rescue.

"Please forgive me, Duncan, but why would you? I've been a complete idiot. You probably never want to see me again."

But he'd left.

Pacing in the bedroom, he was filled with conflict. She was the perfect blend of beauty, brains and miscreant, and her response to his discipline and dark kink had been breathtaking.

The shower stopped.

He glanced at the door.

"May I use your hairdryer?" she asked quietly, appearing in his robe with a towel around her head.

"Top right hand drawer!" Then softening his voice, he asked, "How do you feel?"

"Kind of sick, and very embarrassed. Duncan, am I staying here, or am I going back to my cabin?"

"What do you want to do?"

"Stay, if you'll have me."

"I'll think about it. You need to take some aspirin. You'll find some in the right-hand drawer."

"Okay, and, uh, thank you—thank you for everything."

As she closed the door, he undressed and climbed into bed. He didn't want her going anywhere.

"Brittany, Brittany. You were worth every minute of tonight. I just have to figure where we go from here."

CHAPTER THIRTEEN

THE DELICIOUS AROMA of fresh brewed coffee tickled Brittany's nose, and though her head thumped the pain wasn't terrible. Opening her eyes she found herself alone in the bed, then discovered a small tray with a mug of coffee on the nightstand. Sitting up, she poured in cream, stirred in two teaspoons of sugar, then took a sip.

"Man this is good," she muttered, taking another. "This is so good."

"I'm glad you're awake," Duncan said, ambling in. "How are you feeling?"

"Duncan, hi," she said sheepishly. "Not as bad as I thought I would. I'm loving this coffee."

"I have a new name for you," he declared, sitting on the edge of the bed. "Bratty Brittany, and when Bratty Brittany comes out to play, it's her bottom that's going to pay. You might well remember that."

"Not easy to forget."

"I wasn't sure if you'd have an appetite, but breakfast is waiting."

"I'd love something to eat. I didn't have any dinner last night."

"Oh, you had dinner, but from a wine glass," he scolded. "Come out when you're ready."

"I'm ready now," she said, but climbing from the bed, she added, "Last night, did you say you were throwing away my clothes?"

"I certainly did," he replied, moving into the bathroom to fetch his robe. "Here, put this on. Why would you own an outfit like that?"

"I usually wear a blouse under the top, and the skirt was short because I rolled up the waist."

"I see."

"There you go again," she said with a sigh, wrapping herself in the robe as she followed him into the living room. "Making me feel ten-years old."

"If the shoe fits. Don't worry, I put your outfit in a plastic bag but I haven't had a chance to toss it."

"That's a relief. Duncan, this looks wonderful," she exclaimed, eyeing the breakfast on the table.

"You must not have been as drunk as I thought."

"I have no idea," she said, sitting down and piling scrambled eggs on her plate. "Did I make a complete fool of myself?"

"I only saw you dancing for a minute, and it wasn't pretty. The manager would have stepped in if I hadn't. Apparently Cooper Cross has less than a stellar reputation. How did you end up at The Seven Seas with him?"

"It's no big deal. When I left here I couldn't calm down, so I called him to meet me for a drink."

"You called him? How did you know his cabin number?"

"Sorry, I forgot to mention," she said, buttering some toast. "After you left the bar, Cooper and I bumped into each other while I was waiting for the elevator."

Duncan rolled his eyes.

"Brittany, he would have been watching for you, and when he saw his chance he grabbed it."

"It didn't seem that way."

"You would have ended up in his cabin."

"But I would have said no."

"Do you honestly think he would have taken no for an answer?"

Lifting a forkfull of eggs to her mouth, she suddenly set it back on her plate.

"He kept filling my wine glass and telling me I needed to relax. He was getting me sloshed. I'm such an idiot."

"No, but you do idiotic things sometimes."

"I'm sorry to say that's true," she mumbled, then lifted her tea to down the last swallow. "That was delicious. Thank you."

"Do you want anything else?"

"No, I'm stuffed, but I feel better. My head feels clearer."

"Then let's move to the couch. There's something I need to tell you."

"Sure," she replied, and moving to the sofa, she sat down and looked up at him expectantly. "Aren't you joining me?"

"I will in a minute. Right now I prefer to stand. I think better on my feet. It comes from hours in a courtroom."

"A courtroom?"

"That's the first thing I need to tell you. Yes, I'm an author, but that's not my vocation. I'm a barrister."

"Really? That's Brit-speak for a lawyer, right?"

"Not exactly, but I do argue cases and appear in court. The point is, I have a very busy professional life."

"Why are you telling me this?"

"I'm just a regular man. I'm not a mysterious, literary, James Bond."

"Duncan, there's nothing regular about you. Your work might be regular, but you're not a regular person."

"If you're referring to my—"

"I'm referring to your everything," she exclaimed, interrupting him. "Your personality, and, uh, the other stuff."

"What I'm trying to tell you, is—"

"Duncan, I don't care whether you're a bus driver or the Prince of frickin' Wales."

"My goodness, you really do mean that."

"Of course I mean it. What are you trying to say? Please don't keep me in suspense, just tell me."

"You were right."

"About what?" she asked hastily, just as he was about to explain.

"I am going to buy several gags with your name on every one of them," he exclaimed, throwing up his arms in exasperation.

"I can't help myself."

"Discipline! Regular, strict discipline. That's what you need!"

"Well, duh! I do know that," she quipped, quickly adding, "Sorry."

"I adore your wit, but there's a fine line, Brittany."

"Can we get back to what I was right about?"

"Absolutely. I did use your misbehavior as an excuse to hit the pause button, because, and I'm ashamed to admit this, my fears did get the better of me. A few years ago I hurt someone I loved. I hurt her badly, and myself in the process. Sally was her name. She felt taken for granted, and ultimately she left. It was shocking and inexplicable, and it took some time before I realized she'd been right. The entire episode deeply troubled me for many months. I won't make that mistake again. If we become a couple, I won't take you for granted, not ever."

"Thank you for telling me, Duncan. I have a feeling that wasn't easy. "

"It wasn't, but you needed to know," he said softly, then sitting next to her, he added, "I'm flawed, Brittany, just like anyone else."

The intimacy of the moment engulfed them, and as he placed his arm around her, she curled into his lap.

"Does this mean you changed your mind? Can we spend these last couple of days together?"

"I've been giving this a great deal of thought and I have a proposal. When we dock in Tahiti, how would you feel about coming back to London with me for a week? The first three days will be easy. I always give myself time to adjust before going back to work, but the following days will be my regular life. Would you like to experience it?"

"You're kidding. I don't even know what to say."

"Think about it."

"What's there to think about? Of course I'll come with you. I'd love to."

"Excellent! It will give us a chance to see, uh, what's what."

"I'm so excited. You are the most spectacular man," she exclaimed, throwing her arms around his neck and covering his face with kisses.

"I'm glad you think so, but I'm not sure I'm spectacular. Brittany, one more thing. Do you make a habit of taking off with strange men and getting drunk when you're ticked off? It seemed a very easy thing for you to do. Have you done that before?"

"Um, kind of."

"What does that mean?"

"Going somewhere to dance and have a drink helps me get over things."

"If we have words while you're with me in London, and I truly hope we don't, but if we do, you can't go off galavanting around."

"Sure, no problem."

"I mean it."

"No problem, honestly."

"Now we have to talk about something else, and I must be very strict about this. You will not attempt to manipulate me. You did it once and I punished you, then you turned around and did it again."

"I'm sorry, really, I am, but I have to explain. I saw a documentary about Kate Middleton and Prince—"

"You can stop right there," he said, holding up his hand. "It doesn't matter. You obviously didn't learn your lesson and this must be dealt with. You'll get that spanking over my knee, and it will be meaningful, along with a couple of other things I hope will make you think twice before you decide to pull any more stunts."

"Whatever you say."

"Sir!"

"Whatever you say, Sir."

"Return to your cabin, clean yourself up, and pack an overnight bag. You have fifteen minutes from the time you leave."

"What should I wear back to my cabin?"

"The robe, just as you did before, but I won't be coming with you."

"Should I go now?"

"Yes, and remember, fifteen minutes. Don't be late."

Rising to her feet, she glanced at the clock on the wall, then sending him a nervous smile, she hurried out the door.

CHAPTER FOURTEEN

BRITTANY CHOSE A SILK turquoise skirt and white silk tank top, but wasn't sure if she should wear underwear, putting it on and taking it off twice before finally deciding to leave it on. Hurriedly packing an overnight bag, she moved quickly down the hall, knocking on Duncan's door several minutes before the allotted fifteen minutes.

"You look very nice," he said warmly, ushering her inside. "Go into the bedroom."

He'd changed into a black T-shirt and workout pants, his hair was wet, and she could smell the spicy aroma of his cologne. Moving in ahead of him, she found the room in semi-darkness. He'd closed the drapes, leaving a crack barely a couple of inches wide.

"Put your case on the armchair by the window."

Feeling oddly self-conscious, she walked past the bed and deposited her bag, but when she turned around he had closed the door and was leaning against it, his arms crossed, looking stern and stunningly sexy.

"Come here, Brittany."

"Can I say-"

"No!"

Butterflies fluttering, she hurried the few steps and stopped directly in front of him.

"Your discipline will start with some time alone. You will remain in this room, and you will not watch television, or read, or snoop, nor will you open the drapes. You will not remove your shoes, or any other part of your clothing. I will be checking on you from time to time. Any questions?"

"Uh, no, Sir."

"Behave yourself, young lady. I'll know if you don't."

Softly kissing her, he disappeared into the living room, and with nothing to do but wait, she thought she'd take a nap, but after a few minutes she discovered she couldn't relax. Tempted to risk a quick glance through the teasing opening in the drapes, she went so far as to stand in front of them, but her inner voice told her she'd be crazy to disobey him. Returning to the bed, she propped herself with the pillows behind her back and let her mind wander. Her thoughts drifted to her life in the small town, then shifted to the exciting prospect of her visit to London.

The nanny cam disguised as a clock sat on the desk catty-corner against the far wall. For almost thirty-minutes Duncan watched. Brittany behaved exactly as expected. Closing his laptop, he stood up and stretched, drank some water, then strode across to the bedroom door. As he entered, she jumped to her feet and hurried across to hug him.

"I get it. I didn't at first and it seemed like forever, but when I finally sat down and started to relax my mind took me places."

"I know. You did really well. Take a few steps, turn around, lift your skirt around your waist and remain still."

As she did as he instructed, though not sure what to expect, she wasn't prepared for another wait. As the long seconds ticked by, she bit her lip to keep from moving her feet, and was barely able to resist the need to scratch a sudden tickle on her nose. When she finally felt his fingers slip through the sides of her panties, she let out a relieved sigh. slipping them down, he left them around the tops of her thighs.

"For the next twenty-four hours you will not leave this room," he said softly, running his fingers across her naked backside. "I have told you I'm a strict disciplinarian. If things become too much for you, you will say, *this is too much for me.* Repeat that, please."

"This is too much for me," she managed, finding it difficult to concentrate beyond his tickling fingertips.

"If you say those words I will immediately stop whatever I'm doing and leave. You'll pack your things and return to your cabin. There will be no recriminations, no dramatic goodbyes, no apologies, and we will be over. This isn't a threat, Brittany. If who I am and what I do doesn't fit, there's no point in continuing. I'm giving you an out, and I'm trusting you to be honest."

"Yes, Sir. I understand, and I agree."

He could feel her sincerity, and turning her around, he hugged her tightly, then clutching her hair and tugging it back, he laid his lips on hers. The kiss did not demand or devour, but lovingly lingered, and when he broke away she was breathless.

"Whatever happens," she said softly, "I am in love with you Duncan, and I'll always be grateful that we met."

"And I feel the same. Are you ready?"

"Yes, Sir. I'm ready."

"Your discipline will begin with some unpleasant truths. Raise your hands behind your head, elbows out, kick off your shoes and separate your feet."

Removing her strappy sandals without using her hands wasn't easy, and though she kept hoping he'd offer to help, he stood silently watching her struggle.

"Sir...?"

"You're panicking. Slow down. Think about what you're doing."

Letting out a heavy sigh, she focused her attention on the surprisingly difficult task. Finally succeeding, she smiled up at him.

"Good. Lessons are everywhere. If something challenges you, slow down and take a moment. Eyes on the floor."

Dropping her gaze, his words lingered, but as she reflected he moved slowly around her, reminding her of a great cat circling its prey.

"Brittany, you're a beautiful, intelligent young woman. You are also spoiled and childish, and possess little self-control. You have been without discipline throughout your life, and your constant interruptions show a lack of good manners. Such impolite behavior will not be tolerated."

He paused, allowing his words to hang in the air, all the while continuing to circle her.

"You see your conniving ways as clever, but they are the height of dishonesty. Any further attempts at getting what you want through ridiculous schemes will be severely dealt with. I have a variety of canes in my arsenal, and I will not hesitate to use them when necessary. I can assure you, several strokes from any one of them and you will quickly mend your ways. Are we reaching a clearer understanding, Brittany?"

"Yes, Sir."

And she was.

Brittany had never been spoken to so sternly. When her father had lectured her for a poor grade or some vague misdeed, his voice had been tinged with regret, and he would often apologize for the reprimand.

"I punished you for sneaking into my cabin in an attempt to manipulate me into spanking you. Tell me, Brittany, what did you do?"

"You mean, uh, dressing up and pretending to run into you?"

"Exactly. You contrived another exploit just a short time later. You should be ashamed of yourself, Brittany Carter. Clearly you need a very strict hand, and that, young lady, is exactly what you will receive. My very strict hand."

As his scolding words reverberated through her head, her butterflies transformed into a giant whirling dervish. She thought she could handle anything he dished out, but could she?

"Remember, Brittany, you can leave here any time you choose. All you have to do is tell me."

He knew exactly what was going through her mind; the doubt, the questioning, the conflict. Brittany was made of tough stuff, but she'd never come up against someone like him, nor been on the receiving end of a strong tongue-lashing, though he could deliver worse, much worse. He waited for her signal, the one that told him he could proceed. It would come as a sigh, or the drop of her shoulders, or slight tilting down of her chin. She could take as long as she needed to get there.

Or she might lift her eyes and tell him it was over.

CHAPTER FIFTEEN

TO DUNCAN'S GREAT JOY she gave him all three; she let out a heavy breath, lowered her head, and even though her hands were behind her neck, he saw her shoulders drop. It was the clearest acceptance he'd ever witnessed. A surge of energy rippling through his body, he moved into the closet to retrieve the long, thin polished shoe horn. She'd be covertly watching him, and he wanted her to. Seeing him return with the stinging stick would build her anticipation.

"Lower your arms," he said, carrying it back to her. "Take this and hold it with both hands."

As she took the rod between her fingers, though he could sense her trepidation, he could also detect the sweet aroma of her arousal.

"You must not drop it. If you do, you'll be sorry."

Hearing the quick intake of breath, he suppressed a satisfied smile and ambling past her to the desk, he picked up the high-backed, armless chair, placed it next to her and sat down.

"You were expecting me to tie your wrists and ankles and blindfold you, but one thing you will learn, Brittany, I'm rarely predictable. Lay over my lap."

Leaning forward she wriggled her body trying to find a comfortable position. She thought she'd be stretched across his legs on the bed, or even the couch, and this was an unpleasant surprise. There was no measure of comfort, and he wasn't helping her find any.

"Move further over," he said sternly. "You'll have to squirm to do it."

She did her best, grunting as she gyrated her hips in an effort to move forward, but unable to use her hands to grip the legs of the chair for balance made the process extremely difficult. Feeling his eyes on her wriggling backside didn't help, even if it was still covered.

"Right there," he said sharply, "and keep your squirming to a minimum."

Lifting her skirt and laying it over her back, he began to slap her perfectly positioned posterior. There had been no hesitation, or warning he was about to begin, nor had he run his palm over her naked skin, he'd just started to spank—and spank hard. Repeatedly his hand rose and fell, the smacks falling in no particular rhythm. He'd land a volley of rapid-fire swats, followed by slow, hard smacks, then whisk his hand against the sensitive area where her thighs met her backside. Though she gasped and wriggled and begged him to stop, her pleas went unanswered.

In addition to the stinging spanking, holding the rod proved to be far more potent than having her wrists tied. It not only prevented her from putting her hands behind her, she couldn't grasp the legs of the chair or lay her hands on the floor. His relentless palm continued to pepper her bottom, and no matter how much she squirmed to avoid the scalding slaps, he seemed to be able to hold her in place effortlessly. Unsure how much more she could take, but determined to see it through, she clenched her teeth and told herself it would be worth it in the end. Just as she finished the thought his hand fell quiet.

Duncan stared at her bright red skin. There would be no soothing caress, no rubbing, no tender words, not yet. It took her several minutes to compose herself, but he wasn't surprised. It was a much harder spanking than he'd previously delivered, probably harder than she'd expected, and holding the rod wasn't easy.

"Take the stick in one hand and hand it back for me," he ordered, as she finally settled and sank into his lap.

Not sure whether she should be grateful or frightened, she did as he asked. The moment he took it from her fingers she grabbed the legs of the chair, and though she let out a long, appreciative sigh, her respite was short-lived.

"Off my lap and stand in front of me."

Moving slowly, she pushed herself off his knees and rose unsteadily to her feet.

"Remove your knickers and skirt."

Her panties were still around her thighs, and he watched her nervously pull them off, then reaching to her side, she slid down the zipper of her skirt and let it drop to the floor. Standing up and laying the makeshift cane on the chair, he slid his fingers in her hair, and tugging back her head he locked her eyes.

"That spanking was discipline for discipline's sake, and an example of what to expect if you misbehave. Now you will feel the rod for your dreadful schemes. Being a brat, throwing tantrums, general bad behavior, those are misdemeanors. Schemes are felonies. Do you understand what I just told you?"

"Yes, Sir," she whispered. "May I ask you a question, Sir?"

"You may."

"That spanking, is that something you'll be doing often?"

"Obviously that's entirely up to you," he replied, releasing her hair. "If you require maintenance, then yes, but that's a path we've not even begun to travel."

"You mean, if we end up together?"

"That's exactly what I mean. Anything else?"

"No, Sir."

Stepping aside, he picked up the rod and tapped the chair.

"Bend over, hold the edges of the seat, arch your back and close your legs."

Leaning forward, filled with dread, she followed his instructions.

"Remember what I said. If this is too much, just tell me."

"Yes, Sir."

"Do you think schemes and manipulations are an appropriate way to get what you want?"

"Not anymore, Sir."

He smiled. He'd expected a simple, *No, Sir,* but instead she'd reminded him there was nothing simple about her.

"Your bottom is sore, isn't it, Brittany?"

"Yes, Sir, very."

"Stay as you are and think about your conniving ways. You must also consider how you put yourself at risk with a complete stranger, a man who had already proven to be of dubious character. When I return my rod will teach you just how badly I view these things."

His words sent goosebumps popping across her skin. Her eyes followed him as he moved away, took her bag from the armchair and sat down. She recalled how intensely she'd been attracted to him the moment she'd seen him walking up the gangplank. His confident bearing and squared shoulders had suggested an accomplished man, one who tackled life's challenges with aplomb. For many hours she'd hoped and prayed they'd spend time together. Now her wish had been granted. But she never, not in her wildest dreams, not even after reading Emily's Education, thought she would end up with a stinging crimson backside, holding the seat of a chair, waiting to be punished with a nasty rod. As he settled she quickly averted her eyes. He hadn't forbidden her to look at him, but she wasn't about to take any chances.

Tilting his head to the side, Duncan admired his handiwork, then feasted his eyes on the beautiful, bratty young woman. The craving for discipline and control lived inside her submissive soul, but it was a craving she hadn't fully understood. She was beginning to, but whether or not she would last twenty-four hours remained to be seen. His thoughts shifted to her sentence. The cane, or in this case, the thin polished wood doing the job of a cane, was not to be taken lightly. Three swishes didn't seem enough, and six would be overly harsh. Finally deciding on four, delivered quickly, he focused his attention on Brittany to wait for the subtle signal that she was ready to proceed.

CHAPTER SIXTEEN

WHILE DUNCAN HAD BEEN ruminating, Brittany had been wondering why she could so easily ignore her warning voice before embarking on one of her schemes. She often suffered terrible guilt after outwitting some unsuspecting soul, but she knew she'd never be able to pull anything over on Duncan again. He wasn't just smarter than she and would see it coming, in the unlikely event she was able to pull the wool over his eyes, she'd end up confessing her sins. The result would be a very sore backside, and he probably had other methods of discipline besides turning her bottom the color of a ripe tomato. But the question would have to wait. She was supposed to be thinking about her sins.

Her mind wandered to the scene at the bar, and it occurred to her if something bad had happened, she could have pointed the finger at Duncan, blaming him for upsetting her and causing her to head there to drown her sorrows. Though it had been her choice to meet up with Cooper, she could almost hear the defense. She frowned at the twisted logic, but her hands hurt, and she realized her fingers had been clenched around the chair. Taking a deep breath and letting them fall loose, she unwittingly sent Duncan the signal for which he'd been waiting.

He caught it, and a slight smile curled the edges of his lips. Rising from the chair, rod in hand, he moved forward.

"This will not be pleasant," he warned, "and remember, you can tell me if it's too much."

"Yes, Sir, but I won't, Sir."

"You will receive four cuts, two for your schemes, and two for being so foolish as to call Cooper Cross. You wanted to get out of the cabin and have a drink, fine, but you went too far. Not only that, I suspect you were hoping I'd see you with him. Were you, Brittany?"

"Not consciously, no, Sir."

"Good answer. We often act on a subconscious level, and I believe you. The four cuts will be delivered with a count of three between each. Please refrain from shouting out. You may stamp your foot, but you will not take your hands from the chair. Repeat that please."

"I'm not allowed to shout, I can stamp my feet, but I can't take my hands off the chair."

"Correct. Are you ready?"

"Yes, Sir, though I'm not exactly sure what I'm ready for."

"It will help if you take a deep breath before each strike. I'll be counting to three, so you'll know when to do that."

"Yes, Sir, thank you."

"The first is for sneaking into my cabin and attempting to manipulate me. One—two—take your breath—three."

With a practiced flick of his wrist he landed the stick, eliciting a loud hiss.

"The second, for dressing up like a harlot and ambushing me in the hall. One—two—three."

The strike landed just below the first, causing a bending of the knees and a loud groan.

"The next two for meeting up with Cooper Cross knowing very well he could be trouble. One—two— three."

The third brought the snapping back of her head, and caused her to stamp a foot.

"You're not to put yourself in jeopardy like that again. One—two—three."

The last was delivered to her sit spot, and she gripped the sides of the chair, clenched her teeth, bent her knees, and let out a low, deep growl.

"I'm leaving for a few minutes and you're free to do whatever you wish. I'll return shortly."

Turning her head, she watched him walk out the door, then moving to the bed she flopped on her stomach, but as she rested her hands on her stinging behind, she realized he could have landed the horrible stick a dozen times. He'd decided four was appropriate. He hadn't been cruel, or mean, or unfair. Sinking into the mattress and closing her eyes, though she wasn't sure why, an almost-smile crossed her lips.

Brittany wasn't the only one who needed a break. Duncan had to gather his thoughts. Her craving was so acute he found it surprising she'd never been under the authority of a loving Dominant, but she came from a small town. Those who shared the unique lifestyle had difficulty meeting each other in a large city. He couldn't imagine how hard it would be in a country community. Opening a bottle of Sauvignon Blanc and pouring himself a glass, he sipped the light refreshing wine and thought about the days ahead. He had every confidence she would be next to him on the plane back to London.

"Blast. I need to make her reservation," he muttered, the thought suddenly hitting him, and reaching for the phone he called Joe and asked him to book the seat.

"British Airways, First Class, and make sure they know we want seats next to each other."

"Yes, Mr. Davies, and forgive me if I'm overstepping, but may I say I'm very pleased to hear such happy news. There must be something special about those two staterooms."

"This has happened before?"

"Yes, sir. A couple of times. The same two cabins."

"How extraordinary. I'll be sure and tell Brittany. I hope I'll still need that seat when the time comes."

"I suspect you will," the steward replied, and Duncan could hear Joe's smile as he spoke.

He provided the additional information the steward needed to make the reservation, but as Duncan replaced the receiver he had an unexpected moment of doubt. A few days on a cruise and he'd invited a madcap Southern Belle into his home for a week.

"I've either completely lost my mind, or I really have fallen for her. I suppose love can make one do strange things."

Taking another sip of his wine, he began to think about what he'd do with her once they landed. The Bowler Hat immediately came to mind, and he grinned at the thought of taking her shopping for the right outfit. Then there were the shows at the West End, and indulging in the food court at Harrods. It wouldn't be a question of how to fill their time, but having enough time to do all the things on offer. But his smile began to fade. While the first few days would be all about fun—and salacious sex—on Monday he'd be back at work. Brittany would have to entertain herself until he returned home, and he'd have a brand new case waiting, a case he'd have to peruse after hours in his study.

"I'll worry about that when the time comes," he muttered. "*If* the time comes. It may not. I can't get ahead of myself."

Placing his wine glass on the counter, he returned to the bedroom and found her as he expected. Resting on her side. Moving to the bed he sat down and stroked the hair off her face.

"How are you?"

Opening her eyes, she stared up at him.

"If it was yesterday, I'd probably say something like, how do you think? Now I have no desire to say that. The truth is, I'm not sure how I am, except my butt hurts like hell, and I certainly feel like I've been punished. I was just lying here thinking how I didn't feel any anger from you, just a determination to discipline me for what I'd done. Is that the right word? Determination?"

"I'd say that word is as good as any. Desire maybe. Obligation and responsibility fit as well."

"I am emotional. I want to curl up against you and have you hold me and never let me go, but I guess that can't happen yet, or can it?"

"It can absolutely happen, and it will," he said softly. "There is more to come, but I'm very proud of you. I'm especially proud of everything you've just said."

Reaching for the blanket at the bottom of the bed, he stretched out next to her and covered them both.

"I don't want you getting cold," he murmured, wrapping her up in his arms. "Brittany, I do love how you feel in my arms."

"Duncan!"

"That surprises you?"

"It surprises me to hear you say it."

"Why?"

"I'm not sure. Maybe because I didn't expect you to be so open about your feelings."

"Haven't I already been open about my feelings?"

"Yes, but they were, uh, different."

"Feelings are feelings. I expressed my disappointment and anger, and now I'm expressing how much I adore you. I'll always do my best to tell you what's going on with me, and I expect the same from you, but now it's time to rest, my beautiful Brittany."

"Not your bratty Brittany?"

"Not right now. Right now you're my beautiful Brittany."

"Can I ask you one last thing?"

"Just one."

"Why am I like this? Why are you the way you are?"

"That's a question that has been asked a thousand times by a thousand people, men and women alike," he said with a heavy sigh.

"There's no single answer, and there's no easy answer. Human sexuality, the human psyche, is complex. I've stopped wondering. I've just accepted who I am and the way I am."

"But you were right about why I do some of the things I do."

"You are very spoiled, but you're also very smart. I'll bet you figured out how to get what you wanted when you were just a little girl."

"You're right. My mother would be the one who would scold me and want to punish me, but all I had to do was go to my father and tell him how sorry I was. If I cried a bit that would be the end of any potential punishment."

"And your boyfriends?"

"My boyfriends? Oh, good grief. I don't know why, but every guy I've dated has been scared of me."

"Scared of you, or scared of losing you?"

"How do you know this stuff?"

"Life," he said with a soft chuckle. "The best and cruelest teacher."

"I think you're right. Scared of losing me. Honestly, I don't know why men don't get it. Why can't they take a stand. I got so sick and tired of hearing *whatever you want, whatever makes you happy*. That's all well and good, but after a while it gets boring."

"I'm sure they meant well, and you can be quite fearsome. Not every man is going to put their girlfriend over their knee. They might want to, but it's not PC."

"No, it certainly isn't."

"No more questions. Snuggle up and close your eyes. Round two is coming, and you must rest."

CHAPTER SEVENTEEN

DUNCAN WAS STANDING in a lush green meadow. His dark hair fell to his shoulders in gentle waves, like soft ripples in a pond. Dressed in a shiny suit of armor, but with a crown on his head, a white mist swirled in the air. As she moved forward to join him, her feet not touching the ground, and a familiar melody floated through the air, and the words of the song were whispered in her ear.

These dreams go on when I close my eyes
Every second of the night I live another life
These dreams that sleep when it's cold outside
Every moment I'm awake the further I'm away
There's something out there
I can't resist
I need to hide away from the pain
There's something out there
I can't resist
The sweetest song is silence
That I've ever heard
Funny how your feet
In dreams never touch the earth
In a wood full of princes
Freedom is a kiss
But the prince hides his face
From dreams in the mist
"Brittany. Wake up."
"My prince..."

"Maybe I am, but you still need to wake up."

Struggling to bring herself up from a deep sleep, she opened her eyes and stared into Duncan's handsome face.

"That must have been some dream you were having," he remarked with a soft smile. "You were mumbling something about mists and princes and being in the woods."

"You were a Knight in Shining Armor, literally, then the song played, the one my mother loved."

"What was the song? Do you remember?"

"Dreams in the Mist. I think that's it, and the band is two girls with amazing voices."

"Heart. They were big back in the eighties."

"My mother would sing along and tell me I'd meet my prince one day just like she did, and he'd be a Knight in Shining Armor. Duncan, do you think the dream was right?"

"I hope it was," he murmured, nuzzling her neck. "I'd love to be your knight."

"You are, and I must think that subconsciously as well. I dreamed it."

"Are you ready for Round Two?"

"That depends on what that is," she said with a twinkle.

"Yes, you're definitely ready, but you need some water. I'll fetch it for you."

Watching him walk across to the bathroom she felt her heart swell. She often had mystifying dreams that carried covert messages, but there was nothing hidden in the one she'd just had. Her Dominant prince had walked into her life.

"Here, drink this," he said, returning with a bottle of water, "then take off the rest of your clothes and wait for me on your stomach with your eyes closed. I'll be back in a minute."

"Yes, Sir."

He softly kissed her, and as he left the room she downed several gulps and placed the bottle on the bedside table. Removing her silk top and bra, she settled on her stomach and closed her eyes. It was a few minutes before she sensed, not heard, his return, then the mattress moved and his lips were against her ear.

"Tell me Brittany, what is the bad habit I find annoying and impolite?"

"I interrupt, Sir."

"Yes, you do. When you interrupt it means you're not interested in what the other person is saying, you don't care about their opinion or feelings. It has to stop."

"Yes, Sir."

"Corner time is a gentle way to help you focus, but I have learned corner time doesn't have much of an impact on you, so, young lady, we must move to something else. When we're in London I'll have the proper equipment, but here I have to improvise. Bring your legs together and raise your feet."

After blindfolding her with a black silk sash, he picked up a necktie, wrapped her wrists together at the small of her back and left a tether, then followed suit with her ankles. Knotting the two tethers together created a gentle hog-tie. It was her introduction to bondage, and though not severe, he believed it would make an impression.

"Once you're in my home I'll weave my ropes in various ways, but this position will help you to focus," he said solemnly. "Surrender to this, Brittany, and think about the many times you've interrupted me and others. Think about why you cannot hold your tongue. If your muscles begin to cramp call out to me. Do you have any questions?"

"No, Sir."

"How do you feel?"

"I'm not sure."

"No sense of panic?"

"No, Sir, nothing like that."

"Sink into it. You'll find it can be liberating. Ironic, but it can."

Moving back to the armchair, he settled in to keep watch. He didn't like using neck ties. If she struggled the knots could tighten, causing a problem if he needed to untie them quickly, so he'd left a pair of scissors on the nightstand. Glancing across at the clock on the desk he took note of the time; she'd remain in bondage for fifteen minutes.

For many years Duncan had fantasized about creating a play-room in his house. He had the space, and he'd come close to making his dream a reality during his time with Sally. Thinking of his long ago love, it occurred to him she and Brittany were nothing alike.

"Perhaps that's a good thing," he mumbled under his breath, his eyes focused on Brittany. "Perhaps that's why I'm able to take this leap of faith, because you're so different."

Her upbringing had been far more sophisticated than he would have guessed. She had charmed the Sommelier at The Mermaid, but her demeanor at other times gave no hint of her background, and he wondered if she was ashamed of her family's wealth. Yet she was traveling First Class. Not the behavior of someone who was trying to hide their moneyed lifestyle. Glancing back at the clock, he realized he'd been so lost in his thoughts the time had zipped by. With only five minutes remaining he needed to check on her, and moving quietly to her side he studied her wrists and ankles. There was no sign of the circulation being cut off, the knots appeared to be as he'd left them, her breathing was measured, and she showed no signs of distress. Satisfied, he returned to his chair and continued his vigil.

Though initially tense, after the first few minutes Brittany discovered relaxing made the position more comfortable, and of its own accord her focus shifted. Why did she interrupt? She'd been criticized for it in the past. She decided it must be due to a lack of patience, though she found no difficulty waiting for the time to go by in her present state. She found the contradiction puzzling, but her mind began to fall silent, and she drifted away. When she felt him untying her blindfold, it was as though she was waking up, but she hadn't been sleeping. Her wrists and ankles were quickly freed, and he massaged her muscles as he slowly returned her limbs to their natural position.

"I'm guessing you've done this before," she quipped. "Ooh, I need that rubbing. Thank you."

"Such a cheeky girl," he said with a grin. "Roll on your back."

As he stretched out next to her and brought her into his arms, an unexpected tear dripped from the edge of her eye.

"Why do I feel emotional again?"

"You're releasing negative energy. I don't know how else to put it."

"This is nothing like I thought it would be, well, this part anyway."

"Did you have an epiphany?"

"I did, but I get the feeling you already know that."

"Don't worry about me, just tell me what went through your mind."

"Patience. That's always been a problem for me, but in that fifteen minutes I felt what it means to be patient, and I realized how self-discipline fits into that," then pausing, she asked. "If I start interrupting again, are you going to tie me up?"

"I just might, but you get five gold stars."

"I also felt a weird kind of peace, but now I'm really tired."

"Hungry too, I'm sure. How would you feel about a steaming plate of Fettuccine Alfredo?"

"That sounds absolutely divine."

"I want you to take a hot shower, and by the time you come out the food will be here."

"I'm kind of overwhelmed."

"I know," he nodded, silently adding, *I am too. By you.*

CHAPTER EIGHTEEN

AS THE HOT WATER STREAMED over her, Brittany closed her eyes and leaned against the shower wall. Though drained, a serene energy pulsed through her body. Over the years she had devoured many naughty novels, her head was often filled with salacious fantasies, and she'd spent hours exploring blogs posted by submissive women exploring their unique sexuality. But she had not been prepared for the reality. She loved the pain of Duncan's discipline and the pleasure of his touch in equal measure.

And she loved him. Completely. It wasn't just what he was doing. It was *him*.

Turning off the faucets, she stepped from the shower, toweled off, and wrapping herself up in the bathrobe, she padded back to the bedroom.

"Are you ready to eat?" Standing by a rolling cart, Duncan made a theatrical gesture with his arm. "We have the fettuccine as promised, a green salad, cheesecake, and I ordered you tea instead of coffee."

"Tea! Why does that sound so appealing?"

"Perhaps my English ways are rubbing off. Get into bed and I'll bring you the tray."

"You're spoiling me."

"Good girls get rewarded."

"I like this," she quipped, taking off the robe and climbing between the sheets. "Come along, don't keep me waiting."

"Don't push your luck, young lady."

"But it's what I do best," she said with a giggle. "It's one of the many things you love about me."

"Indeed it is," he said, grinning back at her as he set the tray on her lap.

"Aren't you having anything?"

"Not right now."

"I didn't think it would be like this," she remarked, rolling the creamy Italian pasta around her fork. "I didn't imagine you'd be serving me a wonderful meal in bed, that's for sure."

"There's so much more, Brittany."

"Why did that sound sad?"

"Thoughtful. Not sad. When you've finished you're going to take another nap."

"Another one?"

"Don't you feel tired?"

"Kind of. Is discipline always like this? I mean, things happening then rest?"

"There are no rules, I do what I feel. Now stop talking and eat."

Settling into the armchair, he sat back and watched her enjoy the meal. Her hunger was evident, but he understood her need for conversation. She'd have many questions as the days passed, possibly more than he could answer, and though he'd been a dominant since his teens, he couldn't remember a submissive with such a deep craving for what he offered. Not even Sally.

"That was delicious! Thank you," she exclaimed, laying down her fork and drinking the last of her tea. "And you're right again."

"About?"

"Needing a nap. Wow. I'm really wiped out. What time is it, anyway. I've completely lost track."

"That's what happens. Doing what we do is a complete escape. We stop the world."

"I love it, every bit of it," she murmured, then surrendered to a yawn as he picked up the tray. "Oh, man. I'm really beat."

"That's why I'm leaving you alone. You need to rest, but I'll be here when you wake up."

"Duncan, this is all so amazing."

"It makes me very happy to hear you say that. Sleep well."

Returning the tray to the cart, he rolled it into the living room, switching off the bedroom light on the way, and closed the door behind him.

THOUGH HER BOTTOM WAS sore and her limbs a little achy, she passed into a deep, dreamless sleep until the feel of his arms around her stirred her awake. Surprised and happy to find him next to her, she snuggled against his body.

"Duncan?"

"Yes, Brittany?"

"You're here?"

"Where else would I be?"

Running his hands over her body, he fondled her glorious breasts, caressed her tender backside, and sent his fingers into the slippery wetness between her legs. He'd planned on a long session of teasing and denial, but as he listened to her soft moans and felt her soft submission he changed his mind. She would have the pleasure she'd earned. Rolling her on to her side, he placed his cock at her entrance and thrust forward with slow, strong strokes. The day's decadent events had brought her to a heightened state of arousal, and she could be brought to the brink at any time, but moving his hand between her legs, he rubbed her clit to test the waters. Her soft moans turned fervent, and he could feel the faint pulsing of her inner walls against his cock.

"You are so primed," he whispered, kissing her ear, "and you're going to come so hard."

"I know. I can feel it."

Accelerating his thrusts, he continued his teasing play until she was at the edge, then pulling out he rolled her on to her back. Her eyes gazed up at him, and even in the dim light he could see their sparkling fire.

"I've never felt like this, not ever."

"You're about to feel more."

Though her pussy craved his return, he dropped his mouth to her breasts, languidly kissing them, then hungrily devoured her nipples. Finally raising his head, he slid his fingers in her hair and moved his mouth to her ear.

"Do you want me to fuck you hard, or fuck you gently?"

"I want you to fuck me as you wish."

"Mmm, good girl," he murmured, then traveled his lips to hers.

But it wasn't a gentle kiss, it wasn't a passionate kiss, it wasn't a kiss that relayed their ardent passion, it was all three. As their mouths engaged, he shifted his body, allowing his cock to snake its way back inside her, and with their lips still locked, he thrust forward and began to pump, gathering speed as his climax approached.

"I'm almost there," she suddenly gasped, breaking the kiss.

Her body grew taut, and pulling his fingers from her hair, he grabbed her wrists, pinning them above her head.

"I'm going to fuck you hard," he growled, "and you're going to explode for me. Are you ready?"

"I'm so ready..."

As he pummeled her pussy, her stark nipples brushed against his chest shooting sparks through his loins. Her back suddenly arched, her legs violently closed, and a moment later her cries of orgasmic joy filled the air. His cock felt the demanding clutch of her sex, and erupting in vigorous spasms it jerked out his essence. The intense hours of his discipline culminated in explosive orgasms, until finally groaning as their spasms passed, he fell breathlessly at her side.

"My God," she panted, "I know I shouldn't say this, but—"

"Sssh, just catch your breath."

"I have to. I love you, Duncan, like I never thought I could love anyone, and if it all ends here, yes, it will break my heart, but because of you I know who I am now."

"I love you too, Brittany," he breathed, holding her tightly against him, "I love you from the depths of my soul."

EPILOGUE

THE SHIP HAD REACHED Tahiti.

The day before, Duncan and Brittany had enjoyed leisurely strolls and recovered from the marathon session, but returned to The Mermaid for their last dinner on board. Now standing on the deck, they watched the large cruise ship move into its dock.

"I think Patric was definitely the most colorful character on the ship," Brittany remarked. "I'm glad we had dinner there last night, though I still don't understand why you wanted my nipples hidden."

"I'm not sure Patric would have been able to handle a second showing," Duncan said with a wicked grin, "but we'll be repeating the exercise once we arrive in London, I can promise you that."

"I can't wait to get there. I've wanted to visit London for ages, though I wish it didn't take forever."

"We could always stay overnight in L.A."

"No, I'd rather get there, but be prepared. I'll be totally out of it when we arrive."

"I'll be wiped out too, but we can sleep the whole day. We don't have to be anywhere or do anything except—"

"Except snuggle...oops, sorry," she added quickly, "that was a boo-boo. I didn't mean to interrupt."

"I'll pretend you didn't, but just this once. Now we need to get back to our cabins and make sure we haven't forgotten anything."

"I keep forgetting to ask you," she said as they began walking. "Did you know I was with Cooper Cross the other night, or was I imagining things?"

"You weren't imagining anything, though I do have infallible instincts," he quipped. "Simon called me. You should try and track him down before we leave. You owe him a very big thank you."

"Shoot, I wish I'd known. I'll write him a note and give it to Joe to pass along."

"That's an excellent idea. I hope you learned your lesson."

"You don't have to worry. I'm not planning on an encore."

TWO HOURS LATER THEY were waiting for their flight in the British Airways First Class lounge, drinking tea and sharing a snack, when Duncan unexpectedly jumped to his feet.

"I'll be back in a few minutes."

"Where are you going? Is everything okay?"

"Fine. I won't be long. Maybe you should call your parents while I'm gone. You've put it off long enough."

"You're right. I will."

As he marched away, Brittany leaned back in her chair and stared out at the runway, still trying to wrap her brain around the sudden and unexpected turn in her life.

"I'm living a fairytale," she muttered. "Shoot. I really do need to call mom and dad. God only knows what they'll say."

Reaching for her cell phone, she asked the attendant to watch their carry-on baggage, and walked across the lounge to a private phone booth. Placing the call, her pulse ticked up, and when her father answered she felt her stomach churn. She didn't need his approval, but she wanted it.

"Hi Dad."

"Sweetheart, how are you? On your way home?"

"Not exactly."

"What do you mean? Are you staying in Tahiti for a few days?"

"Not exactly," she repeated.

"So—where are you going—exactly?"

"The thing is, I met this amazing man, and before you say anything he's not just some joker. He's an English barrister, a real gentleman, and I'm very happy. He's not like anyone I've ever met."

"Being from Britain I would imagine that's true," her father said slowly. "You say he's a barrister?"

"Yes. He asked me to stay with him in London for a week. He's flying me there, first class. Like I said, he's not some joker, and—"

"Where in London does he live?" her father asked, cutting her off.

"I'm not sure, but I'm really happy. You'd really like him, he's very educated, and he's—"

"I suppose if that's what you want," he said, interrupting again, "but give me his full name. I want to check him out, and let me know his address as soon as you arrive."

"His full name is Duncan Rhys-Davies, that's R-h-y-s, then a hyphen, then Davies."

"You say he's a lawyer?"

"No, dad, he's a barrister. There's a difference. I don't know what that is yet, but he's a barrister and—"

"You're an adult now, you can do what you want, but make sure he treats you right."

"I want to tell you about him," she said, feeling slightly annoyed. "He has—"

"I'm sure he's a very interesting guy, but if you run into any trouble call me right away. I know some people there. I'll let them know you'll be staying a few days, and they'll be there in a hurry if you need them."

"Thanks, Dad, but I'm sure I'll be fine."

"Call us when you get there. Your mother's out right now, but she'll want to talk to you."

"Thanks for understanding, and yes, I'll definitely get in touch when I land."

"All right sweetheart, I'll speak to you then."

"Wait. Dad, when you interrupt it means you're not interested in what the other person is saying, and you don't care about their feelings or opinion."

"I think that's probably true."

"Don't you care about what I'm saying, or my opinions, or my feelings?"

"What? Yes, of course I do."

"Then why did you keep interrupting me. I've been trying to tell you things."

There was a pause.

"You're quite right. I'm sorry sweetheart, you go right ahead. I'm just in the middle of reading a contract, but it can wait."

"Thanks. I think it's important you know how this all happened."

As succinctly as she could, she told him about meeting Duncan in the restaurant, the creepy blonde who kept staring at her during their dinner at the fine dining restaurant, and how Duncan had enlisted the aid of the Sommelier to have the man removed. It wasn't the whole story, but it was enough.

"This Duncan sounds like a decent guy. I'm glad you made me listen. You stay in touch, and email me pictures, okay?"

"Okay, Dad, thank you."

Walking from the booth sporting a happy smile she headed back to her seat, but Duncan had just returned holding a large box. Feeling a flutter of excitement she quickened her step.

"Were you calling home?" he asked as she sat down.

"I was, it went really well, but I'll tell you about that later. What's in the box?"

"A gift for you."

"Heavens," she said excitedly as he handed it to her. Lifting the lid, she pushed aside the tissue paper. "Wow. A Louis Vuitton handbag. This is incredible. Thank you."

"You're welcome, but you need to open it."

Unfastening the snap, she peered inside and saw a small, oval, wooden paddle.

A hot blush flamed across her face.

"It's a miniature Polynesian oar. When we go out together that's the bag you'll carry, unless it's an evening affair, in which case you'll have an evening bag that can accommodate that lovely souvenir."

"Just like Master Jonas! Duncan, I'm speechless."

"Good, then perhaps I'll have some peace on the journey home."

"I don't think it will last that long," she retorted, then laughed out loud.

"That reminds me. Why did you laugh when I first handed you Emily's Education?"

"Should I tell you? Yes. I must."

As she told him the details of her daydream, and described the cover of the book she'd imagined finding in his cabin, he understood how she had won his heart in just a few days. It wasn't just her sparkling eyes, her sharp intellect and her beauty. Brittany radiated her love of life, and it was contagious.

"Why are you looking at me like that?" she asked as she finished the story.

"Because I love you," he said, leaning forward and lowering his voice, "and you've just given me the title and cover for my new book. I must think of a suitable way to say thank you."

"I think you already did," she replied, holding up her new bag.

"What a devilish mind you have. You even daydream your schemes."

"Not anymore."

"You can fantasize your diabolical plots all you want, just don't act on them."

"I won't, not with you, anyway. I think the flight's about to be called. I'm going to make a quick run to the powder room. I won't be a minute."

Though he smiled as she left, his head was spinning. Was she really his second chance at happiness? How would she respond when he took her to the salacious country estate, Andover Abbey? Would she be able to cope with the hustle and bustle of London after living in a small town?

"So many questions," he said with a sigh. "What I'd give for a crystal ball."

THE END

THE STRICT BRITISH BARRISTER

Book Two

LONDON

CHAPTER ONE

THOUGH THRILLED TO be traveling to London with Duncan Rhys-Davies, after nineteen hours in the air she was utterly exhausted. Leaning against his shoulder on their drive into the famous city she could barely keep her eyes open.

"I don't know how you slept on the flights," she mumbled as another yawn swept over her.

"Practice. I can sleep in a courtroom with my eyes open. Did you get any rest?"

"No, not really, and I'm feeling strange. Wired, but absolutely wiped out."

"We'll be home soon, but you should try to stay awake until the sun goes down. It will help you adjust."

"Not a chance," she muttered, yawing again, "but I'm sure I'll sleep until morning."

"I hope you're right. We only have three days before I have to start thinking about going back to work."

"I'll be fine," she assured him, nestling into him and closing her eyes.

As she molded against his shoulder, he thought back to their extraordinary meeting on the ship. Finding a beautiful young woman hiding in his stateroom was the last thing he'd expected, and her obvious desire to be spanked had been even more surprising. In the salacious days that followed, her fervent need to submit had bordered on astonishing. In her sweet, Southern Belle style, she had seduced him as much as he'd seduced her. Unable to call their time together a whimsical shipboard romance and say goodbye, he'd invited her to join him for a week in London. The spontaneous gesture was out of character. He wasn't the spontaneous type. As the car pulled to a stop in front of his house, he withdrew his keys from his carry-on bag. The driver had moved quickly to open the car door, and as she climbed out, he heard her grumbling about needing a shower and a bed.

"I'll open the front door. Please bring the luggage and leave it in the foyer," Duncan said to the driver as he followed her. "I have to pop upstairs, but I'll only be a minute."

"Yes, Sir."

Brittany had already climbed up the steps and was leaning against the door. Hurrying to join her, he unbolted the locks, ushered her inside, and moved quickly in behind her to turn off the alarm.

"Duncan, this is great," she murmured, staring around the foyer. "I really like the black and white tile floor, it's so British, not that I know much about British things, but it looks like pictures I've seen, and television shows too. I'll bet you have really good tea here. Tea and crumpets. I've always wanted tea and crumpets. I'm surprised they didn't have crumpets on the ship. Aren't you supposed to smother them with honey and butter?"

"Brittany, you're babbling," he said with a grin. "Come upstairs with me."

"Do you have a shower in this house?"

"Of course," he replied patiently, noticing she was unsteady on her feet, "but you need to focus on putting one foot in front of the other if you're going to get there safely."

With an arm around her waist he walked her slowly up to the second floor, then guided her down the hallway to the double doors that led into his bedroom.

"Here we are," he declared, pushing them open. "I'll clear out some drawers for you."

"That looks inviting," she muttered, spying the dark mahogany, heavily carved, canopied bed. "It's positively royal, and wow, those are amazing," she added, lifting her gaze to the ceiling beams.

"The sooner you take that shower, the sooner you'll be able to lie down," he said smoothly, moving her toward the bathroom.

"Oh, my gosh!"

Her tired eyes widened as she entered. Staring at the white marble counter, the wide mirror in the ornate silver frame, and the unique bathtub encased in highly polished wood, she let out a small gasp.

"I've never seen anything like this. I don't even know what to say."

"I'm particular, Brittany, as you will learn, but that's a conversation for another time. Towels are in this cabinet," he continued, stepping towards a row of cupboards, "and you'll find anything else you might need in the drawers. Feel free to help yourself."

"You're...um...even more than I thought," she said softly, then letting out a sigh, she added, "Sorry, my brain isn't working very well."

"You poor thing, you're wiped out. I have to deal with the driver. Get undressed and put your clothes in that hamper, then take a shower. I'll join you in a minute."

"Duncan," she said wearily, gazing up at him, "this feels like some kind of dream."

"I hope it's a dream come true."

"It sure feels like it."

"Get undressed, or must I spank you already?" he teased with a grin. "I'm sure you'll feel much better after you've washed away the grime from the trip."

"Spank me? No, I'm too tired to be spanked."

"You may be too tired to be spanked, but I'll never be too tired to do the spanking," he warned, wagging his finger at her, then planting a quick soft kiss, he strode from the room.

Peeling off her clothes, she stepped into the large stall and stood for a moment, slightly bewildered.

"I know I'm not thinking clearly, but what the hell?" she muttered, staring at the chrome holes in the marble walls. "Am I about to be body-sprayed?"

Reaching forward to turn on the faucets, she spied two of them labeled, STEAM. Realizing the shower doubled as a steam room, but too tired to experiment, she turned the regular knobs and hoped for the best. To her relief water splashed over her from a waterfall spout above her head, and closing her eyes, she stood for a moment, relishing the joy of the hot spray. When she heard Duncan return, she wiped the steam off the glass and waved as he began to undress.

"Care for some company?" he asked, opening the door and stepping in.

"That was quick."

"I had incentive," he replied with a grin, taking her into his arms.

"I can't find any soap, or even a spa dish."

"That's because I don't have either, but I do have shower gel."

Reaching past her shoulder he pushed the wall. To her amazement the marble tile turned inward revealing a shelf holding several plastic bottles.

"Here you'll find everything you need. Bath gel, shampoo, conditioner, shaving gel, and what's this?" he said with a frown. "Ah, yes. I bought this just before I left. Lemon-basil Foaming Lotion. I thought it sounded rather appealing."

Lifting the face cloth from the rack behind the products, he pumped out the exotic gel and began to move it across her shoulders.

"I love that smell," she murmured. "Good choice."

"I'm glad you approve. Turn around and place your hands on the wall."

"I...uh..."

"You're not going to start being difficult already, are you?"

"No, no, it's just, I'm so worn out."

"Stop worrying. I'm going to give you a quick wash and put you to bed."

"I've never had a man wash me before. It's weird."

"Everything is weird, as you put it, if you choose for it to be. Behave or I shall make good on my threat and spank you."

"No you wont, you're not that mean," she retorted, though half-heartedly, then did as he said, turning around and resting her palms on the smooth marble. "Mmm, it does feel good," she admitted, as he moved the soft, foamy towel across her skin.

"Of course it does. Close your eyes, take a deep breath and relax."

Moving the soapy washcloth down her back, he slipped it quickly into the cleft between her cheeks, and though she uttered a small cry of protest, he dallied for a moment pulling it away, wringing it out and hanging it back on its holder.

"Poor, tired, girl," he crooned, pumping more gel into his hands.

Rubbing his hands together and creating copious suds, he slid his palms across her breasts.

"That feels good too," she moaned, closing her eyes and leaning against the wall.

Lightly pinching her nipples, he slipped his other hand between her legs to rub her clit, evoking a loud groan.

"As I suspected," he said softly. "You're a passionate soul, Brittany, your body will always give you away. You're wetter than the water dribbling down your skin."

"It's almost as if you know me better than I know myself."

"Perhaps I do," he whispered. "Be a good girl and let yourself go."

Pushing his finger gently into her channel, he sought out the hidden button deep within. Her sudden bleating told him he'd found it, and rubbing her clit with one hand as he massaged the magic spot with the other, he quickly brought her to a shuddering climax. Holding her until she slowly lifted her head, he reached behind her and turned off the faucets.

"Do you feel better?"

"Much, thank you, Duncan, but I swear I could pass out."

"Come on, I'll towel you off."

Taking her hand, he led her from the stall and sat her on the edge of the tub, then began wiping her off.

"There's a hair dryer in the middle drawer," he said, wrapping the bath sheet around her.

"I'm not sure I even have enough energy, to dry my hair I mean."

"Do your best."

"I really do need to sleep. I can't stay up. I just can't."

"All right, Brittany, I'll turn the bed down for you. Hopefully you'll just take a nap and wake up."

Grabbing a towel of his own and wrapping it around his waist, he left the bathroom and ambled across to his bed. As he moved the decorative pillows to a nearby chair, and pulled down the covers, he heard the sound of the dryer.

"You're going to be up at midnight, and be completely washed out all day tomorrow," he muttered to himself. "Ah well, there's nothing to be done about it."

Wandering across to his antique chest of drawers, he pulled out one of his soft, cotton T-shirts, and was about to leave it on the bed for her, when he heard the dryer switch off. A moment later she appeared in the doorway wearing his robe.

"Not a hundred percent dry, but close," she said, padding across to the bed. "Is that T-shirt for me?"

"It is, unless you'd prefer to sleep naked."

"Honestly, I don't care," she sighed, pulling off the robe and crawling between the sheets.

"If you wake up in a couple of hours, try to get out of bed. You really do need to adjust. Going to sleep now isn't the best plan."

"I have to," she replied with a frown, puffing up one of the pillows. "Aren't you joining me?"

"No, I'll finish my shower, then run out to do some errands."

"I don't know how you can stay awake."

"I'll check on you when I get back," he promised, pulling the bed covers over her.

He stood over her as she closed her eyes and rolled on her side, then heading back to the bathroom, he dropped his towel and returned to the stall. Soaping Brittany's gorgeous body and bringing her to a climax had left Duncan with a raging erection. Standing under the steaming water and stroking his rigid cock, he imagined her wrists bound above her head and her nipples clamped. In mere moments he groaned through a powerful orgasm, then leaned against the wall and let out a satisfied sigh.

CHAPTER TWO

THE WEATHER DURING the cruise had been warm and sunny, and though Duncan had enjoyed the tropical conditions, he found it comforting to return to the London drizzle and grey skies. It was May, in the low sixties, and as a few drops of rain splattered against the windows he broke into a smile. He was home.

Dressing in comfortable slacks and a sweater, he moved quietly past his sleeping beauty, softly closed the door, and trotted down the stairs. Grabbing his trench coat from the hall tree, and his umbrella from the antique stand, he headed off to the local shops. After sitting in an aircraft for too many hours he needed the walk, and striding purposefully down the street he thought about the days ahead. He was due back in his office on Tuesday, and assuming Brittany would still be bone-tired the following day, he'd have Sunday and Monday to whisk her around the city. He wanted to share his favorite restaurants, and continue the salacious play they'd enjoyed on the cruise.

"But where do we go from there?" he muttered as he turned the corner and the local shopping area came into view. "I can't think about that. I won't. One way or another things will develop."

Stepping inside the small, family owned grocery, he picked up a basket and began to search out the crumpets.

"Duncan, welcome home," the portly, middle-aged shopkeeper said. "You're so tanned. You must have had good weather."

"Thanks, Charlie, and yes, I did. The sun was out almost the entire time."

"The wife wants to take a holiday to the tropics, but it's so far away. I keep asking her, why travel all that distance when we have France and Spain at our doorstep? What do you think, Duncan? Is it worth the hours in the air and the extra cost?"

"It is for me. Papeete is truly a different world, and when I'm at sea my life here at London feels a million miles away."

"A cruise. I admit that does appeal to me. She keeps talking about that as well. Can I help you find something? You seem to be searching."

"Crumpets!"

"They aren't with the bread. They're on the other side next to the cakes."

"Thanks. Is there a brand you'd recommend?" Duncan asked as he wandered through the aisles.

"I only carry Warburton's. Can't go past Warburton's, at least according to the wife."

LOST IN AN ALIEN DESERT, Brittany wandered aimlessly up and down the pink sand dunes, the sun blazing overhead. Her Chanel sunglasses provided little protection from the glare, and opening her bag, she searched out her bottle of water. Not only did she discover the water bottle was gone, the bag itself was completely empty.

The desert suddenly transformed into a crowded department store. It was hot, there were people everywhere, and she was sure if she couldn't find a place to sit down and have something to drink she would faint. The throngs crowded around her. She couldn't breathe. She was suffocating...

Bolting upright, her eyes popped open. With her heart thundering in her chest, she stared around the strange room in complete panic. A couple of seconds ticked by before she remembered she was in

London with Duncan. Taking a deep breath, she tried to calm herself.

"Man, that was weird, and I'm so hot," she mumbled, throwing back the bed coverings. "Water—I've got to find some water."

Stumbling out of bed, she made her way unsteadily into the bathroom, splashed her face, then dipping her mouth under the spout she let the water flow. Finally straightening up, she stared at her reflection. Her complexion was blotchy and her eyes were red. Wishing she had a bottle of water to leave on the nightstand, and finding no glasses on the counter to fill, she padded back into the bedroom and noticed the T-shirt Duncan had offered sitting on a chair. Tossing it over her head, she started off in search of the kitchen. As she made her way unsteadily down the stairs, she admired the collection of black and white, artfully framed blowups of famous stars from Hollywood's golden era. Marilyn Monroe, James Dean, Humphrey Bogart and Lauren Bacall were among them. Finally reaching the foyer, an elegant living room sat to her left, and a doorway to her right. The closed door stirred her curiosity, just as Duncan's cabin had done during the cruise. Unable to resist, she wrapped her fingers around the brass handle and pushed it down. The door floated open, and peering inside she caught her breath. Standing against the wall like a proud, wooden creature, was an extraordinary piece of furniture.

Slowly moving forward, she stood in front of it and ran the tips of her fingers across the reddish-brown, highly polished, glossy wood. The piece was at least six feet high, the upper half was barrel-shaped, like a roll-top desk, but it was unlike any roll-top desk she'd ever seen. Adorned with heavily carved panels, it also boasted winged horses flanking a finial above a sloped ledge at the top, and intricate carvings danced in front of her eyes wherever they fell.

"It's called a Wooten."

Spinning around, Duncan stood in the doorway holding a bag of groceries in each hand.

"I...uh...I was looking for the kitchen. I woke up dying of thirst."

"And you thought the kitchen would be next to the front door?" he asked, raising his eyebrows.

"Sorry. I'm still a bit out of it."

"As it so happens I'm headed to the kitchen myself. I just picked you up some crumpets."

"You did?"

"I did. Come with me."

Hurrying after him as he walked across the foyer and into the living room, she discovered it flowed into a formal dining room, and a swinging door led into a pristine kitchen decorated in white and grey.

"Are you all right?" Duncan asked, studying her as he placed the bags on the kitchen island. "You look flushed, or is that embarrassment?"

"I'm fine," she replied, "and I guess I deserve that."

"I guess you do, but are you sure you're fine?"

"I do feel strangely hot. In fact, that's what woke me up. I came down to get a glass of water."

"Let me feel your forehead," he murmured, walking across to her and placing his palm on her brow. "Heavens, girl, you're burning up."

"I am? It's probably just the long flight."

"I don't think so. Get yourself straight back to bed. I'll bring you some tea and aspirin in a few minutes."

"Duncan, that's really sweet of you, but—"

"No arguments, Brittany," he said firmly. "You're getting sick. If we're lucky we can nip it in the bud."

A shiver rippled through her, but she wasn't sure if it was his sexy authority, or a chill from whatever was ailing her.

"Okay. I'm going, but what's a Wooten?"

"As you saw, it's a desk, but a very unique one. I'll show it to you later. Now go up to bed. I'll be there shortly."

"Okay, I'm going, and thank you."

"For what?"

"Taking care of me."

"It's my pleasure. Now, scoot."

Moving back through the house and up the stairs, when she entered the bedroom she spied her purse and suitcase. Though still feeling hot and weak, she dug out her soft cotton aqua nightgown and toiletries bag, and carried them into the bathroom. Switching out Duncan's T-shirt for her nightie, she wiped her face with a damp cloth, applied some moisturizer and brushed her hair, but she still looked terrible. Ambling back into the bedroom, she discovered Duncan standing next to his dresser holding a tray.

"How do you feel, Brittany?"

"A bit warm and kind of achy, but I think I was dehydrated."

"Your fever isn't from dehydration. I think you're getting the flu, and we have to stop it before it takes hold."

"You might be right," she said with a frown, touching her fingers to her throat. "I'm getting a tickle."

"I have some soup and aspirin for you, and I'll stay in the guest room until you're past this. No point in both of us being sick."

"I'll stay there. You shouldn't have to give up your bedroom."

"I want you in here," he insisted, carrying the tray over as she climbed back into bed. "Besides, I can't be bothered changing the sheets. Finish this soup and toast, then take the aspirin and the pill. It's homeopathic and very effective. It will stop the bug before it takes hold. I'll be back with a hot cup of tea."

"Thank you, Duncan. I'm so sorry. I can't believe I'm getting sick. What a bummer."

"My goodness, you don't have to apologize," he said gently. "It's unfortunate, but it happens, especially after such a long journey. Not to worry, you'll be good as gold in no time."

"Good as gold," she repeated, managing a smile. "Such a lovely saying. I know you're very strict, but you're also very sweet and thoughtful."

"The two go together, at least with me. Enjoy your soup. I won't be long."

TROTTING DOWN THE STAIRS, Duncan entered his office and moved across to his desk. The magnificent antique had been left to him by his great uncle. It didn't have a scratch or mark on it, and swinging it open, he lowered the writing panel to reveal the many drawers and receptacles. Retrieving a file he wanted to review, he carried it into the living room, tossed it on the coffee table, fired up the fireplace, then headed into the kitchen.

As he set the water to boil, dropped the tea leaves into the tea pot, and the bread into the toaster, he found himself smiling. While it was regrettable Brittany was unwell, there was something charming about her sitting in his bed sipping chicken soup. The toast popped up, and smothering it with blackcurrant jam, he finished making the tea, poured it into a cup, and added the milk and sugar. Carrying the plate with the toast, and the cup and saucer, carefully up to his room, he walked in and found her leaning back on the headboard with her eyes closed. The soup bowl was empty and the pill had been taken. Placing the tea and small plate on the nightstand, he picked up the tray from her lap.

"That was so good," she mumbled, opening her eyes. "Thank you."

"Do you want to go back to sleep?"

"Yes, definitely, but is that tea? I'd love some tea."

Opening the nightstand drawer, he withdrew a plastic bottle and tipped out two small pills, placing them next to the lamp.

"These are Melatonin. If you wake up later and it's nighttime, slip them under your tongue. They'll help you fall back into sleep and regulate your body clock. Try not to worry. I'm sure you'll feel better in the morning."

"I hope so," she said with a sniffle. "I'm so looking forward to running around London with you."

"It will happen, I promise. If you need me, pick up the phone and call my mobile. It will be easier than yelling down the stairs."

"Good idea, but I doubt I will. I'll be going back to sleep the minute I finish this wonderful tea."

"I'll check on you later, and I'm not going to kiss you, but I'll make up for that when you're better."

"You'd be an excellent doctor," she said, gazing up at him. "You have an outstanding bedside manner."

"I thought about going into medicine, but I was worried it would take the romance out of life."

"Funny you should say that. I've often wondered how doctors can be normal around people outside their office. I didn't say that very well. I really do feel muddled."

"Get some rest," he said softly. "I'll see you later."

As he walked out the door she reached for her toast. The sweet, tangy jam melted in her mouth, and washing it down with the hot, rich tea, she slipped under the covers and closed her very tired eyes.

DOWNSTAIRS IN THE LIVING room, lounging in an over-stuffed chair in front of the fire with his feet up on an ottoman, Duncan was reviewing documents of an old case. Reading snatches of legalize for a few days helped his transition back into the heady practice of law, not always easy after writing naughty novels. His client had been accused of embezzling. Duncan had known the man for many years and had been convinced of his innocence. After gathering a team of skilled investigators, the truth had been discovered, and his client and longtime friend had been cleared.

The guilty party had been revealed in a dramatic moment inside the courtroom. It was the stuff of Law and Order. Reading the file again was just what he needed to get his head out of his erotic books and inspire him to return to work, but he was abruptly interrupted. Mozart jangled in his pocket. Retrieving his phone and seeing the name on the screen he quickly accepted the call.

"Jane, lovely to hear from you. How are you?"

"Glad you're back, I missed you terribly. Are you awake enough for dinner later?"

"Of course. The usual place?"

"Perfect, see you there around six. You can tell me all about your trip."

"Excellent. See you there."

He ended the call, then sat for a moment, thinking of Brittany upstairs in his bed. Not wanting to disturb her, he decided to leave her a note on the off-chance she woke up.

CHAPTER THREE

STIRRING FROM A DEEP, dreamless sleep, Brittany rolled on her side and stared at the clock. 7:04 p.m. With a long stretch and heavy yawn, she reached up and switched on the lamp. Her teacup and small plate were gone, and an envelope with her name scrawled across the front was resting in their place. Tearing it open she found a small pill, along with a note.

If you're reading this between 6 p.m and 8 p.m., I'm with a friend for dinner. The pill is another dose of the homeopathic remedy. You need to take it along with the Melatonin. On the dresser are some copies of Horse and Hound that might help you relax and drift back to sleep. I've also left you a sandwich and a glass of milk in case you're hungry. I'll poke my head in when I get back.

L & K,

Duncan.

"You left me a sandwich and a glass of milk?" she mumbled. "You're so thoughtful."

Slipping from the bed, she padded into the bathroom, freshened up, and was about to return for her snack when she noticed a door at the far end with a fluffy mat in front of it. Her warning voice whispered she should think twice before exploring, but her curiosity won out. Turning the handle, she gently pushed, and as the bathroom light splashed into the room, she spied a row of hanging suits and shirts. She'd found his closet! Locating the light switch on the wall just inside the door, she flicked it on.

"Wow, there are closets, and there are closets!" she exclaimed, stepping inside. "This is incredible!"

The room was large and meticulously organized. Running the length of the wall to her left were suits and sport coats arranged by color. Against the narrower back wall, shoes in cloth bags sat in cubbyholes, and at the end of the room on the right was a door which appeared to lead into the hall. To her right were drawers, open shelves, and a floor to ceiling mirror. The crowning glory was an island in the center. Ambling past his suits and shoes, she checked the door. As she'd guessed, it opened into the passage above the stairs. Continuing around the room, she idly pulled open a drawer next to the mirror. A collection of cufflinks sat alongside a bowl of many keys, each sporting a different colored string. She couldn't imagine why he'd have so many, but losing interest, she shifted her gaze to the island. Telling herself she'd have just a quick look, she walked across to the unique piece of furniture, and slowly slid back the top drawer. It was obviously where he emptied his pockets. There were scraps of paper with scribbled telephone numbers, business cards, and odd coins in a dish, but her eyes fell upon a photograph of Duncan with a woman on a snowy mountain. Their skis leaned against their shoulders, they had their arms around each other, and they were both smiling. Turning the picture over she read the notation.

Happy V'day. Love you, Jane.

"V'day? Oh! Valentine's Day! But that was just a couple of months ago."

Peering more closely, she shook her head. The woman was gorgeous.

"I really wish I hadn't seen this," she grumbled. "I knew he wasn't a monk, but shit! He sees this picture every day!"

Regretting the discovery, and wishing she was as beautiful as the girl in the photograph, Brittany carefully put it back and closed the drawer. Letting out a heavy sigh and trying to shake off the jealousy, she was about to leave when she noticed a cabinet at the bottom of the island with three locks running down the side.

"I'll bet the keys in the bowl are to open this!" she exclaimed. "That's so smart! It would take forever to try them all, and only he knows which are the right ones because of the color of the strings."

She suddenly put her hand to her head. A giddy spell had swept her up. Realizing she needed to go back to bed, she returned to the bedroom, stopping at the dresser to pick up the sandwich and milk. Climbing between the sheets, she finished the snack, popped the pill, and dropping the Melatonin under her tongue, she turned off the beside lamp and curled under the bedcovers. As she drifted back to sleep an image of Duncan floated through her mind. He was standing at the bedroom door, his arms crossed and a frown on his face.

"Bratty Brittany, such a naughty girl. On the cruise you poked around my stateroom and were properly punished, but now you've been snooping through my things here. What am I going to do with you? You need to be taught a much stronger lesson. Clearly the first one didn't take."

Not asleep, but not fully conscious, the vision had been frighteningly real.

DUNCAN HAD JUST PAID his taxi and was walking up the front steps. Oftentimes a taxi was more convenient than driving, especially on a Friday night. Though the rain had diminished he was still wet, and stepping inside, he pulled off his trench coat and hung it on the antique hall tree to drip into the porcelain bowl at the base.

The house was quiet. Abruptly overcome with a long yawn, he climbed the stairs looking forward to bed. Reaching the landing, he moved to his bedroom and peered inside. The ghostly glow of the digital clock illuminated the outline of Brittany's sleeping body, but he noticed the glass of milk had been drunk and the sandwich eaten.

Though he could have entered his closet at the end of the passage, he crept across the bedroom to the bathroom to collect his toiletry bag. Gently closing the door behind him, he switched on the light and gathered what he needed, but as he turned to leave, he paused. The white, fluffy mat in front of his wardrobe was out of place.

Moving quickly forward, he opened the door, flicked on the light and looked around. The drawer that held his cufflinks and cabinet keys sat slightly open. Shaking his head, he strode across and pushed it closed.

"Bratty Brittany, what a naughty girl you are," he said softly. "Repeating the sins of the ship? Apparently so. I'll have to give this some thought."

Crouching down at the back of the island, he prodded what appeared to be a solid panel. There was a soft click, and it swung open to reveal a safe. The front cabinet with the three locks was a decoy. If his home was ever burglarized it would draw the thief's attention, but if the perpetrator was successful and managed to open it, they'd be in for a very unpleasant surprise.

Inside was some cash and pieces of paste jewelry, but the jewelry was a booby trap that triggered a spray of purple dye. It was impossible to remove without the necessary solution, and it carried a foul odor. As much as he hoped Brittany wouldn't go so far as to open a locked cabinet, it would certainly teach her a lesson if she did.

Unbuckling his Rolex wristwatch, he placed it carefully next to his other timepieces, then closed the safe door and back panel. Leaving the closet and ambling down the hallway to the guest room, he stripped off and slipped into bed. As he turned out the light, a wicked smile crossed his lips. Brittany would be better soon, and he would enjoy showing her the error of her ways.

IT WAS EARLY MORNING when Brittany woke up. The tickle in her throat was gone and the body aches had passed. Padding into the bathroom, she was about to take a shower when she decided on a hot bath instead. Turning on the water she noticed some bath gel in a glass container on the counter. Dropping in some dollops, she watched it bubble into foam, then moving back to the bedroom she opened her suitcase. She'd packed for a tropical cruise, not damp London weather. Finally pulling out a long-sleeved shirt, some light sweat pants, and a pair of athletic socks that would be comfortable to wear around the house, she carried them with her into the bathroom. Clipping her hair up, she slipped into the tub and sank gratefully into the hot, foamy water.

"Brittany?"

Duncan's voice came with a gentle knock on the bathroom door.

"Come in."

"You look happy," he said as he entered. "You also look a whole lot better."

"I am happy, and I feel great. It must have been those pills you gave me and that wonderful sleep."

"I'm very pleased to hear it."

"Why don't you join me? There's plenty of room in here. You have a very big tub."

"That's an invitation I can't resist," he said, quickly undressing. "Scoot forward. I'll sit behind you."

Climbing in, he separated his legs, and she leaned back against his chest.

"Oh, this is lovely," she purred as his arms came around her. "I could stay in here all morning."

"Your pussy is so wet" he whispered, sliding a hand down her body and exploring her sex, "and I don't mean from the water. Such a randy girl. Randy and naughty."

"Randy?"

"The British word for horny, which I truly dislike."

"I've never cared for it much either. I like randy much better."

"Brittany, turn around to face me, and put your legs around my waist, but be careful," he warned, reaching out to help her.

"This isn't so easy."

"There. You've done it. Now stroke my cock. If you do it well I'll take you to bed and ravage you."

"Ooh, I'll do it well, I promise," she purred, wrapping her fingers around his shaft.

Determined to please him, she vigorously rubbed his manhood as he kneaded her breasts, tweaked her nipples, and occasionally teased her clit. The minutes ticked by, their salacious play bringing them both to a fevered pitch. Just when she was about to beg him to take her to bed, he gripped her wrist.

"Stop. Dry off, go back into the bedroom and wait for me, but I want to find you in a provocative pose."

"Yes, Sir," she replied breathlessly.

Overjoyed, she carefully climbed out of the tub, and hurriedly toweling off she tried to think of a position that would please him. Leaving the bathroom, the pose came to mind. Climbing on the bed, she rested on her elbows and knees, arched her back, and spread her legs wide apart.

"I like it," he announced, finally entering, his turgid cock sheathed in a condom, "but presenting your ass guarantees you're going to feel the sting of my hand. Is that what you want, Brittany?" he asked, climbing on the bed behind her and smoothing his hand over her naked cheeks.

"If it pleases—"

He landed a volley of quick, sharp smacks, cutting her off.

"What do you say?" he asked, teasing her entrance with the tip of his member.

"Ooh, thank you, Sir. Please will you fuck me?"

Clutching her hips, he thrust inside her, and began to pump with strong, slow strokes.

"I'm going to fuck you until you're wailing into that pillow."

"Sir, it won't take long," she gasped, "especially when you say things like that!"

"You'd better ask permission," he said firmly, pausing to deliver several quick, sharp slaps.

"I will, I will."

Basking in the joy of being under his control once again, relishing the same hot intensity they'd shared on the cruise, she buried her head in a pillow and let out a wail. His fingers dug into her skin, his cock accelerated, then he paused to tease her clit. She thought she might faint from the pleasure, and as her orgasm loomed, she looked over her shoulder with pleading eyes.

"Sir," she bleated, "please may I come?"

"Are you sure you're ready?" he asked, sending his hand beneath her to tweak her nipple. "Do you promise to be good?"

"Yes, Sir. I promise."

Clutching her hair, he tugged her head back, and grasping her waist with one hand, he let loose, pummeling her with abandon.

"Come for me now," he commanded, suddenly feeling his climax approach. "Now, Brittany!"

As the delicious tingles sparked through her body, she dove her fingers against her clit, rubbing furiously, hoping to extend the glorious sensations. He continued to pump zealously, and only when the waves of her orgasm began to wane did she hear his groans as his climax shuddered through him. Finally slipping from her depths, he collapsed on the bed. Breathless and drained, she dropped on her stomach beside him.

"Duncan, that was incredible," she panted, snuggling against him and closing her eyes. "You are amazing."

"We, Brittany, we are amazing together," he murmured, and letting out a heavy breath, he joined her, drifting in the post-orgasmic bliss.

IT WAS BRITTANY WHO stirred first, propping herself up on an elbow and kissing him.

"I feel wonderful," she said softly as he opened his eyes. "You fixed me."

"I hope so, but I'm not going to push our luck. We'll stay in today, and if you're still feeling this good tomorrow we'll venture out."

"Are you sure we can't go out today?"

"I'm sure. It's cold and damp. Those pills can stop the flu taking hold, but if you're not careful it could come back."

"You're probably right," she said with a sigh, then pausing, she added, "Um, Duncan, I, uh, there's something I need to confess."

"I'm listening."

"Please don't be mad."

"No promises, but I'll do my best."

"Last night when I woke up, I, uh, I kind of went into your closet."

"Kind of?"

"Sorry. I did go into your closet."

"It's a wardrobe," he corrected her, "and I'm aware of that."

"You are? Why didn't you say anything?"

"I fully intended to, but a naughty, naked, sexy siren lured me into her bathtub."

"I'm so embarrassed."

"That's an improvement," he remarked. "On the ship you were full of excuses for sneaking into my stateroom."

"Are you going to punish me?"

"Of course, but you were honest. I'll be merciful."

"You sound like a King!"

"I am your King, but I won't cut off your head unless you do something really bad, like, burn the toast."

"I'll remember that," she said with a giggle. "Thank you for being so understanding."

"Thank you for telling me. I'm going to rinse off and think about your punishment. I'll be back in a minute."

He climbed from the bed, and as she watched him stride across the room, she felt her heart swell.

"Dammit," she said under her breath. "I'm falling hard. Really hard."

CHAPTER FOUR

OVER A FULL ENGLISH breakfast, which Brittany ravenously devoured, Duncan listened attentively as she chatted about her life back in South Carolina. Taking his last bite, he laid down his fork and studied her, a grave expression crossing his face.

"I've decided on your punishment," he declared. "Your curiosity isn't a bad thing, but you must learn to control your impulses."

His unexpected announcement startled her, and trying to quiet her butterflies, she stared back at him with a pained expression.

"Why do you make me feel ten years old?"

"Probably because you act like a ten-year old sometimes. As I mentioned, your discipline will be less severe because you told me what you did, but Brittany, no more snooping! If you want to know something, just ask."

"You're right. I'm sorry. I could have just peeked inside the door and stopped there."

"Exactly. First, you're going to wash and dry all these dishes. I'll be in the living room working, so you'll have to find your own way around this kitchen to find out where everything goes, though you might enjoy that," he added, raising an eyebrow. "Second, you were so interested in my desk you'll spend the remainder of the morning cleaning it. If it takes longer, so be it. Third, you will, of course, be spanked. Any questions?"

"No," she replied with a sigh, "though it's not exactly how I imagined my first day here."

"You're not complaining are you?"

"Maybe," she replied, with the hint of a grin.

"You are a very cheeky girl, but it suits you."

"It does?"

"Yes, it does. Now start clearing up these dishes, and you need to take another pill. I think I will too. An ounce of prevention can't hurt."

As Brittany began to carry the dishes to the sink, Duncan retrieved the homeopathic medication from his vitamin cabinet.

"One now," he said, handing it to her, "and you should have another one tonight."

"Thank you. Uh, Duncan," she said softly, wrapping her arms around his neck, "do you realize you haven't kissed me since we got here?"

"Yes, I am very aware of that, and I won't, not until I know you're one-hundred percent better."

"This morning you—"

"This morning I was very careful," he said, cutting her off, "but you're probably right. I laid in the sheets you slept in, and you snuggled next to me. I'm probably kidding myself that I haven't been exposed to your nasty germs."

"So...?"

"So, nothing. I'm still paranoid."

"I certainly don't want to kiss someone who doesn't want to kiss me," she retorted indignantly. "Maybe I'll find myself another handsome Londoner to do the honors."

"And maybe I'll kiss your bottom with my wooden spoon. I'm off to start a fire in the lounge. Get to work, young lady."

Disentangling himself from her arms, he moved through the dining room into the comfortable lounge, turned the gas fireplace on high, and retrieved the laptop he'd left charging overnight. Sinking into his easy chair near the fire and listening to Brittany putter in the kitchen, a satisfied smile crossed his lips. He adored her, and in spite of their uncertain future, he was glad he'd brought her back with him. Opening his computer, he clicked into his email, and his happy smile turned into a frown. An endless stream of messages waited a response. Reading each in turn, he deleted those he could, answered the ones needing an immediate reply, and downloaded the rest into their respective files to reply to later. He was almost finished when Brittany entered the room.

"I'm finished!" she declared, then abruptly began to giggle. "I was thinking, why don't you buy me one of those naughty maid's outfits?"

"That is an excellent suggestion," he agreed with a grin. "Will I find the counters clean, the dishes put away and the sink spotless?"

"Yep, it's all done, but when can I go shopping? I know I'm only here for a short time, but I have nothing to wear for this weather, not even a proper jacket."

"I'll see what I can find to tide you over. I should have something to keep you comfortable in the house."

"That would be great, but when we finally go out, I'm not sure what I'll do."

"Point taken. I have a cream cable-knit jumper, or rather sweater as you call it, that should fit. It got caught up in some laundry and shrunk. I planned to give it to a charity shop, but I just haven't had the time. Do you have a pair of nice jeans?"

"Yes! I totally forgot about them."

"Your jeans and that jumper will be find for the place we're having lunch tomorrow."

"Awesome. Where are we going?"

"It's a surprise, and don't you have more work to do?"

"You mean the desk?"

"Under the sink there's a bottle of wood oil. It's clearly marked, and there are clean rags in the—"

"I saw them."

"In the cabinet next to the door that leads into the laundry," he finished, raising his eyebrows.

"Sorry," she said softly. "Yes, I saw them."

"Also in that cabinet is a small, black, square box, and in that square box are some cotton swabs. Grab the oil, rags and a handful of the swabs, and meet me in the office."

"Okay," she said with a smile, then pecked him on the lips. "Sorry. I couldn't help myself."

"You're lucky my computer is on my lap. Scoot."

As she hurried away, he closed his laptop, set it on the coffee table and headed into his office. Making sure the magnificent Wooten desk was locked, he moved to a small closet and he retrieved a handheld vacuum cleaner.

"I have everything," Brittany declared, entering the room.

"Use this to clean the outside," he said, showing her the small vacuum. "It will suck away the dust in the nooks and crannies. After you've done that, take a swab, dab it into the oil, and—"

"Are you saying I have to move a Q-tip into the crevices of all the carvings?"

"Indeed. When I was a boy, taking care of this desk was a great source of pride."

"But it's so big I'll never finish."

"Not if you don't get to work. You can take a tea break in an hour."

"If I survive that long!"

"If at least two of those panels aren't done when I return, you'll be finishing the job with a hot bottom. No slacking off!"

"You're so strict."

"You keep telling me I am, so I suppose I must be," he retorted, but he couldn't suppress his grin. She was a brat and a diva, but she was also the cutest, sexiest girl he'd ever met.

Returning to the living room, he finished his emails, the last one from his publisher asking when he'd be receiving the new manuscript. Duncan answered by sending it off, then made an online reservation at The Crafty Fox, the country pub he planned to take Brittany the following day. It offered delicious food in a comfortable, relaxed atmosphere, allowed horses to graze in the adjacent paddock, and dogs to stay with their owners on the patio. The pub was one of his favorite places to unwind, and he always found it a welcome break. Brittany's hour was almost up, and closing the laptop, he headed into the kitchen to make the tea. Just as he set the water to boil, his phone rang. Lifting it from his pocket, he broke into a smile and accepted the call.

IN DUNCAN'S OFFICE, Brittany stood back from the desk and admired her work. The areas she'd polished were glowing. Not only had the chore been much easier than she'd expected, she'd actually enjoyed it. Wanting to show off her work she ambled into the living room, and though Duncan wasn't there, she could hear him talking in the kitchen. Moving off to join him, as she walked through the dining room and neared the swinging doorway, she caught the tail end of his phone conversation.

"I missed you too, Jane, very much, but don't worry, I'll see you on Monday and we'll work everything out."

The words swirled through her head. Her stomach churning, she leaned against the wall and tried to tell herself not to jump to any conclusions. Except for the picture in the drawer, there was no evidence in the house of a woman's presence. Jane could be anyone, even if the inscription on the photograph suggested she was more than a casual friend. The sound of the whistling kettle broke into her worried thoughts, and doing her best to regain her composure, she moved through the door. Duncan was dropping tea leaves into the pot. Seeing him sent her heart racing. The thought that she might be nothing but a quick, secret fling was almost too much to bear.

"Weren't you supposed to be waiting for me?" he asked, lifting his gaze.

"The desk looks so beautiful I wanted to show you, the top half, I mean," she said haltingly, "and the hour is almost up."

"You've done the top half already? That was fast. Properly I hope."

"Of course!"

"Did you find it tedious?"

"At first, but the carvings are so beautiful I started to feel cleaning such an amazing piece of craftsmanship was an honor."

"You have just made my day," he said with a smile, walking towards her and opening his arms.

She paused. It was a nanosecond pause, but it was still a pause.

"Brittany, is something wrong?" he asked, as she sank against his chest.

"No."

"Are you sure?"

Brittany squeezed her eyes shut, wincing as her insecurities took hold. How could she ask about the photograph in the drawer, or tell him she's just listened to his conversation? She decided she couldn't, at least, not yet.

"I, uh, think I just need a cup of tea."

"You're not feeling sick again, are you?"

"No," she said hastily, "I feel really good. I think it might be a—wow, am I really here?—thing. I'm in London with you. It's a big deal. The reality is sinking in."

"Understandable, and yes, it is a big deal. Take a seat at the table. I have something else that will help put a sparkle back in those eyes."

"You do?"

"Crumpets, with butter and honey."

In spite of her misgivings, a spontaneous smile danced across her face.

"Crumpets? I can't wait."

But as he moved to the island and she sat down, she had the overwhelming feeling he knew she'd just lied. She told herself she had no choice.

"Go ahead, try one," he said casually, returning to the table with the plate of crumpets and teapot. "They really are delicious."

Lifting a crumpet from the plate and taking a bite, she rolled her eyes.

"Oh, wow, I knew they'd be good, but these are incredible. I want one every day for the rest of my life. No, I take that back, I want two every day for the rest of my life. Why don't we have these in the States?"

"That, Brittany, is a very good question."

"Seriously, they are unbelievable."

"I have to agree. I don't eat them often or I'd never stop. I'd turn into a dumpling."

"I can't imagine you ever becoming a dumpling," she said with a giggle. "I'm sure I'll be fine to go out tonight. Can I change your mind?"

"Nope, but I do have something planned. Something I'd like to do very much."

"Sounds intriguing," she said, trying to push her fears to the back of her mind as she devoured the remainder of the crumpet.

"I want to curl up on the couch with you, sit in front of the fire and have a picnic dinner. Wine, smoked salmon, crackers, artichoke dip, all kinds of tasty, sexy things, and talk until we're all talked out. I want to know about your family, what you want to do with the rest of your life, what your dreams are, the places you've visited, and the places you want to visit. Then I want to take you to bed and kiss every part of your delectable body."

She let out a heavy sigh. Her handsome, sexy Brit had just out-lined a night she'd dreamed of since the day they'd met on the ship.

"I would absolutely love that. I want to learn about you too," she murmured, then pausing, she added, "Anything and everything you want to tell me."

"You already know I'm a barrister and write naughty novels, and I know you're a gorgeous creature with an overactive curiosity, but not much else, and that has to change."

Sipping her tea, and gazing at him across the table, she felt her insecurities beginning to fade. Brittany believed Duncan's feelings for her were genuine, and matched her own. But she still wanted to know exactly who Jane was, and she was determined to find out.

CHAPTER FIVE

THE ROMANTIC EVENING had drifted by like a dream. Wearing only comfortable robes, Duncan had fed Brittany a variety of delicious morsels, and over a bottle of velvety red wine they had talked, laughed, and pondered profound questions. Jane's name hadn't been mentioned, and Brittany's concern continued to fade as the evening progressed. When the rain started, adding to the intimacy in the late night hour, she curled into his lap.

"You're like a cuddly kitten," he murmured, running his fingers through her hair.

"If I was a kitten I'd be purring. I never want this evening to end. I know that's a cliche, but I mean it."

"I'm sure we'll make many more memories, and now, my sexy, precious girl, I'm taking you up to my bed."

"What about all this?" she asked, waving her hand at the coffee table.

"That can wait. I have more important things to do."

"It's been such a wonderful night. The food was amazing—the wine—everything."

"It was a wonderful night for me as well," he said, shifting her off his lap and helping her to her feet, "but it's not over yet."

Ambling up the stairs and into the bedroom, he moved behind her, lifted her hair to softly kiss her neck, then sliding the robe down her arms, he let it puddle around her feet.

. "Duncan," she breathed, turning to face him, "I love how you touch me."

A momentary furrow crinkled his brow, then placing his hands on either side of her face, he lowered his mouth against hers, devouring her lips and demanding her response. Their passion ignited, and suddenly pulling back, he scooped her into his arms. The bed was only a few steps away, and laying her down, he fell next to her, moving his lips to her neck, then down her chest to consume her breasts. Moaning her pleasure she reached for his cock, and as her fingers wrapped around him, he lifted his head and let out a low groan. Quickly slipping out of his robe, he pulled off the sash, grabbed her wrists, deftly tying them together above her head.

"I think you need to be reminded who's boss," he growled, darting his lips to her ear. "Leave them there."

"Yes, Sir."

But she'd barely managed the words. The sudden bondage had sent her butterflies fluttering and a flood through her sex. She watched, spellbound, as he kneeled between her legs. Dropping his hand against her pussy, he teased her clit, then plunged his finger inside her soaked channel.

"Who's in charge?" he demanded, thrusting it in and out.

"You are, Sir," she bleated breathlessly.

"Do you want my cock?"

"Desperately."

"Beg."

"Fuck me, please, please, take me, ravage me, slide your cock in me, please, Sir."

Clutching her hips, he pulled her into his pelvis, and placing himself at her entrance he pushed forward. He was taking her, utterly and completely, and she loved it. She loved his power, his control, and his steel will.

"Your body is mine. I'll fuck you as I want. Quick, like this," he growled, pummeling her pussy, "or like this," he muttered, slamming his rod with slow, strong strokes. "In my bed, you belong to me."

His words swirled around her head, words she'd never heard before, words that rang true, words she realized she'd been longing to hear her entire life. As the endless minutes ticked by, he ravaged her ruthlessly, taking her to the brink, then backing off, building her orgasm like a ticking time bomb. She knew it would explode, but when was up to him.

"You've been a good girl," he said huskily, lowering his body on top of her. "Good girls get rewarded."

She wanted to speak, she wanted to thank him, she wanted to let him know how much she treasured his praise, but his mouth was on hers in a crushing kiss, then abruptly he moved his lips to her ear.

"You're going to come now, and it's going to be big. Scream as much as you want."

Straightening up, he gripped her waist.

His thrusts began slowly, but rapidly gathered speed. Her climax rose up inside her, drew closer, then seized her. Electric sparks sizzled through her body, shooting hot, scintillating sensations through her limbs. Wailing her pleasure with each new wave, his lips fell against hers swallowing her cries. Her arms flew over his head and around his neck, her bound wrists urgently clutching him against her, until the spasms waned and she fell limp beneath him. Every part of her tingling, she felt him untie her wrists, then wrap her up in his arms.

"Dream happy dreams," he whispered. "I'll see you on the other side."

As she drifted away, Duncan willed his heart to stop its wild thumping. The splattering of the rain against the windows usually lulled him to sleep, but he couldn't rest. Brittany was unlike any woman he'd met.

WHEN DUNCAN WOKE THE following morning and stared at the clock, he couldn't believe it read 10:32 a.m. Then he could. The jet lag, the bottle of wine, and their long, late night had taken their toll. Feeling Brittany stir next to him, he pulled her into his arms as she groggily opened her eyes.

"I hate to tell you this, but we need to get up."

"No, please, no."

"I promise our lunch will be worth the effort. I'm going to take a shower, but by myself or we'll never get out of here."

"Do we have time for a cup of tea before we leave?"

"Spoken like a native Brit," he said with a chuckle, slipping from the bed and walking across to his dresser. "We'll have a cuppa and some toast, but I don't want to ruin our appetites. The place I'm taking you has great food. Here's the jumper," he declared, taking it from a drawer and placing it on the bed. "You really do need to get in the shower as soon as I'm done."

"I will," she murmured, sitting up and releasing a yawn. "As much as I love being in bed with you, I can't wait to get out and about."

Thirty minutes later they were in his Audi zipping down the motorway heading into the English countryside. The sun peeked through picturesque clouds, and listening to the CD of a local rock band, the miles sailed past. In spite of Jane's lurking shadow, and the unpleasant knowledge Duncan would be meeting her for lunch in a couple of days, Brittany couldn't recall ever feeling so happy.

"We're almost there!" he declared, turning down the volume as he exited the motorway.

"Wonderful. I'm starving."

"That's the fresh country air! We can sit outside if you want. If we're lucky we might be visited by a horse or two. I'm taking you to an old country pub where dogs and horses are welcome."

"That's fantastic. Thank you so much for bringing me here."

"I'm very glad to do it. I try to get to this place at least once a month."

"It's gorgeous out here," she said wistfully, staring at the distant hills. "I'd love to live in an area like this."

"We're almost at the village. I should warn you, the pub is supposed to be haunted, but England is full of ghosts. My parents live in a house that was built in the eighteenth century, and they swear they share it with a little girl."

"Ooh, I just got chills."

"I don't believe it, but there are more things in heaven and earth..."

"That's for sure. Look at us!"

Her spontaneous remark struck him.

"Yes, look at us," he repeated, glancing across at her.

Entering the small country town, he pulled into a parking space, then took her hand as they ambled down the street towards a white building with paned windows, and an overhead sign featuring a laughing fox.

"Why is the fox so happy?" Brittany asked.

"Because he's cunning and always gets away."

"Oh, I like that!"

Duncan pushed open the door, and a robust, middle-aged woman bustled forward to greet them.

"Duncan, how lovely to see you."

"Hello, Doris, this is my friend, Brittany. She's visiting from South Carolina."

"You've come a long way. Isn't it good that the weather cleared for you? Still a bit nippy though. I'll take you to your table and bring you a pot of tea."

Escorting them to a secluded booth, she placed the menus on opposite sides of the table, but as she walked away, Duncan slipped into the bench seat next to Brittany.

"Remember, we're British, so no hijinks," he said with a wink. "Lest you forget, you're still due a spanking."

"I am?"

"You know you are. I don't always deliver immediately, but I always deliver."

Though his comment sent her butterflies fluttering, the photograph of him with the gorgeous girl suddenly burst into her mind. Unable to stand the unanswered question another minute, she decided to take the plunge.

"Duncan, can I ask you something?"

"You can ask me anything, and why do you look so serious?"

"Do you have, uh, someone else, like a girlfriend?"

"Where on earth would you get that idea? Do you honestly think I would have asked you to come here and stay at my house if—"

"Sorry, sorry," she said hastily, cutting him off. "I'm sorry, it's just..."

"Brittany, I thought you understood I'm single. Where did that come from?"

"I, uh..." she began hesitantly, searching for an answer, "you're really good-looking and successful. It's hard to believe you're not attached."

"I'm not," he said firmly, "and since we're on the subject, is there someone special waiting for you back in South Carolina?"

"No, not even close."

"Good, that's settled."

She believed him. His ski bunny valentine was history, but his lunch date with her remained an annoying mystery.

"Here you are," Doris announced, arriving at the table carrying a tray. "I've brought you some scones with whipped cream and raspberry jam. I'm sure Duncan will agree you have to try them."

"I would most definitely agree, and we're in no hurry. I thought we might sit outside for pudding and coffee later. I told Brittany some horses might stop by."

"Oh yes, you must," Doris said earnestly. "The Tottenham's will probably ride in, especially with the sun being out."

"Will you reserve us a table on the patio? What time do you think?"

"They usually arrive around two-thirty. I'll make sure to save you a good spot. Just wave when you're ready to order."

"Thank you, Doris, we will, but you know what I'm having."

"Roast beef, Yorkshire pudding and roasted vegetables!"

"That sounds amazing," Brittany piped up.

"Check the menu before you decide," Doris suggested. "We have quite a few specialities."

"You should pile on plenty of the jam and cream," Duncan said solemnly, reaching for a scone as Doris walked away. "Scones in the States are not scones. I don't know what they are, but they're not scones. Open wide and bite off half."

Sinking her teeth into the soft dough, she let out a moan and rolled her eyes.

"That's unbelievable. I want one of those every day for the rest of my life."

"Along with a crumpet?"

"Yes, along with a crumpet," she replied earnestly, then placing her elbow on the table and resting her chin in her hand, she let out a sigh. "I'm dreaming. Things like this don't happen to me."

"Apparently they do," he said softly, moving his arm around her waist. "I'm wide awake, so you must be as well. Oh, no!"

"What's wrong?"

"I've just snagged my watch buckle on the back of your jumper, or rather, my jumper. Bend over my lap so I can get it off."

"Excuse me?"

"It's the only way I'll be able to see what I'm doing. Lean over."

"But my face will be in your crotch."

"Your face, my crotch," he said with a chuckle. "You won't hear me complaining."

"Duncan!"

"I have to get this thing unstuck! Bend over, but move slowly."

"Good grief, this is so embarrassing."

"Embarrassing would be if I spanked you while you're there."

"Oh, dear God, no!"

"I will if you don't hurry up."

"Okay, okay."

Though initially horrified, she found the absurd situation amusing and began to giggle.

"Are people staring?" she asked, looking at him over her shoulder.

"Absolutely. There's a man two tables away giving me the thumbs up!"

"Now you're just teasing me."

Though it was only a few minutes, to Brittany it felt like forever, and when he finally told her she could sit up, her face was covered with a hot, red flush.

"I need a shot of whiskey," she declared, running her fingers through her hair, "and you should sit across from me."

"I'm perfectly comfortable where I am, thank you."

"Why do you have such a wicked look in your eye?"

"That's classified."

"How reassuring," she quipped sarcastically, shooting him a look as she reached for her teacup. "I can't even begin to imagine."

"You probably could if you tried hard enough," he retorted, sporting a devilish grin, "though you might not want to."

He had just decided a flogging was in her future.

CHAPTER SIX

AFTER ENJOYING THEIR long, leisurely lunch, and promising Doris they'd return for coffee on the patio, Duncan took Brittany's hand and led her outside. The sun was still beaming its warmth, and with a soft breeze wafting around them, they headed down the quaint village street.

"There's an interesting antique store I want you to see," Duncan said as they ambled past the charming shops and gazed in the windows.

"I love antique stores. You never know what you might find."

"Then you'll really enjoy this place. It's like walking into another world."

"Getting away with you is like being in another world," she remarked softly, leaning against his shoulder.

The store was only a few doors down, and as Duncan ushered her inside, Brittany stood and stared.

"This is amazing. Why do I feel as if I should be whispering?"

"I know what you mean," Duncan murmured, leading her slowly through the many collectibles and old pieces of furniture. "Look up there. What do you think of her?" he asked, pointing to a portrait of a beautiful, dark-haired young woman with a mischievous expression.

A chill pricked Brittany's skin.

"Good grief. That could be me."

"She sprang to mind the moment I met you. The likeness is uncanny."

"May I help you?"

As Brittany turned and found an elderly gentleman, her first thought was a Charles Dickens' novel, but when their eyes met, he caught his breath.

"What can you tell me about that painting," Duncan asked, gesturing to the portrait, "and how much are you asking for it?"

Though the man quickly composed himself, his surprise remained evident.

"I'm afraid I don't know much," he replied. "I've been meaning to research the artist, but I'm not very good with the computer. I believe he's French. May I say," he continued, moving his eyes back to Brittany, "you bear a remarkable resemblance."

"That is why we must come to terms," Duncan said solemnly.

"I quite agree," the man said with a nod, and still staring at Brittany, he murmured, "Extraordinary, quite extraordinary."

A price was quickly negotiated, and they left with the painting carefully packaged. Depositing it safely in the car, they hurried back to The Crafty Fox. True to her word, Doris had kept a table open for them on the patio, and Brittany was delighted to discover three horses grazing in the paddock across the fence.

"This is wonderful," she exclaimed. "I can't believe I'm in a restaurant next to horses. I absolutely love this."

As Doris delivered dessert—flaky pastry filled with custard, coated with melted chocolate and topped with a scoop of vanilla ice cream—Brittany let out a sigh and shook her head.

"This is too much, I'm sorry, Duncan, but I have to live here. I'm leaving South Carolina and moving into this pub. You can visit me on weekends."

"That would work," Duncan said with a poker face. "I'll arrive on Friday, make mad, passionate love to you all weekend, and deliver your weekly spanking on Sunday night. Speaking of which, you won't be spanked when we get home."

"You've changed your mind?"

"Oh, no, I haven't changed my mind. I won't be spanking you, I'll be introducing you to my flogger."

"S-sorry, what did you just say?"

"You heard me. Finish your pudding. I'll be back in a minute."

"You can't just leave after saying something like that."

"Of course I can. I won't be long."

As he rose from the table and disappeared inside, the people who owned the horses entered the field. Brittany watched as they tacked them up and climbed on for the ride home.

"Ready?"

She turned and looked up at him, then shook her head.

"I'll never be ready to leave this place, and I want that dessert every day for the rest of my life."

"Of course you do," he said with a chuckle.

Sighing heavily she pushed back her chair and stood up from the table.

"You're actually going to flog me?" she asked in a breathy whisper.

"Yes, I'm actually going to flog you."

"I don't know what to say."

"You don't have to say anything, you just need to know it's going to happen. Come on. We need to hit the road."

Leaving the pub and walking to the car, Brittany's butterflies fluttered in her very full stomach, and settling into her seat, the pending discipline consumed her thoughts.

"Is the flogger because I went into your closet, sorry, wardrobe?" she asked as he climbed behind the wheel.

"Not because you went in, but because you opened my drawers. I'm also going to paddle you for keeping me waiting this morning."

"Paddle me? It was only five minutes."

"Five minutes, five swats," he said calmly.

She remained quiet as he pulled away from the curb, but as he drove through the village, she reached across and touched his arm.

"Duncan, sorry to ask, but have you brought other, uh, people here?"

"My sister, Catherine, I've brought her here, but no-one else."

"I don't know why it's important, but I'm glad," she said softly. "This was one of the best days of my life."

"It's not over yet, and for the record, I'm glad too. I loved every minute."

THOUGH BRITTANY ATTEMPTED to calm her nerves on the drive home she had little success, and as Duncan turned down his street, then rolled the Audi into his garage, her heart began to beat like a bass drum.

"I'm not going to take you out to sea and make you walk the plank," he remarked, turning off the engine and sending her a warm smile.

"No, you're just going to take a paddle and a flogger to my backside!"

"Actually, a flogger then a paddle, and your look of dread will not change my mind. You deserve it. I would have thought you'd learned your lesson on the ship when I spanked you for breaking into my stateroom."

"I didn't break in, I sneaked in."

"Semantics. Get inside or I'll add a few extra swats with a very special hairbrush."

"Just how many of these lethal weapons do you own?"

"Stick around a while and you'll find out."

He climbed from the car, retrieved the painting, and headed to the door that led into the kitchen. Though it took her a minute, she grabbed her bag and followed him in.

"That shoulder bag, what do you keep in it? I've never understood about women and their bags."

"I feel safer having everything with me, and it's not just a shoulder bag, it's a Ralph Lauren Shopper."

"It's quite beautiful. Make sure you don't leave it anywhere."

"Not a chance. This bag is my third arm."

"Go up to the bedroom and take off your clothes. I have to turn off the alarm."

"You want me to wait for you completely naked?"

"Yes, Brittany, completely naked."

Pulse racing as she climbed the stairs, she entered the bedroom, and thinking it might help to calm her nerves, she decided to take a quick shower. As she foamed the lemon-basil gel in her hands and rubbed it over her body, she thought about the moment she'd first seen Duncan on the ship. She'd been captivated by him.

"I still am," she mumbled, rinsing off and stepping from the stall.

Quickly rubbing herself dry, she ran a brush through her hair, then wrapped a towel around her chest. Taking a deep breath, she closed her fingers around the door handle, paused for a moment, then opened the door. To her delight the bedroom was bathed in candlelight, but then she saw a thick rope hanging from one of the thick ceiling beams. With a fresh wave of nerves she moved across to the bed, only to find a pair of fur-lined, leather shackles and a blindfold. Her stomach flipping, she picked up one of the cuffs and ran her fingertips across the soft lining.

"Sit on the edge of the bed," Duncan instructed, walking up behind her.

Startled, she turned around and found him wearing only black shorts, the bulge of his rampant cock clearly outlined.

"Sit on the edge of the bed," he repeated. "Drop your eyes and stretch out your arms."

Keeping her gaze to the floor, she did as he directed, and her heart racing, she watched his feet take the last few steps towards her. He stopped, ran his fingertips down her arm leaving goosebumps in their wake, then reaching past her, he picked up the leather manacles. As he slipped the first around her wrist and buckled it closed, she felt her thumping heart skip. When he added the second, a warm flood washed between her legs.

"Close your eyes."

She paused, then lifted her gaze to stare at him for one last second, wanting to memorize how he looked in the candle's flickering light before squeezing them shut. Her breathing had quickened, and as the soft foam pressed against her cheekbones, she almost smiled. She loved being blindfolded.

"I've changed my mind. You'll be paddled first for being so willful," he whispered, his lips against her ear. "Then you'll meet the thick, leather tongues of my flogger."

A surge of energy fired through her body, and as he brought her to her feet, for a moment she couldn't find her balance, but his arm moved around her waist and he guided her forward.

"I don't believe we need this," Duncan muttered, tugging off the towel. "Are you ready?"

"Yes, Sir," she said with a quiver, though not sure she was.

"I'm going to raise your arms and attach your wrists to the rope."

Though she felt oddly removed from the reality of what was happening, when he finished securing the cuffs, she could hear the sound of the rope sliding across the wood above her head, the tinkle of the chrome rings on the cuffs where they touched, and Duncan's measured breathing directly behind her. The paddle and flogger were about to punish her backside. Taking a deep breath, she anxiously waited.

WHEN BRITTANY'S ARMS were above her head and almost straight, Duncan wound the rope around the leg of the heavy dresser against the wall, securing it with a slip knot. His implements sat on top, including a pair of nipple clamps and a glass of ice. Picking up the oval-shaped paddle, he stepped behind her and lightly tapped it on her cheeks.

"Brittany, are you listening?"

"Yes, Sir."

"These are your rules. You will not speak without permission. If you feel faint or distressed, your safe word is red. Clear?"

"Yes, Sir. My safe word is red."

"You may wriggle and you may cry out, but no shrill screaming. Do you have any questions?"

"No, Sir."

"Open your mouth."

She parted her lips, and he placed the paddle's leather handle between her teeth.

"Bite down, and don't let go."

As she bit into the soft leather, he smoothed his hand over her bottom, then landed a hot slap, quickly followed by another. Falling into an easy rhythm, his palm bouncing unrelentingly across her backside, he knew she'd find a strange solace in the leather handle between her teeth.

"Nicely warmed up," he muttered. "I'll take the paddle now."

Wiping the handle on the towel she'd worn from the bathroom, he began fondling her breasts.

"I nicknamed you Bratty Brittany because you truly can behave like a spoiled brat," he declared, tweaking her nipples. "I have no issue with you wandering the house, but to open drawers? No! That crosses a line and deserves the appropriate punishment. Do you agree?"

"Yes, Sir."

"You sound sorry."

"I am, Sir."

"Are you sorry because you got caught, or sorry for being a nosy parker?"

"Being a nosy parker. I felt guilty, Sir. That's why I confessed."

"My paddle will spank away your guilt. If you hadn't told me, you'd get a dozen swats, not the six you're about to receive."

"Thank you, Sir."

"After each swat you'll say, I deserve another, Sir. I was a naughty nosy parker," he instructed, sliding the paddle over her cheeks. "Do you understand?"

"Yes, Sir."

"Are you ready?"

"Ooh, yes, Sir."

He delivered the first smack, adding enough force to offer a biting sting.

"Ow, ow. I deserve another, Sir, I was a naughty nosy parker."

"I agree," he said sternly, landing the paddle on her opposite cheek.

"Ow! I deserve another, Sir, I was a naughty nosy parker."

"You certainly do deserve another. Going through my drawers! Shameful!"

As the hard swat landed on top of the first, she stamped her feet and let out a squeal.

"Permission to speak, Sir?"

"Do you deserve another?"

"Yes, Sir."

Duncan had to smile. It was not the first time a misbehaving female had attempted to pause her discipline by asking permission to speak. He struck the paddle harder, evoking another stamp of her feet.

"Ooh, ow, I deserve another, Sir, I was a naughty nosy parker."

"And what happens to nosy parkers, Brittany?"

"They're punished, Sir."

Dispatching the paddle with an upward flick of his wrist, he whisked it against her sit spot. She wriggled as she wailed, but quickly blurted out the phrase,

"I deserve another, Sir, I was a naughty nosy parker."

"I'm not sure that was sincere," he said slowly. "You were in a hurry and want this to be over. Say it again, and mean it. "

Brittany cringed. There was no fooling him.

"I deserve another, Sir," she repeated. "I was a naughty nosy parker."

Moving to her opposite side, he snapped the leather paddle upwards and caught the bottom of her cheek. She let out a howl, then a deep groan.

"A well punished bottom, that's what your snooping cost you, and now I'll leave you to suffer through that hot sting. I'll be back in a few minutes."

"Permission to speak, Sir?"

"Very well."

"Thank you, Sir," she mewled. "It was very wrong of me, and I'm glad of the discipline."

Her softly spoken words touched him, and moving his arms around her, he dropped his lips to her neck.

"What a good girl," he crooned, kissing and nuzzling the sensitive skin. "Are you saying you learned your lesson?"

"I did, Sir, I really did, and I'll never give in to temptation like that again."

Moving his hands to her scorched behind, he began to rub away the burn.

"I wasn't going to do this for a few minutes, but I believe you're truly sorry," he said tenderly.

As she felt herself melt against him, she wanted to whisper the three magic words, but she couldn't quite get there.

CHAPTER SEVEN

LEAVING WITH A WHISPERED promise to return with a surprise, he had brought back a glass of ice. Taking a cube and sliding it over Brittany's burning bottom, though writhing as she gasped in shock, the soothing chill evoked a grateful moan.

"Precious girl," he whispered, softly sucking her neck as he slipped his fingers into her pussy. "You are positively dripping."

Moving another ice cube across her breasts making her catch her breath, he popped it into his mouth and sank his lips around her nipples. To the sound of her utterances of surprise and pleasure, he drew in her puckered cherry tips, sucking and twirling the cube until it completely dissolved.

"I have another surprise for you," he whispered, pinching her nipples in quick succession. "Don't go anywhere."

She let out a strange bleating sound as he quickly retrieved the clamps, and holding her tit flesh firmly in his hand, he placed the first at the base of her nipple and slowly released.

"Ooh, Sir, Sir..." she panted urgently. "Please, Sir, what is that?"

"I should scold you for speaking without permission, but I know you're devoid of thought right now," he murmured, moving on to her second breast to repeat the process.

She moaned loudly, and he knew she was aching for his touch between her legs. Answering her unspoken plea, he cupped her sex, then slid his middle finger deep inside her drenched pussy. As she let out a cry of joyous relief, he began thrusting it in and out and thumbing her clit.

"Sir, Sir, I'm close," she panted, writhing against his hand. "Please, Sir, may I come? Please, Sir?"

"You reached your orgasm so quickly," he remarked, withdrawing his hand. "How have you survived without this in your life?"

"Sir, I don't know."

But her frantic, impassioned reaction had fired his own fever. Pulling off his boxers, he tossed them aside, then stepped back to savor the exquisite sight. Her luscious body shone in the glow of the candles, drips of water glistened where the ice had melted, and he could glimpse the erotic dew between her thighs. He softly stroked himself, but only for a moment.

The flogger beckoned.

Retrieving it from the dresser, he draped the long, leather straps over her shoulder, letting them slink across her breasts, then moving to her side, he glided them away and lightly flicked them against her bottom. Hearing a short gasp, he flicked them again, but with a little more energy, but the third time he swung his arm, her soft wail filled the room. To his utter joy, she thrust out her backside for more. Raising the flogger, he swished the tongues through the air, delivering them across the center of her cheeks. He waited for the wail, the cry, the moan, but she was silent. Worried, he moved quickly to her side.

"Brittany?"

"Please," she whispered, "please don't stop, Sir, I beg you."

Her ardent plea sent fresh energy coursing through his loins. Clutching her hair, he jerked it back, and sinking his lips on her mouth, he kissed her with dark, rabid hunger.

"My precious girl," he growled as he broke away. "You fill me with fire. I want to devour every inch of you."

Stepping back and lifting the flogger, he snapped it against her bottom. Her deep howl echoed through the dimly lit room. Walking slowly from side to side, flashing the flogger every few seconds, her yowls transformed into a single sound, changing in pitch and volume but never ceasing. When he finally lowered the whip and stepped behind her, smoothing his palm over her radiating backside, he placed his mouth against her ear.

"Talk to me."

"I...feel...weak...I need you."

Thrusting his fingers into her pussy, he was met with an avalanche of moisture, and a long, deep moan.

It was time.

Moving in front of her, he held her breast and opened the first clamp. She whimpered. Gently rubbing the bud to relieve the sharp pain, he moved to its twin, but as he took it between his fingers, she bleated out an odd whimpering sound.

"What is it?"

"They hurt, but the hurt feels so good."

"How have you lived without this?" he asked again. "You poor, starving girl."

"I don't know. I've been so frustrated for so long. I never thought..."

She stopped short, swallowing hard. He knew she was fighting a swell of emotion. Her call had finally been answered, and not only was she filled with relief and gratitude, he guessed she probably couldn't believe it, perhaps even afraid to.

"I'm here now," he murmured, slipping off the blindfold. "Look at me. The lonely hours of frustration are over."

Their eyes met, glimmering in the candles' flickering flames.

Time stood still.

His fingers clutched her hair.

"Dammit, Brittany," he muttered, a deep frown crossing his brow, then dove his mouth on hers.

Smoldering feelings surged to the surface, and their urgent kiss expressed what lived in their hearts. Swept up in the all-consuming moment, their tongues danced, their muffled moans echoed through the room, until longing to hold her properly, he broke away to unbuckle her shackles.

"Make sure you lower your arms very slowly," he warned, but she fell against him, and immediately scooping her up, he carried her to the bed, placing her on her stomach. "Are your shoulders cramping?" he asked, gently kneading them.

"No, Sir, but your massage feels amazing."

Little by little he moved her arms to her sides, all the while rubbing her muscles to make sure they didn't spasm.

"Please, hug me," she suddenly begged. "I need you to hug me."

Stretching alongside her, he was about to hold her when she abruptly shifted to her side and placed a hand at the back of his neck. Pulling him into a kiss, she clung to him, pressing her body against his.

"Please, Duncan," she begged breathlessly, gazing up at him, "please make love to me?"

Moving her on her back, he quickly sheathed his engorged member, rested on top of her, and allowed his cock to find its way into her hot, wet channel. He stayed buried for a moment, relishing the feel of her, then began thrusting with slow, strong, powerful strokes. Their gaze locked, her fingers were digging into his arms, and as he accelerated, she let out a fervent wail.

"I'm there! Please say yes."

"Yes."

The single word was all he could manage as his explosive climax shuddered through his loins. Groaning in unison, the convulsions gushed through them until the last spasm waned. His flaccid member slipping out, he fell next to her, utterly drained.

BRITTANY HADN'T FELT him roll off her body.

Brittany was somewhere else.

Brittany was soaring.

She was floating high above the Earth in a magical world.

The mountains were purple and pink, and covered with a shimmering golden haze.

"Come back to me, precious girl."

Though she could hear the voice of her beloved Duncan, she didn't want to leave the serene, mystical heaven, but she could feel his hands stroking her body, and his lips kissing her face and neck. She tried to blink, but her eyes were so very heavy, then without warning, they popped open.

"There you are," he purred. "You had me worried for a minute."

"I was in the most amazing place. It was like a dream, but it wasn't a dream."

"You were in subspace. I promise I'll explain everything to you in the morning, but now you need to sleep."

"I do," she murmured, "I'm so tired."

Pulling the covers over them, he hugged her into his chest and let out a heavy sigh.

"What was it Bogart said in Casablanca?" he muttered softly. "Of all the gin joints in all the towns in all the world, she walks into mine. Brittany Carter, of all the ships cruising all the oceans of the world, you walked onto mine."

SHE WASN'T SURE WHAT stirred her from the deepest sleep she'd ever known, but as Brittany slowly pulled herself awake, she became aware of Duncan's hand on her shoulder. Rolling on her back, she found him standing beside the bed.

"You've been out of it all morning," he said, leaning down and giving her a hug.

"That was the best sleep I've ever had in my life, and I don't think it was because I was recovering from jet lag."

"I don't think so either. I've brought you a cup of tea, and toast with marmalade."

"That sounds divine. What time is it?"

"Almost ten-thirty. That's why I woke you. If you want to go out, you need to start getting ready."

"I definitely want to go out," she replied, slowly sitting up and letting out a yawn.

"Then drink your tea. I found another jumper, and a pair of black slacks still in their dry cleaning bag. I dug out a parka as well. They're Catherine's. She has a few things in the spare room in case she stays over. I've left them on the chair next to your suitcase."

"She won't mind me borrowing them?" Brittany asked, reaching for the tea cup on the nightstand.

"Of course not, Catherine's a peach. I can't wait for you to meet her."

"Last night was like an amazing dream."

"You were incredible."

"Me? I didn't do anything."

"You did everything, more than I ever expected."

"You'll have to explain that."

"I will, but right now I have to make a couple of calls. Come down when you're ready, but try not to take too long."

Kissing her gently, he headed downstairs to his study.

Though he had no desire to make the call, he needed to contact Nigel Chamberlain, his Head of Chambers. Being a Q.C., Duncan carried a great deal of responsibility, and Nigel would be waiting to hear from him. Picking up his landline, Duncan reluctantly punched in the number.

"Good to have you home," Nigel began. "I trust you're ready to jump back into the fray."

"Absolutely," Duncan lied.

"We can expect you tomorrow, I trust. Booted and suited and ready for bear."

"Yes, Nigel, of course."

"Excellent. I'll see you for breakfast at the club around eight-thirty."

"I may be meeting with a new client," Duncan said hastily, thinking on his feet.

"That's what I like to hear. Who is he?"

"A referral. I don't know much myself at this point."

"Then I'll see you in chambers."

"Yes, you will, Nigel. Goodbye."

Putting down the receiver, Duncan stared at the phone. He'd just told a blatant lie to his Head of Chambers. Standing up, he thrust his hands in his pockets and began to pace.

"That tea and toast hit the spot," Brittany declared.

Looking up, he saw her standing in the doorway dressed in the forest green, turtleneck sweater, black slacks, and her long hair falling around her shoulders. She took his breath away.

"Wow, you are beautiful, Brittany. Huh. I like that. Beautiful Brittany, your good twin."

"So Bratty Brittany is my evil twin?"

"Exactly," he murmured, walking across to hug her. "You look so ravishing I want to take you back upstairs."

"Don't tempt me. By the way, I took my dishes to the kitchen, washed them and put them in the cupboard."

"Aren't you a good girl," he said with a wink. "Do you need anything else before we go? Unfortunately I have a lunch obligation, but I don't plan to eat very much. I want to take you to an early dinner at one of my favorite restaurants."

The mention of his lunch date sent a shadow across her heart.

"That's a shame," she said, hoping she sounded casual. "Do you think you'll be very long?"

"Not if I can help it. I'll drop you at Harrods and let you shop. I'll probably be about an hour."

"How will we meet back up?"

"I'll ring you, or you can ring me if you want, but just in case something unexpected happens I'll give you a key to the house," he said, stepping back to his desk and picking up an envelope. "It's in here, along with the address in case you forget, and instructions for the alarm. I'll have to go into the office tomorrow, so you'll be able to come and go as you please."

"Great. Thanks."

"Do you have Catherine's parka?"

"It's hanging on the coat rack by the back door. I assumed we'd be taking your car."

"Yes, we will. I'll bet you're looking forward to shopping at Harrods."

"So much," she said with a forced grin. His lunch with the mysterious Jane was all she could think about.

Reaching the garage and climbing into the car, unsettled and not sure what to do with herself, she pretended to rummage through her bag.

"Back to work for me tomorrow," Duncan remarked with a grimace, backing out onto the street. "I hope you won't be too bored."

"I should buy one of those naughty maid's outfits. I can clean the house all day and you can imagine me doing it."

"I'd never get any work done."

"Is your lunch with a client?" she asked innocently.

"I'm meeting Catherine. I would have invited you, but it's not just a casual get-together."

"Really? Catherine?"

"But you will meet her soon, and that's a promise."

"I'd like that," Brittany replied, fighting the desire to demand an explanation.

"Brittany, are you feeling all right? You seem on edge, or am I imagining things?"

She couldn't answer him. Consumed with confusion and filled with anger, she was afraid to speak.

"Brittany?"

"What? Sorry," she muttered, "I was just thinking about gifts I should buy for mom and dad."

"To be honest," he said quietly, stopping at a traffic light, "I hate the thought of you leaving."

His comment brought a lump to her throat, and staring across at him, a wistful smile crossed her face.

"To be honest, I do too."

But with heat filling the back of her throat, she wondered how she could believe a single word he said. He wasn't meeting his sister. He was meeting Jane.

CHAPTER EIGHT

DUNCAN HAD BOUGHT THREE hours of parking close to Harrods. It was an extravagance, but taxis could be a hassle, and he had thoughts of driving Brittany around the busy city after lunch. Holding her hand as they strolled towards the famous department store, he couldn't shake the feeling something was bothering her.

"Here you are," he declared, stopping at one of the many entrances. "A million square feet of shopping space."

"Good grief. Will I get lost?"

"You might," he said with a grin. "Beware of the food court. There are way too many scrumptious treats."

"Thanks for the warning."

"I'll call you on my way back and you can tell me where you are."

"Ah, good suggestion."

"Bye, Beautiful Brittany," he murmured, pulling her into his arms and hugging her warmly. "Try to behave yourself."

"I'll try, but I can't promise," she replied, fighting the temptation to add a sarcastic comment about the lunch he was having with his beautiful valentine.

"I'll take your confession later," he said with a wink, then turned and began walking down the street.

She was about to step inside the store when out of the blue, an idea floated into her head. She could follow him. She knew it was bad, very bad, but she needed answers! Staring after him, trying to think of a way to prevent from being seen if he should look over his shoulder, a tall, heavyset man wandered by. Falling into step behind him, to her dismay Duncan turned the corner. Though she prayed her cover would follow, the large man continued straight ahead. Pausing her step, she peeked around the building. Her eyes picked up the flash of Duncan's trench coat as he crossed the street. Waiting until he was further down the block, she continued her pursuit, but keeping pace wasn't easy. He was a swift mover, and she was almost out of breath when she saw him enter a jewelry store. Darting inside a restaurant on her side of the street, she ordered coffee in a take-away cup. Grateful for the respite, she kept watch through the front windows as she sipped her drink, but when a cab stopped directly in front of the jeweler blocking her view, she thought she'd have to risk stepping outside.

She was not prepared for what happened next.

As the taxi pulled away, Jane stood on the footpath, appearing even more glamorous than her picture.

Brittany watched helplessly, her heart breaking, as Duncan stepped from the jewelry store and opened his arms. Jane moved into them, they hugged, then to Brittany's horror, they started across the street towards her. Panicking, she hurried to the counter and asked if there was a powder room.

"Yes, madame," the young waitress replied. "Through the dining room to the back door and across the courtyard. You can't miss it."

Pulse racing, she walked swiftly past the tables, opening the back exit to find an artfully decorated courtyard with dining tables. Darting towards the ladies room on the opposite side, she'd just entered when she heard the sound of Duncan's voice. Quickly closing the door, she leaned against it and caught her breath. Finally gathering her wits, she discovered the powder room was just as beautifully appointed as the restaurant and the patio. The counter was marble with a brass sink, over which hung a large, ornate mirror, and a small couch sat against the wall. But she also noticed a high window overlooking the courtyard. Standing on her toes, she peered through the glass. Duncan and Jane were in clear view, and to her relief, Duncan's back was facing her, but she couldn't believe her eyes as he produced a small, black velvet box and presented it to the beautiful Jane. The gorgeous woman lifted the lid, pulled out a ring, placed it on her engagement finger, and jumping from the table, she threw her arms around his neck. Stumbling backwards, Brittany caught herself just as she was about to fall, and staggering to the small couch, she flopped down and clutched her stomach.

"No, no, it can't be true," she sobbed, copious tears springing from her eyes. "What a total fool I've been. All those things he said were just bullshit. I've been played. Totally and completely played."

Flooded with heartbreak, she covered her face with her hands. When the bitter sobbing began to pass, she stumbled to the wash basin, splashed her face with water, and stared at her reflection.

"I'll go back to his house, pack my suitcase, but then what? I can't just go out to Heathrow and pray there's a seat available. Claridges! That's where I'll go. They can make my travel arrangements for tomorrow. I'll have an amazing dinner, then get plastered at the bar."

Satisfied with her plan, she took a deep breath and began to repair her makeup, but when her phone jangled, her heart stopped. Taking a deep breath, she decided what to say, then lifting it from her bag, she accepted the call.

"Hello, beautiful Brittany. Have you enjoyed yourself?"

"Sure, yes," she managed, moving to peer out the window.

"I'm on my way back to Harrods. It's about a ten minute walk. Where are you?"

His table was empty.

"I'm in the food court. I couldn't resist. Meet me there."

"The food court's a big place. Where exactly?"

"Tell me where you want me, and I'll find it."

"The sushi bar."

"Okay, I'll see you there."

Ending the call before he could engage her in any further conversation, she rushed through the courtyard, but slowed her pace in the dining room. Stepping outside, peering up and down the street and seeing no sign of him, she hailed a cab.

"Where to Madame?"

Fishing in her bag she found the envelope, pulled out the paper with his address, and read it to the driver. As the taxi headed down the block, she fought back a sudden wave of emotion. She didn't want to shed another tear over him, but she couldn't stop the heavy droplets spilling down her face.

STANDING IN THE BUSTLING food court, Duncan's worry grew. Brittany was not by the sushi bar, nor anywhere else he could see. Pulling his phone from his pocket, he typed a quick text.

In food court by Sushi. Where are you?

Waiting impatiently, he stared at the screen.

Nothing.

His frowned deepened.

"Damn and blast. I knew you were on edge," he grunted. "What the hell happened, and where are you?"

His phone beeped.

A response.

Both relieved and anxious, he opened the message.

Pet department.

Confused, and sure something wasn't right, he set off. The only pet department was a small concession on the second floor called Mungo and Maud. Striding briskly through the store, he arrived at what was left of the once-famous, Pet Kingdom. Brittany wasn't to be found, but he wasn't surprised. Grabbing his phone, he was about to text her again, but changed his mind and called her. Her phone went straight to voicemail.

"Brittany, please call me and tell me what's going on. Obviously something is horribly wrong. Where are you? I'm very worried."

Exasperated, he headed to one of his favorite haunts. A bar that offered a quiet lounge where he could nurse a drink and ponder the strange turn of events. Stepping outside, he was met by an unexpected, blustery wind. Glancing at the sky, grey clouds threatened. Thrusting his hands in his pockets, he strode forward, but just as he reached the bar his phone beeped. Anxiously retrieving it, he opened the message.

Not much fun, is it, being led on a merry dance that takes you nowhere? The gig is up, you bastard. I saw you and Jane. I'd wish you and your future bride a happy life, but I'm not that forgiving. God help that poor woman. You missed your calling. You should be an actor. You gave me an Oscar winning performance!

As if the Gods were underscoring the moment, a clap of thunder roared overhead and the skies opened up. Frustrated and angry, he pushed through the door, marched into the lounge, pulled off his coat, and dropping into a chair he typed his reply.

Whatever you THINK you saw, you jumped to the wrong conclusion. I'm not marrying anyone, I'm not engaged, and everything that happened between you and me was real. I can explain about Jane. I'm at The White Carriage. It's a bar near Harrods. I'll be here for an hour, then I'll go home.

Watching the message disappear, he slumped in his seat.

"You look like you've had better days."

Looking up he saw Daphne, a waitress who had served him many times.

"Without a doubt. I need a drink, but I need something hot."

"Irish Coffee!"

"Perfect, with a double shot. Thanks."

Dropping his phone on the table, his head swirled with questions. Why had she followed him? She'd been upset in the car, but from what? And how did she see him give the ring to Jane? The courtyard had been virtually empty.

"Are you so obsessive you followed me? Is that possible?" he muttered. "I didn't get that feeling from you, but if that's how you are, that's not good. That's not good at all."

"Your coffee, sir."

Startled, he looked up.

"Why so formal?" he asked, as Daphne placed the mug in front of him.

"We have a new manager. He told me I'm too friendly with the customers."

"That's ridiculous, and I need a friendly face today."

"Why are you so worried? I don't think I've ever seen you like this."

"I've hurt someone, someone very special, but it was...well, the thing is...she was somewhere she shouldn't have been, and she saw something she completely misunderstood."

"That's too bad. My mother always says the only way to fix something is to talk, but then you have to listen."

"Those are wise words. Tell your mother thank you."

"I hope it all works out, Duncan," she whispered, then in a regular voice, she added, "Let me know if you need anything else, sir."

It made him smile, and as he watched her walk away he felt calmer. Picking up his coffee he took a sip, then sighed, as the warm, comforting liquid slid down his throat.

BRITTANY HAD TOLD THE taxi driver to wait. Fighting more tears, she'd thrown the few things she'd unpacked into her suitcase, then hurried back to the cab and directed the driver to Claridges. Now in the small office that served as the check-in counter, her eyes puffy and red, she tried to avoid the sympathetic look of the impeccably dressed clerk. His kindness made keeping her composure even more difficult.

"I'll only be here a couple of nights," she managed, "and I'd like a small suite if you have one."

"I do, but I'm going to upgrade you to our Mayfair Suite. I'm sure you'll find it most comfortable. There's a butler on the floor. Might I suggest our crumpets—"

"Crumpets?"

"Yes, they're excellent, as are our scones—"

"With cream and raspberry jam," she muttered, the lump at the back of her throat burning with a white hot heat threatening to suffocate her.

"Yes, that's how I like them too."

Pain shredding her heart, she couldn't stop the large tears falling from her eyes, and landing with a silent plop on the top of the wooden counter.

"I'm so dreadfully sorry," the young man said, his brow crinkling. "I didn't mean to upset you."

"It's not you," she sniffled. "I'm the one that's sorry."

"My name is Harry Guilford," he said warmly. "If there's anything I can do..."

"I just need to g-get to my room," she stammered, silently adding, *but if you have a needle and thread, perhaps you can stitch up the huge hole in my heart.*

"Yes, of course. Everything's in order. Do you have just the one piece of luggage?"

"Uh-huh."

"Here is your key. Your suitcase will be delivered to your suite momentarily, along with some refreshments compliments of the hotel."

"You've been extremely kind," she mumbled, finally lifting her eyes to meet his. "I really am very grateful."

"If you need anything, ring down and ask for me, Harry Guilford. Perhaps you should visit our spa. We have an excellent masseuse."

"Thank you. I might do that."

She was about to suggest he call her Brittany, but a porter appeared, and with a slight nod of his head, he announced he'd be showing her to her suite. Picking up her bag, she followed him through the elegant foyer to the lift, and when she was ushered into her suite, the room took her breath away. For a fleeting moment Duncan took a back seat, but as the porter explained the various amenities, her thoughts returned to Duncan, and how much she wished they were in the beautiful room together.

"Will there be anything else, madame?"

"Uh, yes. Where would you suggest I go for a drink later?"

"There's The Fumoir, decorated in a 1903s theme, or Claridges Bar, very beautiful with a huge chandelier. They offer a light menu if you care for something to eat."

"Thank you," she said, reaching into her bag and retrieving a five-pound note. "You've been most helpful."

"Thank you very much, madame."

As he left and closed the door, she carried her bag into the bedroom and pulled out her cell phone. Dropping on the bed, tired and filled with despair, she stared at Duncan's text. She'd read the message as she'd entered the check-in office, but she'd been so upset she'd barely processed the words.

Whatever you THINK you saw, you jumped to the wrong conclusion. I'm not marrying anyone, I'm not engaged, and everything that happened between you and me was real. I can explain about Jane. I'm at The White Carriage. It's a bar near Harrods. I'll be here for an hour, then I'll go home.

She read it through several times, then placed her phone on the nightstand.

"Wrong conclusion?" she muttered angrily. "I saw what I saw. You gave her a ring, and she put it on her finger!"

Swinging her legs off the bed, she stood up, ambled into the bathroom and stared at the tub.

"A long hot soak, and maybe I won't wait until tonight. Maybe I'll get totally plastered right now."

CHAPTER NINE

SITTING IN HIS EASY chair, sipping a large scotch in front of the fire and listening to the rain splash against the windows, Duncan had never felt so out of sorts. Idly glancing around the room, he noticed the portrait of Brittany's eighteenth-century lookalike leaning against the wall waiting to be unpacked.

"Now is as good a time as any, I suppose," he muttered, placing his glass on the side table and pushing himself out of the chair.

Ambling across the room and picking it up, he carried it into the kitchen, cut the string and ripped off the protective wrapping. The dark-haired girl stared at him, whimsy flickering in her eyes.

"It's astonishing how much you look like her. Damn and blast, Brittany, what have you done to me, and where the hell are you?"

Taking it back to the living room, he propped it up on the sofa, and picked up his scotch.

"Here's to you, Bratty Brittany," he declared, raising his drink, "and of course, you too, Beautiful Brittany. Why did you follow me? We should be enjoying an early dinner in a lovely restaurant. No! You should be here and over my knee getting your glorious bottom spanked. I'm living a Shakespearean tragedy, and I think I might be slightly drunk."

Leaning forward, he studied the artist's name.

"F. Benoit. Let's see if there's any information about you and this lovely creature you painted."

Retrieving his laptop, he settled back into his easy chair, and typed in the artist's name. There were many results, but he clicked on the headline that read, Francois Benoit, Biography and Best Known Works.

Francois Benoit - 1853-1892.

Though famous for his depictions of life in the French countryside, in later years Benoit turned to painting portraits of the French nobility, most especially, the love of his life, Babetta Babineaux. Their relationship was reportedly tempestuous, but nonetheless, he went to his grave calling her, fille Précieuse.

"Fille Précieuse? That's precious girl!" Duncan breathed, a sudden chill pricking his skin.

He thought back to the night before, how she had thrust out her bottom for the flogger and cried out her euphoria. For years he had hoped to find a woman who would respond as she had, and who would touch his heart.

"I miss you," he murmured under his breath. "This house feels empty without you."

Reaching for his phone, he opened up her message.

Not much fun, is it, being led on a merry dance that takes you nowhere? The gig is up, you bastard. I saw you and Jane. I'd wish you and your future bride a happy life, but I'm not that forgiving. God help that poor woman. You missed your calling. You should be an actor. You gave me an Oscar winning performance!

Something wasn't right, but he couldn't put his finger on what was bothering him. Going through it again, the answer continued to elude him, and he decided to read it out loud.

"Not much fun, is it, being led on a merry dance that takes you nowhere? The gig is up, you bastard. I saw you and Jane. I saw—Jane!" he exclaimed. "How did you know her name was Jane? I've never mentioned the name Jane."

Suddenly sober, he jumped from his chair and began to pace.

"How, Brittany? How did you know her name? I need to clear my head. A shower. I'll take a shower, then eat. The answer is right in front of me, I can feel it."

Grabbing the portrait, he carried it up the stairs and into his bedroom and placed it on the chair near the window. With one last look, he moved into his wardrobe to undress, but opening his top drawer to clear out his pockets, he saw the photograph. Picking it up, he turned it over and read the scribble.

V'day, love you, Jane

"Oh, for pity's sake. You saw this and assumed she was, or is, my girlfriend. Dammit, Brittany, I want to hug you and kiss you and spank you all at the same time. But how did you know I was meeting her for lunch, or did you just follow me out of curiosity? Regardless, I have to find you. I don't know how, but I must."

PERCHED ON A STOOL inside the dimly lit Fumoir bar, Brittany was on her third Kir Royal Champagne Cocktail. Flirting with Keith, the handsome bartender, had helped to distract her, but she'd read Duncan's message yet again. With a frustrated sigh, she placed her phone on top of the bar, trying to decide if she should call him.

"I think I need one more of these," she mumbled, pushing her glass towards the barman.

"I'm pleased to make it for you, but may I suggest you have a bite to eat?"

"A bite to eat," she repeated. "I haven't had anything to eat all day. Wait, that's not true, I had a piece of toast and marmalade this morning."

"Toast and marmalade? That's it? All day?"

"Yep, that's it, all day, and it's been the worst day of my entire life. I don't want to talk about it, any of it, but may I ask you something?"

"Be my guest."

"Do you have a girlfriend?"

He laughed out loud, then nodded his head with a grin.

"Yes, I'm spoken for, but thank you. I'm immensely flattered."

"Oh, no, I didn't mean that," she sputtered. "I was asking as a general question."

"My apologies. Yes, I do. Her name is Priscilla."

"Okay, great, perfect. If you were somewhere you shouldn't be, and saw Priscilla doing something horribly wrong, and she told you later she could explain, what would you do? Did that make any sense?"

"I think so. Would I give her the chance to explain what I thought I saw, even though I was somewhere I wasn't supposed to be? Is that what you're asking me?"

"Yes, that's it exactly."

"Definitely. Do you know how many people are convicted for crimes they didn't commit?"

"Huh, I hadn't thought about that. Maybe I should call him."

"It's usually a good idea to give people the benefit of the doubt. Aren't we innocent until proven guilty?"

"This is just one big mess," she said, throwing up her hands. "I don't know what to do."

"Have some dinner. I'm sure it will help to clear your head."

"Your friendly bartender is probably right."

The comment came from behind her, the voice mature and upper-crust. Turning around she found a dapper, grey-haired man with a neatly trimmed mustache and glasses, wearing an elegantly tailored three piece suit.

"Hello, I'm Charles Rutherford," the man said with a smile. "I don't have anyone to dine with this evening either. It's not much fun having dinner by one's self."

"Are you staying here?" Brittany asked, wondering if he was someone important. He looked and acted like an upper-crust English gentleman.

"I am."

"Me too. Nice to meet you—Charles? That's what you said, right? Sorry, but I'm just the tiniest bit buzzed."

"Yes, Charles, like our Prince. No apology necessary. May I ask your name?"

"Brittany."

"Nice to meet you too, Brittany. I don't suppose you'd care to join me for dinner, would you? No strings, of course. Just two ships passing over a dining table. We can chat about your dilemma, whatever it might be."

"I don't want to chat about it."

He paused, then said,

"Chat about what?"

For a moment she was confused, then abruptly understood the joke.

"Ha! Very good," she said with a giggle, and slipping off the barstool, she reached for her bag. "I'd love to have some company. Thank you. Bye, Keith. Maybe I'll come back for a nightcap."

"I'll be here."

"That's a large purse you have," Charles remarked as they ambled off.

"I carry it everywhere. I like to have it with me so nothing happens to it. I don't trust safes in hotel rooms."

"Very wise."

Feeling lightheaded as they moved through the foyer, she looped her arm through his elbow.

"I hope you don't mind. I'm not myself tonight."

"I don't mind at all. I take it you're visiting from America."

"South Carolina, and I feel as if I've been gone for ages, but it's only been a couple of weeks."

"Brittany, I've just had a thought. There's a charming little French place around the corner. The food is simply marvelous. What do you say?"

"That's a splendid idea. Isn't that what you say here? Splendid?"

"It is," he said with a chuckle, guiding her through the lobby towards the doors.

"I might need my coat."

"It's only two minutes away, not even that, and I have my brolly if the wet stuff starts up. Are you game?"

"Absolutely," she exclaimed as they stepped outside. "This cool air feels so good."

"I agree, but we should walk a little faster so you don't get chilled."

"This is fun. I'm so glad I ran into you. Does this restaurant have sole? I love Sole Almondine."

"They do, but if you're at loose ends tonight, does that mean you're staying at Claridges by yourself?"

"Sadly, yes. I was on a cruise and met the most wonderful man, but it's become complicated. I thought I'd made a terrible mistake, but now I'm wondering if it was me who made a terrible mistake! Wait, what did I just say? That came out all wrong. My head is all fuzzy. I'm not feeling very well. Are we almost there?"

"Yes, but it will be faster if we go through this alley," he said, quickening his pace and turning off the main street. "I know the owners. We can enter through the kitchen and I'll introduce you to the chef. He's a friend of mine."

"I hope it's not far. I'm starting to feel really cold."

"No, it's not far. You'll soon be eating that Sole Almondine. The kitchen entrance is just around here."

They turned a second time, but they'd reached a dead end.

"Where is—?"

A blinding pain suddenly sliced through the side of her head. Tumbling to the ground, she hit rough, wet concrete.

"Charles, help me."

But her whimpered cry received no response. Bewildered and overcome, it took her a few minutes before she struggled to sit up, and gingerly touching her head, she knew before she studied her fingers they were wet from blood.

"Charles...?"

But she was in cold, empty darkness. Fighting panic as she scrambled unsteadily to her feet, she staggered to peek around the corner. Though the alley was empty and foreboding, like a beacon of hope, she could see the busy street. Darting her eyes to the ground, she searched for her bag, then realized the man had lured her down the dark lane to rob her. Shaking from cold and fear, tears cascading down her cheeks, she stumbled through the alley, her hands scraping against the rough side of the building as she grabbed at it for support. Finally reaching the street, she lurched towards the hotel wondering if she'd make it, but the alert doorman recognized her immediately and rushed down the street to help her.

"My goodness," he said urgently, removing his coat and placing it around her shoulders.

"He hit m-my head," she managed. "He hit m-my head and t-took my b-bag."

. "You're safe now. I've got you," he continued, placing an arm around her waist. "We'll take care of you. Don't worry."

"I'm so g-glad you s-saw me," she mumbled, shivering and sobbing as she leaned against him. "C-can you f-find Harry G-Guilford?"

"I certainly can," the doorman replied, moving her through the lobby and into an office. "He's still on duty. I'll get him here right away."

He sat her on a couch, and as she wrapped her arms around herself, she heard him call Harry and order a pot of tea.

"That silver-haired man you left with, did he do this?" the doorman asked, sitting next to her.

"Yes. M-my b-bag. It has m-my money, p-passport, everything."

"What's happened?" Harry asked, bursting through the door.

"She was attacked," the doorman replied, rising to his feet. "I've got tea on the way."

"Thank you, Thomas. Good man. Ring the doctor and the police, and fetch a blanket. Don't worry, Miss Carter," Harry continued, sitting next to her. "A cup of tea is on its way. My goodness, what a state you're in."

"Tea, it f-fixes everything," she blubbered. "That's what you s-say here, right?"

"We do, and it does," he said warmly. "Is there someone you can call? Do you have any friends here?"

"M-my phone. I just remembered, I left it on the counter in the bar. The Fumoir. There is someone. A f-friend, he's a b-barrister."

"I'll fetch it for you," the doorman said, handing Harry a blanket and taking back his jacket still around Brittany's shoulders.

As he headed out the door, a young woman arrived with a pot of tea and a plate of pastries.

"I'm so terribly sorry this happened to you," Harry said softly. "We do our best to keep our eye out for predators, but they can slip past."

"It's not your fault. It's me. I'm so stupid sometimes."

"Here, have a sip of hot, sweet tea, it will help," he said tenderly, pouring her a cup. "It's a medicine unto itself."

Hands shaking, Brittany took the cup, and sipping the comforting drink, her thoughts were consumed with Duncan. She didn't care about Jane, or the explanation, or anything. She just needed him to be there with his arms wrapped around her.

SITTING AT HIS KITCHEN island, Duncan had just finished a bowl of tomato-basil soup and a toasted cheese sandwich when his phone rang. Staring at the screen, his heart skipped.

"Brittany, I'm so glad to hear from you."

"Uh, excuse me, is this Mr. Rhys-Davies?"

"Yes," Duncan replied, his heart leaping a second time. "Why are you on Brittany's phone? What's happened?"

"My name is Harry Guilford. I'm an assistant manager at Claridges. I'm calling for Miss Carter. She's all right, but she's been the victim of an assault and is asking for you. Can you—?"

"I'm on my way."

CHAPTER TEN

HASTILY RUMMAGING THROUGH the contents of Brittany's bag, Bert Willis, aka Charles Rutherford, couldn't believe his luck. Not only did he find a wad of travelers checks and a slew of credit cards, he discovered an envelope containing a piece of paper with a high-end address, along with a key, and what was obviously an alarm code. Starting up his 1994 Volvo sedan, he headed off, but knowing where it was he had two concerns. Parking, and making his score before the girl reported her assault to the police. As soon as that happened, the alarm code and locks would be changed.

But lady luck smiled on him a second time.

As he cruised past the house, an Audi backed out of the garage and sped away. It appeared the home would be ripe for the picking, then reaching the end of the block, someone left a parking space on the opposite side of the street. His tires squealed as he spun his car around, and quickly slipping into the tight spot, he let out a grateful sigh.

"This was meant to be, but I've gotta hoof it. Fifteen minutes and I'm out."

Realizing he had nothing to carry any ill-gotten gains, his eyes fell on Brittany's bag. Tipping it upside down and shaking out the contents, he jumped from his car and walked swiftly to Duncan's front door. The key slid easily into the lock, and moving inside he saw the alarm box, but it wasn't beeping.

"In too much of a hurry to set it? Ha!"

Seeing the living room on his right, the stairway in front of him, and a closed door to his left, he chose the door. Walking in and flicking on the light, his eyes fell on the antique Wooten desk. He let out a whistle.

"I've gotta get some boys and come back for this!" he declared, then immediately began rifling through the many shelves, alcoves and drawers, pocketing a Mont Blanc pen, a sterling silver letter opener, and a check book. Looking around the room to make sure he hadn't missed anything, he noticed a cricket bat mounted in a glass case on the wall.

"What have we got here?" he murmured, stepping closer. "Ha! Jackpot time. This I've gotta have."

The bat carried the autographs of celebrated players from the sixties, and as he read the names he shook his head in disbelief.

"Frank Misson, Dennis Amiss, Ian Redpath, blow me down. Does that say Butch White?"

Running his fingers along the bottom of the glass case he found a latch. Pressing it gently, it popped open. Lifting the bat from its holders, he carried it to the door and rested it against the wall ready to pick up on his way out, then swiftly made his way up the stairs. The double doors at the end of the hallway beckoned. Hurrying forward and entering the bedroom, his eyes fell upon a stunning portrait of a beautiful young woman. He paused. She looked remarkably like Brittany, but it couldn't be her. The painting was clearly an antique.

"Too big and awkward to move, but I'll come back for that one day. Now where's the bloody wardrobe?" he grunted, scanning the room. Walking quickly into the bathroom, he spied a fluffy mat at the base of a door. Striding across and pushing it open, he broke into a grin. "I knew it!"

Moving inside and stepping up to the square, wooden island, he slid open the top drawer and stuffed his pockets with the loose change, bank notes, and a gold money clip, but as he closed it, he spotted the cabinet with the three locks.

"Well, well, look at this. What a joke. My six-year old nephew could pick those."

Reaching into the inside breast pocket of his jacket, he pulled out an item he carried with him at all times. A zippered leather wallet containing the tools of his trade. Selecting a long, thin, steel rod, he played with the top lock.

"You beauty," he said with a chuckle as the lock clicked open.

The second was equally cooperative. He checked his watch.

"One to go, then I have to sling my hook, but I know there's stuff in here, and I'm not leaving until I get my hands on it."

DOING HIS BEST NOT to panic, Duncan swerved through the London traffic, coming to an abrupt stop in the front of the hotel. Anticipating his arrival, Thomas had kept the area clear, and quickly escorted Duncan through the foyer to the office where Brittany was waiting. Duncan had to swallow back his shock. Totally disheveled, pale and traumatized, she was giving her statement to a police officer, and a doctor was closing his bag.

"Duncan! Thank God you're here," she whimpered, her eyes brimming with fresh tears.

"I'm Harry Guilford," Harry announced, stepping up to meet him.

"Thank you for everything you've done," Duncan said, quickly shaking his hand, then moving to sit next to Brittany. "My poor girl," he murmured, putting his arm around her shoulders. "You're shaking."

"Excuse me, sir," the police officer said politely. "If you could just give me another minute, I'm almost finished."

"Yes, of course, my apologies."

"Miss Carter," the policeman continued, "how tall was he?"

"Not overly tall. Probably five-eleven."

"Is there anything else you can tell me about this man? Anything at all?"

"One thing did just occur to me. He smelled like I do when I leave a salon. The scent wasn't cologne. It was more like hair spray."

"Thank you, Miss Carter. I'm going to speak with the bartender. If you think of anything else please call the station," he said, offering her a card. "I have your mobile number. I'll be in touch when we have something to report."

"Do you think you'll catch him?"

"There's a good chance. Try not to worry."

"Doctor, how is she?" Duncan asked as the policeman left.

"Very fortunate. I'm Doctor Blake, by the way."

"Duncan Rhys-Davies. Nice to meet you, and thank you for coming."

"Brittany, you have no concussion, and except for a headache you should be fine. Take a couple of these if you need them, and keep those scrapes on your hands clean."

"You can give them to me," Duncan said, reaching for the pill bottle and the doctor's card. "I'll be taking care of her."

"Good. She shouldn't be alone, and don't hesitate to get in touch if there are any problems."

"Thank you very much," Duncan said, rising to his feet. "Please send your bill to me. Here's my business card."

As Harry escorted the doctor from the room, Duncan sat back down and brought Brittany into his arms.

"You poor thing. When we get home you need to tell me how this happened to you."

"I should never have left the hotel with a stranger," she whimpered. "I'd been drinking. I wasn't thinking straight. This is a nightmare. My bag had all my stuff. My money, my passport, everything."

"Nothing that can't be replaced, but it may not come to that. You heard the policeman. He sounded confident this thug will be caught."

"Miss Carter, I'm so dreadfully sorry," Harry declared, walking back in. "This should never have happened. The security of our guests is a top priority. We have CCTV in and around the hotel. I'm sure this chap, whoever he is, will be apprehended very quickly, and the hotel will find a way to make this up to you."

"Please call me Brittany. From the moment I arrived, you've been amazing."

"Will you be staying? I can arrange—"

"Excuse me for interrupting," Duncan interjected. "Brittany will be coming home with me, right, Brittany?"

"Yes, definitely, yes."

"Then please allow me to have your suitcase packed and brought down," Harry offered, then taking a breath, he added, "I don't mean to overstep, but may I say, I'm so pleased this horrible ordeal appears to have ended happily."

"Yes, thank goodness," Brittany replied with the shadow of a smile. "I can't say I'm glad it happened, but I'm very grateful with how things have worked out."

A SHORT TIME LATER Brittany's suitcase arrived, and Harry escorted them out to Duncan's car, but before Duncan pulled out into traffic he reached for Brittany's hand. Holding it gently, he brought it to his lips.

"My precious girl, I've been so worried."

"Are you very angry?"

"I was, but now I'm just incredibly relieved, and I can't wait to get you home."

"Duncan, I believe what you said in your text, and I'm sorry. I jumped to the worst possible conclusion."

"You should never have witnessed what you did. When you're feeling better I'll explain the whole thing, then you can tell me what happened tonight," he said, releasing her hand and pulling away from the curb.

"There's nothing much to tell. I'd had three glasses of champagne, and I know that doesn't sound like much, but I'd had nothing to eat all day and the alcohol went straight to my head. Anyway, this very well-dressed man came up and asked if I'd like to join him for dinner. I was so upset and muddled, I said yes."

"But how did you end up in an alley?"

"He said it was a short cut to a French restaurant, and we could go in through the kitchen because he knew the owner and the chef."

"If you didn't have a bandage on the side of your head, I'd tan your gorgeous bottom."

"Yes, I know," she murmured. "I was stupid."

"You must be starving, or has the drama killed your appetite?"

"I don't feel hungry, but I feel shaky. Maybe not eating is one of the reasons."

"I'll rustle something up. Maybe soup and a crumpet. How does that sound?"

"That sounds wonderful, and I'm desperate for a shower."

"I'm sure you are," he said, slowing down and turning into his garage. "That's strange. The lights are on in my office. I didn't go in there when I came home." Closing the garage door behind him, he was about to climb from the car when a disturbing thought crossed his mind. "Brittany, where's the envelope I gave you, the one with my address and the key?"

"It was in my...oh, no! My bag. Does that mean—?"

"Do you have that card the police officer gave you?"

"Yes, right here," she said, pulling it from her pocket.

"Get in touch with him, tell him you're in the garage at my house, and the man who attacked you might be inside. I'm going to pop my head in and see if I hear anything."

"Duncan! No! Wait for the police to arrive."

"I'm just going to step in the hallway. Ring him and stay put."

As he left the car and disappeared into the house, she grabbed her phone and placed the call, only to discover she had no signal. Quickly climbing out, she walked around holding the phone in the air, but having no luck, she opened the door a crack and peered down the hallway. Everything was quiet. His office was the closest room, and creeping down the passage, she moved inside and locked the door behind her.

NOT HEARING ANYTHING when he'd entered the house, Duncan had poked his head in the office. With the display case open, and the cricket bat leaning against the wall, he didn't know if the thief had left it behind or was still in the house. Stealthily climbing the stairs, he entered the bedroom just as Bert successfully opened the decoy cabinet and discovered the cash and jewelry.

"You little beauty! I knew I'd find something in here!" Bert exclaimed.

Duncan froze.

"Money and a diamond necklace! I knew it would be worth the—aargh! What the fuck? My eyes. My bloody eyes."

Knowing the intruder had tripped the booby trap and been blasted with the dye, Duncan darted into the bathroom and looked through the open door. Bert was scrambling to his feet, his face purple, his eyes squeezed shut, and his arms flailing wildly. Though the door from the wardrobe into the hall had no lock, the door leading from the bathroom did. Creeping up and closing it, he pushed in the button at the back of the handle.

BLINDED AND STUMBLING around in search of something to wipe the stinking mess from his eyes, Bert happened to stagger against a row of hanging shirts. Feeling the soft cotton fabric, he wiped it urgently across his face. He was finally able to squint, and desperate to splash his eyes with water he headed for the bathroom.

"Why is this locked?" he growled, pulling on the handle. "Bloody hell, did I lock it? I don't even remember closing it."

He'd dropped his wallet of tools in front of the cabinet, and as he turned to fetch them, he noticed the second door. Lurching across the small space, he was relieved to find it unlocked.

Duncan waited on the other side, but Bert was a tough, career criminal. As he entered the hallway, Duncan tried to push him against the wall, but in spite of his stinging eyes, Bert plunged his fist into Duncan's stomach. Doubling-over and toppling to the ground, Duncan tried desperately to breathe, while Bert bolted down the stairs, but as he reached the foyer he realized he'd left behind Brittany's bag with all his takings.

He paused.

"It's not smart to mess with a country girl from South Carolina."

Spinning around, he saw his pretty, petite victim swinging the cricket bat. Before he could react the heavy wood landed between his legs.

Letting out a roar of pain, he grabbed his crotch and fell to the floor.

"If you fucking move I'll flatten your balls into pancakes and stuff them up your ass."

Staring at him rolling on the floor in abject agony, she knew he wasn't going anywhere, and desperately worried about Duncan, she threw the bat aside and raced up the stairs calling his name. Reaching the landing and hearing a groan, she turned and spied him curled up on the carpet.

"Duncan, oh, my, God, Duncan," she said breathlessly, running to his side. "Are you okay? What did he do?"

"My phone. Call Catherine," he managed, his voice a hoarse whisper, then suddenly grabbed her arm. "Brittany, please don't go back next week."

But the sound of sirens interrupted them, and seconds later the police burst into the house.

"We're up here," she called, "at the top of the stairs."

"I want you to stay," Duncan panted. "Brittany, I love you."

"Duncan," she murmured, her eyes filling with tears, "I love you too. I love you so much it hurts."

CHAPTER ELEVEN

CATHERINE WAS STRETCHED out on her couch having a glass of wine and watching television when her phone chirped. She loved birds, and her ring tone sounded just like her budgies. Muting the television and lifting it off the side table, she was slightly alarmed to find Duncan's name on the screen. Rarely did he ring her in the evening.

"Hi, I hope everything's all right."

"Is this Catherine?"

The voice was soft and feminine.

"Yes, who's this? Why are you ringing on Duncan's phone?"

"He asked me to call you. My name is Brittany Carter."

"Brittany? Yes, he's mentioned you. Has something happened?"

"He'll be fine, but he was attacked and taken to the hospital. The police are driving me there now."

"Attacked? Oh, no. Where? How? Which hospital?"

"Mercy General. He ran across an intruder in the house."

"Tell him I'll be there shortly, and thank you."

Catherine hurried to her bedroom to change. Duncan wasn't just her older brother, he'd been her protector and confidant throughout her life. When they were children, he was the one who would comfort her when she scraped her knee. He helped with homework through school, and offered sage advice when she began dating. Jumping in her car and zipping through the traffic, she pulled into the emergency parking area and jogged across to the entrance. Pushing through the doors, she immediately spotted a police officer and an attractive, dark-haired young woman deep in conversation.

"Excuse me, I'm Catherine, Duncan's sister. Are you Brittany?"

"Yes," Brittany replied, rising to her feet and staring at her in shock.

The beautiful woman calling herself Catherine looked exactly like Jane.

"How is he?"

"He'll be fine," Brittany managed, completely bewildered.

"I'm Sergeant Jeffries," the police officer interjected. "He was punched in the stomach. We thought it best to have him checked out."

"Absolutely. Can I see him?"

"He'll be out in a few minutes," the officer replied. "Brittany, as I was saying, I'll return your things as quickly as possible. It shouldn't take too long."

"Thank you for everything. I'm so glad you arrived when you did."

"Just doing my job, and now I'd best be going, I have loose ends to tie up before I can call it a night."

As he strode from the waiting room, Brittany sat back down, and Catherine settled in the chair next to her.

"It looks like you've been hurt too," she remarked. "That's quite a bandage on the side of your head, and your hands are scraped up. What happened?"

"It's a long story and I'll explain, but first, may I ask, do you also go by the name Jane?"

"My goodness, yes I do, but only Duncan calls me that. If he didn't tell you, how did you know?"

"I happened to see it on a photograph, and I wasn't sure I should ask him about it, but why does he call you Jane?"

"The story's a bit embarrassing. He'd get in trouble for calling me Jane when we were growing up, but that didn't stop him. Jane is short for Plain Jane."

"I don't understand. You could be a supermodel."

"I'm not sure about that, but thank you. There was a time when quite a few boys were chasing me, and Duncan thought I was getting a bit full of myself, so he'd tease me and call me Plain Jane."

"I can totally see him doing that," Brittany said with a grin.

"You look very pale. Are you sure you're all right? Maybe you should see a doctor too."

"I'm fine. This has been quite a night."

"I can only imagine. I was panicked driving over here. Duncan has always been my Knight in Shining Armor. If anything ever happened to him..."

"He's become my Knight too," Brittany murmured with a sigh. "He's the most amazing man."

"Yes, he is. Can you tell me what happened?"

"I don't know where to begin."

"Just the highlights. You two can fill me in on the details later."

"Okay, let's see, we had a misunderstanding and I bolted, got a bit drunk at Claridges, and ended up in an alley being mugged. In my bag was Duncan's address and a key to the house. The hotel called Duncan to pick me up, and while he was gone my attacker broke in. He was still there when we got back."

"That's quite a story."

"Everything that happened is my fault," Brittany groaned. "I just hope I can find a way to make amends."

"When it comes to misunderstandings there's usually plenty of blame to go around."

"I don't think that's the case this time."

"Miss Carter?"

"Yes, doctor," Brittany said anxiously, jumping to her feet as the doctor approached. "How is he?"

"He can go home. He'll feel almost normal in the morning. He just needs a good night's rest, and from the looks of it, so do you. You're very pale."

"I'm exhausted and starving, but I'll be fine."

"There you are," Catherine exclaimed, Duncan appearing in a wheelchair being pushed by an attractive nurse.

"Catherine," he said with a smile, though his voice was solemn. "Thank you for coming."

"What did you think you were doing, fighting with a criminal like that?" Catherine demanded. "Honestly, I feel like punching you myself."

"He took me by surprise. I admit it wasn't my finest hour."

"I'm sorry, I didn't mean to yell. You just scared the hell out of me," she said earnestly, kissing him on the cheek. "I'll bring the car around."

"Aren't we a pair," Brittany remarked as Catherine hurried away. "I guess we're going to be looking after each other." Then lowering her voice, she murmured, "I understand about Jane now, well, almost everything."

"I knew you would when you saw her, but we'll talk later."

"I see a car pulling up," the nurse announced. "I'll wheel you out there."

"I can walk."

"I'm sure you can, but I have to follow the rules."

"I can't wait to get home," Brittany said with a weary sigh as they started to the door. "We both need a very long sleep."

DURING THE DRIVE HOME, Brittany filled in the details of her harrowing ordeal in the alley, and Duncan revealed how he thought he'd have the element of surprise over the thief.

"He was so fast. I swear he must have been throwing the punch walking out the door."

"The whole night sounds like one big nightmare," Catherine remarked. "You're both very lucky. Um, Duncan, why is there a policeman outside your door."

"Maybe he's waiting in case that creep has partners," Brittany suggested.

"Good guess," Catherine said, rolling to a stop. "I'm coming in. I'll fix you two a cup of tea and some supper."

"You don't need to do that," Duncan argued. "It's late. You should go home."

"Nope, you need me. Shoot, there's nowhere to park. I'll just leave the car here. That policeman can keep an eye on it."

"A cop watching an illegally double-parked car," Brittany piped up from the back seat. "I love it, but, uh, I need to go inside. I don't feel so good."

"After everything you've been through it's a wonder you're still on your feet at all," Duncan replied, gingerly unfastening his seat belt. "Maybe you should come in, Catherine. She hasn't eaten all day, and I'm not up to puttering around the kitchen."

"You couldn't have stopped me anyway, but I'm glad we're in agreement."

They climbed from the car, but as they walked up the steps, Catherine flashed the young constable a warm smile.

"Evening, everyone. The Sergeant asked me to stay here until you returned. We couldn't lock the place up, and we didn't want to just leave it."

"How very kind of you," Catherine said, lightly touching his arm. "Would you mind terribly watching my car for a few minutes?

There's nowhere to park, and I have to make sure these two are settled before I go home."

"Be happy to, Miss," the constable replied as Brittany and Duncan moved inside.

"Thank you ever so much. Here are the keys in case you need them."

Standing in the foyer, Duncan discreetly dropped his lips to Brittany's ear.

"Plain Jane in action."

"I see what you mean."

As Catherine walked in and closed the door behind her, Duncan poked his head in his office to check on his priceless desk. To his great dismay he discovered the cricket bat was missing.

"The police must have put it somewhere," Brittany said tentatively. "That's what I used on him, the mugger I mean, Charles, or whatever his name is."

"You did what?" Duncan asked, staring at her in shock. "I thought the police caught him on his way out. What the hell happened?"

"Can I explain over a cup of tea? I really don't feel right."

"I'll put the kettle on," Catherine said quickly, "and I'll tell our fearless guard I'm making him a cup as well. That should keep him happy."

"I'm dying to hear about this," Duncan continued. "You actually clonked him with my cricket bat? How the blazes did you do that?"

"Let's wait until Catherine comes back so I don't have to repeat myself. I'm wiped out. If I wasn't so hungry I'd go right up to bed."

"You," he whispered, pausing to gently pull her into his arms, "are the most astounding woman I've ever known."

Resting her head on his chest, Brittany closed her eyes and melted against him.

"I could go to sleep right here. I'm so sorry I took off this morning."

"You can explain tomorrow, but right now all I want to do is hold you."

"Stop with the canoodling," Catherine declared, walking back inside. "You both need a cup of tea and something to eat, then bed."

"All right, Miss Bossy Boots," Duncan retorted, his arm still around Brittany as they followed her to the kitchen.

"Sit down and I'll get cooking. Brittany, tell us what happened with the cricket bat."

As Catherine made a pot of tea, scrambled eggs and buttered toast, Brittany explained how she'd used the bat to incapacitate her attacker by targeting his most vulnerable area.

"You're so brave," Catherine exclaimed. "I wouldn't have had the courage to do something like that. Okay, Duncan, your turn. How did you end up getting punched in the gut?"

"I'll tell you, but first, Brittany, I'm speechless. Didn't his purple face scare you?"

"I wasn't looking at his face. I was totally focused on landing the bat where I needed to. Once he was on the ground nothing mattered except finding you."

"You can stay with me any time," Catherine said, dishing out their supper. "I'd feel very safe with you in my flat."

"That's unbelievable," Duncan mumbled, then frowning, he added, "I should probably call Nigel. There's no way I'll be going to the office tomorrow, but it's so late."

"I'll call him," Catherine offered. "I'll make sure he's convinced you were a gallant hero and ended up in hospital for your trouble."

"Thanks, that would be great. In fact, embellish the story. I need a few uninterrupted days with this precious girl here."

"I'd love that," Brittany said softly. "Thanks, Catherine. Those eggs were delicious."

"Time for bed," Duncan declared, moving across to peck Catherine on the cheek. "Thanks for coming," he said gratefully, then whispered, "May I tell Brittany about the ring?"

"Sure," she replied quietly, then picked up a mug of tea. "I'm taking this to our friendly policeman. You two go to bed. I'll lock up and set the alarm before I take off."

Leaving the kitchen together, they separated in the foyer, Catherine heading to the front door, while Duncan and Brittany started slowly up the stairs.

"I can't deal with a shower," Brittany murmured. "I'm collapsing the minute I see that bed."

"Good plan. If you passed out I wouldn't be able to pick you up."

Entering the bedroom, she peeled off her clothes and crawled between the sheets. Duncan quickly followed, but not before finding the pain killers the doctor had given him and insisting she take one. Finally curled up with the lights out, she snuggled against him, letting out a long, exhausted sigh.

"I meant what I said, precious girl. I love you."

"I meant it too."

But the words had barely escaped her lips before sleep had swept her away.

CHAPTER TWELVE

WAKING IN THE MORNING with Brittany nestled against him, Duncan relished the feel of her soft, warm, yielding body, but the dangerous chain of events had been sent into motion because of her snooping. Though he cared for her deeply, her impetuous behavior had to stop, and she needed to trust him enough to talk to him if she had questions or concerns. Gently extricating himself from her limbs, he moved quietly across to the bathroom, softly closed the door, and started the steam in the shower stall. He didn't use the expensive feature often, but when he did he was grateful he'd incurred the added expense. In the midst of a difficult case, or dealing with an impossible client, ten minutes in the hot fog would relax his body, clear his head, and oftentimes, he'd find answers to confounding problems. Settling on the bench seat, he closed his eyes and leaned his head against the marble wall. He had residual pain in his stomach, but it wasn't bad, and as the wet heat cloaked him, visions of Brittany flashed through his mind's eye. The way she'd writhed in pain and pleasure as his flogger swished across her glorious bottom, her charming blush whenever he said something provocative, and the sound of her sweet, soft, southern accent.

I have to have this every day for the rest of my life.

Her repeated comment made him grin.

Abruptly Brittany's image moved away and Catherine appeared, standing with her fiancee, Robert Logan. Robert was a venture capitalist with tremendous ambition. Though a couple of years younger than Duncan, he had already accumulated significant wealth. Duncan's eyes popped open.

"Catherine! Why did you come to me for help with your ring, and not talk to him? Were you afraid? Damn! Is that why Brittany didn't ask me about the photograph? She told me she'd sneaked into my closet, but she didn't tell me everything. I know I can be strict, but am I so strict she's actually scared?"

Turning off the steam and starting the shower, he braced himself for the cold that would burst from the overhead waterfall spout. The shock lasted only a moment, then the water became warm and comforting. Shampooing his hair and soaping his body, he rinsed off quickly, then stepped from the stall feeling clear-headed and invigorated. Toweling himself off, he pulled on his robe, and ambled back into the bedroom to sit on the edge of the bed.

"I'm glad you're still sleeping," he murmured. "You need the rest, but when you wake up we need to clear the air about some things. It's in my nature to take charge, but I don't want you to fear me so much you're afraid to talk to me, not the way Catherine's afraid to talk to Robert. I won't have that, and I don't want it for my sister. It's up to her of course, but now I'm concerned, very concerned."

Brittany hadn't stirred, and though the conversation had been one-sided he felt better, but as he was about to leave she mumbled something.

"Hey, precious girl. I'm sorry. I didn't mean to wake you."

"I'm not sure you did, but Duncan, I'm still so tired."

"Stay in bed. There's no reason for you to get up. How's your head?"

"No headache, I'm just so tired," she repeated. "I couldn't leave this bed even if I wanted to."

"Go back to sleep."

"Can I ask you something?" she murmured, her eyes still half-closed as she stared at him.

"You can ask me anything."

"I need to know. I'm sorry, but I won't be able to rest until I do."

"Go ahead, though I can guess."

"What I saw in that cafe, the engagement ring..."

"It was too big. Catherine was supposed to have it sized, but she waited too long. It fell off her finger in the sink. The platinum band was badly damaged in the garbage disposal."

"Oh, no."

"Her fiancé had been pestering her to take it into his jeweler, and she panicked. This happened the day before I left on the cruise. When she called me she was very upset, so I took it to a place I knew could make it right. Fortunately Robert, that's her fiancé, travels a great deal and he'd left on a two week business trip. When I gave it back to her, she took it straight to his jeweler to finally be sized. I promised her it would be our secret, so—"

"So you couldn't tell me why I wasn't able to join you for lunch."

"That's right, but last night she said it would be okay."

"Duncan, I'm so embarrassed, and so sorry about everything."

"You just get the rest you need," he said, moving the covers over her shoulders. "We can do our postmortem when you're up and around."

"I don't know why I'm still so wiped out."

"You went through a major drama. Now go back to sleep" he murmured, softly kissing her, "and have sweet dreams."

As she let out a sigh and closed her eyes, he wanted to slip off his robe and crawl in next to her, but resisting the temptation he headed into his closet. Dressing in comfortable clothes, he walked downstairs, brought the fireplace to life, made a pot of tea, then placed a call to Catherine.

"How are you?" she immediately asked. "How's the stomach?"

"It's okay, but I need to ask you something very important, and I want you to be straight with me. Deal?"

"Sure, fire away, but remember I'm at work."

"Close your door."

"This sounds serious. Sure, hold on."

Catherine was an executive at a high-profile public relations company. Their clients were some of the richest and most famous in London. It was through her work she'd met Robert Logan.

"I'm back. What's the question?"

"Why were you afraid to tell Robert what happened to your ring?"

He heard a quick breath.

"Um, I, uh—"

"When you start a sentence like that, it means you're looking for a way to fudge your answer," he said, interrupting her. "Just tell me. You know I'm on your side."

"Duncan, it's nothing you need to worry about."

"I've worried about you since the day our mother brought you home from the hospital, and that's not going to change. I'll worry more if you don't tell me what's going on with you two."

"Okay. I'll tell you. He's developed a temper. I was afraid if I told him what happened to the ring it would set him off."

"I see," Duncan murmured, forcing himself to stay calm. "How does this temper manifest itself?"

"He yells, and..."

"And, what?"

"Sometimes he throws things."

"How often does he get angry enough to throw things?"

She paused.

"How often, Catherine?"

"It used to be just once in a while, but it's becoming more frequent," she said quietly, then hastily added, "He doesn't lose his temper every night, it's not like that."

"What sort of things does he throw?"

"I feel like I'm in the witness box and you're questioning me."

"That's good. Take the emotion out of the story and just tell me the facts. What does he throw? Give me an example."

"Do I have to?"

"No. You don't have to do anything, but you can't ignore what's happening because it's uncomfortable."

"Uncomfortable?" she repeated. "Duncan, uncomfortable is a pair of shoes that don't fit right."

"Are you saying he throws breakables?"

"Yes. It's, uh, extremely disturbing."

"So his temper scares you?"

"It didn't used to, but now it does."

"Has he ever directly threatened you?"

"No, but when he gets crazy that's how I feel. Threatened. Do we have to keep talking about this? It's upsetting me."

"Back to the courtroom," he said, though softening his voice. "Take the emotion out of your answers."

"I'll try."

He suddenly wanted to be with her. He wanted to hold her hand and give her a hug.

"Just one more question. Are you scared all the time?"

"Duncan, the truth is," she began, her voice cracking, "I'm walking on eggshells. I know he's under pressure at work, there's some jumbo deal he's working on, but I never know what might set him off. A look, or how I ask him if he'd like to eat out or stay in, it could be anything."

"Catherine, what you choose to do is your call, but marriage is a big step, and you need to be one-thousand percent sure. It's one thing to respect your husband and have the kind of fear that's built into that respect, but to fear, to truly fear, that's no way to live. You've got six months before the wedding. Use that time wisely."

"Duncan..." she murmured breathlessly, "I don't know what to do. I'm scared to end things, and I'm scared not to."

"You know I'm here. You can come by any time, stay here any time. Having Brittany in my life changes nothing. Understand?"

"Thank you. I...uh...I need to hang up now."

"I know you do."

"Bye."

"Bye."

The call had shaken him, and pouring himself a second cup of tea, he leaned back in his chair.

"If that guy touches a hair on your head, I'll follow Brittany's example and take my cricket bat to his groin."

Gathering his wits, he placed a call to Nigel, fully expecting him to be unavailable. To his shock, Nigel picked up the call.

"I understand you tangled with a burglar and ended up in hospital," he exclaimed. "Heavens, man, are you all right?"

"I am, and I apologize for having to do this, but I need the rest of this week to take care of some things."

"No doubt, no doubt."

"Nigel, this, uh, event, for lack of a better word, has given me a new perspective. I want to lighten my workload. I don't want any more eighteen-hour days."

"Ah, I see. You've been a workaholic for as long as I've known you. We all burn out at some point. I did. We'll talk next week."

"I appreciate this very much."

"You may be one of our stars around here, but you're human. Sometimes we lose sight of that. Don't hesitate to ring if you need me."

"Thank you, Nigel."

Ending the call, Duncan picked up his cup, wandered into the living room, and sat on the couch in front of the fire.

"This all started with that cruise," he mumbled. "I thought my life was perfect when I boarded that ship, then I met you Brittany Carter, and all hell broke loose." Staring at the flames, a soft smile crossed his lips. "I must be crazy, but if I could do it over again I wouldn't change a damn thing."

CHAPTER THIRTEEN

DRIFTING IN A BOAT on a pink lake, Brittany studied the thick, grey fog in the distance. The sun was warm against her skin, and a slight breeze ruffled her hair. The still, glossy water reflected the imposing mountains on either side, reminding her of the photographs she'd seen of Milford Sound in New Zealand, and the Fiords in Norway.

The craft abruptly picked up speed. It was taking her to the fog which now appeared dark and gloomy. She searched for the oars, but there were none. The fog loomed closer, towering over her like a ghostly mountain. Her fear became terror. If it swallowed her up she'd be lost forever. Miraculously Duncan appeared beside the boat, and slicing through the water like a dolphin, he used his wake to guide her towards shore. Just as the menacing cloud threatened to engulf her, Duncan wedged the boat into a sandbank, and rising up like a Greek god, beads of moisture twinkling like diamonds against his skin, he swept her into his arms. Carrying her effortlessly as he splashed his way to shore, he settled on a fallen tree trunk and flipped her over his knee.

"What did I tell you about climbing in that boat and going off by yourself?" he scolded, pulling up her skirt and whisking down her knickers.

"I felt like I had to," she replied earnestly, staring at him over her shoulder with pleading eyes.

"You were almost lost in the fog. I would never have found you," he continued, delivering hot slaps on her exposed flesh. "You know how much I care about you. I cannot allow this reckless behavior to go unpunished."

The spanking began with gusto, his hard hand landing rapid-fire swats, evoking kicks and loud squeals.

"You knew it was wrong when you climbed in and let it take you into the lake," he declared, blistering her cheeks with a volley of rapid-fired smacks before pausing to squeeze her cheeks. "Why? You must tell me why."

"Because I was scared."

"Scared? But you seemed so happy at the picnic table. What scared you? I told you I'd be right back."

"That's why I was scared. I was scared because you left and I was afraid you'd never come back. I was scared nothing was real, and how could an amazing man like you possibly love a plain girl like me, just a plain girl from a small Southern town. That's why I got in the boat. To sail somewhere safe."

"Brittany," he said tenderly, "you must have faith in me. Do you hear me, Brittany? Do you? Do you hear me, Brittany?"

Waking with a start, her eyes flew open. Duncan was gripping her shoulders, his worried face staring down at her.

"Brittany, you were having a bad dream."

"I, uh, yes, oh, my gosh."

"Take some deep breaths, then you can tell me about it," he said, holding her tenderly.

"I will, but please make love to me? I need you," she begged, her hands urgently unbuttoning his shirt.

"But what about your head?"

"I'm fine, really. Please?"

Hastily removing his shirt, he rose to his feet and pulled off his slacks.

"My precious girl," he murmured, resting on top of her.

"You still have your underwear on."

"I will make love to you, but on my terms," he said firmly, pinning her wrists on either side of her head. "My boxers stay on until I decide to take them off."

He saw the flicker in her eyes. She needed his control.

"You wanted me to take charge. It calms you and makes you feel safe."

"It does. I don't know why, but it does."

Moving his lips to her neck, he sucked in her skin, then leisurely kissed his way to her shoulder and the hollow of her neck. As he slowly moved down to her nipples, she arched her back and raised her chest to meet his mouth.

"Remember the clamps?" he whispered, clutching her breasts.

"Yes, Sir."

"One night, very soon, I'll spank you and finger you until you're gasping, then I'll put those clamps on you, but make them tighter and attach chains. They'll be attached to a belt around your waist, and when you wriggle—"

"Oooh, you're making me crazy!"

"And when you wriggle, they'll tug, and nip, and make you very, very wet."

Lowering his teeth to her cherry tips, he nibbled and sucked, not stopping until she was writhing beneath him.

"I want you so badly. Please, Sir, please will you take me?"

Wordlessly he straightened up, slid off his boxers, then pressed his fingers into her slick slit.

"Are you wet enough?"

"Yes, Sir—I mean, if you think so, Sir."

"You caught that just in time," he growled, placing himself at her entrance. Plunging inside her, he gripped her waist and began stroking vigorously. "Is this want you want?" he panted. "You want me to fuck you like this?"

"Whatever pleases you," she said breathlessly, "but, ooh, yes, Sir."

Accelerating his strokes, he rammed his rod without pause, then abruptly stopped.

"Sir, ooh, Sir," she whimpered. "I was right on the edge."

"I know."

Clutching her seat cheeks and resting his head next to hers, he pumped with quick, abrupt thrusts until her cries were once again at a fever pitch, then backing off, he tongued his way from her neck to her mouth, crushing her lips in an all-consuming kiss, and began slow, teasing strokes.

"Please, Sir," she begged as he broke away.

"Please what?"

"Ravage me and let me come. Please, I can't stand it."

"This time," he promised. "Come when it hits."

Kneeling up between her legs, he clutched her hips and pulled her into his pelvis, battering her sex with his rigid cock, keeping himself at bay until she let out her euphoric cry. The tingling waves of pleasure pulsed through his body, and groaning loudly, he released his essence, but even as his drained member slipped from her depths, her euphoric cries still filled the air. Kissing her breasts until they finally abated, he rolled beside her, holding her until their breathing settled.

"Duncan?"

"Yes, precious girl?"

"Is your stomach okay?"

"It must be. I didn't even think about it," he murmured, pulling the covers back over them. "Do you want to tell me about your dream?"

"Yes, but not yet. For the moment I just want to lie here with you. Is that okay?"

"So much more than okay," he said with a contented sigh. "There's nothing else I'd rather be doing, and nobody else I'd rather be doing it with."

DUNCAN WASN'T A MAN who lolled in bed, but the events of the previous day had taken their toll. With his office situation under control, his conversation with Catherine behind him, and Brittany's warm body next to him, he allowed himself the luxury. He sank into the mattress, his mind rested, and he was cloaked in an unfamiliar depth of peace. When she finally moved, throwing her arm across his chest and lifting her lips to nuzzle his neck, he rolled on to his side and gazed down at her.

"How are you this morning?"

"Is it still morning?"

"I have no idea, and amazingly, I don't care."

"Me either. Have you ever not cared?"

"Never."

"How does it feel?"

"I'm not sure," he replied thoughtfully. "Different, in a good way, but definitely different. Have you ever not cared?"

"Um, I don't think so. Back home, the minute I wake up I jump on my computer to see how much I sold overnight."

"Do you miss your business?"

"I don't at this minute, but I have been wondering how things are going. I've been very neglectful. Have you called your office?"

"Indeed I have, and put things off for the week. I need to be with you," he said solemnly, his fingertip smoothing away a stray lock of hair. "I've done some serious thinking, and I'm making some changes. I don't want to spend the rest of my life at the beck and call of my clients. But enough about me. How's your head?"

"It hurts, but not a headache hurt. The injury hurts."

"You're so lucky. It could have been so much worse."

"I think he missed. I think I was supposed to be knocked out."

"I suspect you're right. Do you want to stay and rest a bit longer?"

"I'd love to take a shower, but I can't get my head wet, and you have an overhead waterfall."

"The guest room down the hall has a handheld shower."

"It does? That's great."

"While you're doing that I'll make us some porridge."

"Porridge," she repeated, her eyes lighting up. "I've never had porridge."

"You'll love it," he said with a grin, climbing from the bed and pulling on his boxers. "First, though, I need to show you something."

"Right now?"

"No time like the present."

As she slipped out of bed, he took her hand and led her to the bathroom, helped her on with his robe, then opened the door to the wardrobe.

"Duncan! Holy smokes!"

The beige carpet was covered in the purple dye, with a sharp outline where Bert Willis had laid her Ralph Lauren bag.

"The dye temporarily blinded him. That gave me time to lock the bathroom door, but as I explained, there was no lock on the door leading out into the hall. I could have had him trapped until the police came. It was an oversight I'm going to correct, though hopefully I'll never have to use it."

"What about this carpet? I guess you'll have to replace it."

"I might go with hardwood floors. You can help me decide, but there's something else I want to show you. I never want you to feel that you have to poke around for answers about me or my life. We're going to have a talk about that, and some other things too, but I hope this will show you I have no secrets. Obviously writing my naughty novels under A.S. Cane is a secret from the world, but otherwise my life is an open book. You can ask me about anything, including my former girlfriends. Okay? Got that?"

"Okay, and yes, I understand."

"Come with me," he said, guiding her around the dye to the opposite side of the island.

Kneeling in front of what appeared to be its solid back, he pushed against the corner. The panel swung open revealing his safe.

"So the locked cabinet on the other side is a decoy. This is where you keep your valuables."

"Exactly," he said, spinning the dial and opening it up. "It's also where we should put your passport and anything else you care about. The only other person who knows about this is Catherine, and the company who installed it of course."

"And all those keys in the bowl?"

"A red herring. If someone saw those they'd think what you probably did. It would take forever to try them all. That's what I call the convincer."

"Wow."

"I doubt that creep will be back, but he might have friends. I need to come up with something else. Speaking of which, I also have to reset the alarm and change the locks to the front door. He only had the key for five minutes, but I'll still feel better knowing the key he had no longer works."

"This is all my fault," she mumbled. "I can't say sorry enough times."

"That's one of the things we need to talk about," he said gently, "and deal with."

"Deal with?"

"Yes, deal with, but later. Go and take your shower."

"Duncan, you're being awfully good about all this."

"The most important thing, my precious girl, is that you're all right."

"No, the most important thing is that you're all right."

"We're both all right," he crooned, hugging her. "By the way, I have something interesting to tell you about your portrait, or rather, the girl in the portrait."

"You do? I can't wait!"

"You know the guest room is just down the hall. Use that door, and I'll see you in the kitchen shortly."

As she padded away, he closed up his safe, and being careful not to step in the purple mess, he dressed quickly and headed downstairs to make the porridge.

CHAPTER FOURTEEN

SITTING AT THE KITCHEN island next to Duncan, Brittany finished the last of her porridge, laid down her spoon, and leaned against his shoulder.

"I feel so much better. Thank you. That was delicious."

"Are you feeling up to a talk?"

"Is anyone ever up for a D and M?"

"What's D and M?"

"Deep and meaningful."

"I think I'll use that in one of my books," he said with a grin, "but if you're not in the mood..."

"I was only joking. I'm definitely in the mood."

"Let's sit in front of the fire."

"That sounds like a very good idea."

Ambling into the living room she settled on the couch, but Duncan remained standing.

"Aren't you going to join me?"

"Not yet. As you know I'm a lawyer, and Catherine says when I talk to her about her problems she feels as if she's in a courtroom. I don't mean to come across as insensitive, but leaving emotion out of things and dealing with just the facts—"

"Excuse me," Brittany said, interrupting him, "but that's what people are, a jumble of emotions. You can't just eliminate them."

"I don't eliminate them, I cut through them. I'll ask you questions, and I want you to imagine you're under oath and answer truthfully."

"Nope, this is ridiculous."

"Excuse me?"

"I can't promise I won't get emotional."

"You can try!"

"Don't get your knickers in a twist," she retorted, raising her eyebrows. "Or should it be, don't get your boxers in a bunch?"

"I swear, if you didn't have that bump on your head you'd be over my knee."

"Why? Because I'm disagreeing with you?"

"You, Brittany Carter…" he muttered shaking his head and breaking into a broad smile.

"Why are you grinning like that?"

"I just remembered something I read when I was researching that portrait, but never mind that for the moment. Will you please do this my way?"

"Fine. Go ahead," she said, holding up her right hand. "I swear to tell the truth, the whole truth, and all that jazz."

"Seems a pretty young woman from South Carolina wants a spanking!"

"Sorry," she said with a giggle. "I couldn't help myself. Go ahead."

"You need to be serious now," he said soberly. "This isn't a joking matter."

"Okay. I'm paying attention."

"Brittany, are you afraid of me?"

"Heavens, no. I wouldn't be here if I was. I feel butterflies when we talk about punishment or before a spanking, but that's not scary in a bad way."

"I'm very pleased to hear it," he said with a relieved sigh. "You admitted going into my closet, but didn't mention the photograph. Can you tell me why?"

Dropping her eyes, she shifted uncomfortably on the couch.

"Take the emotion out," he pressed, lowering his voice.

"I see what you mean about pushing past feelings," she said quietly. "I felt jealous, and I was too embarrassed to ask about it. Then I overheard you on the phone saying you missed her and you were meeting up for lunch. You called her Jane, not Catherine. I had no idea you were speaking with your sister. At that point, any thoughts about mentioning the picture flew out the window."

"I see," he murmured, sitting down next to her. "Will you tell me about the dream now?"

"It brought my biggest fear into focus."

"And what's your biggest fear?"

"I'm not, uh, enough, for you."

"Explain."

"You're really handsome, you're a barrister, you're accomplished and sophisticated, and I may come from a good family and have my own business, but I'm not like you. I feel so ordinary next to you. That also crossed my mind when I saw that photo in your drawer. Catherine's so beautiful."

"Brittany! You can't be serious! You knocked out a violent criminal with a cricket bat, the same criminal who had whacked you on the head in a dark alley just a short time before! And you're not just brave, you're incredibly sexy. Any man would be thrilled to have you at his side, especially this man."

"Duncan, I don't know what to say."

"Say you'll let go of all these insecurities and stay with me for a while longer. I've got a plan, and I'd love you to be a big part of it. I want to transition out of my law practice and start a publishing company. I have a concept for a system that would give authors real options. I see a void I believe I can fill. I've been thinking about this for a couple of years, and I think now it's time to take the leap."

"My gosh, that's a big deal."

"Yes, it's a really big deal, and obviously I must take things one step at a time, but let's see how we get along for a while. Of course, if you want to go back—"

"I don't want to. I feel so at home here, and I want to be with you."

"Brittany, what I do, the flogger, spanking you, being strict with you," he said gravely, "are you sure that's what you want?"

"One-thousand percent," she whispered. "Sorry, but my emotions have come back like crazy. I don't just want what we have. I need it. I can't pretend I won't be difficult. I'll probably throw a tantrum now and then, but at the end of the day—"

"At the end of the day," he said softly, putting his arm around her, "you'll have me to hold you, and spank you, and most of all, to love you."

"Duncan, you always know the right thing to say."

"Not always, but I try. I'm going back to the kitchen to clean up our dishes," he said, kissing her lightly and rising to his feet. "You stay here. I'll be right back."

"Then I want to go to Harrods," she called after him. "I need some clothes."

But when Duncan returned he found her stretched out and sound asleep. Realizing she still needed time to recover from the trauma, he covered her with a blanket, retrieved his laptop, and settled into the easy chair. She continued to nap through the rest of the afternoon, and as they watched television after dinner, he noticed her yawning and insisted on an early night. Holding her tenderly as she snuggled into his body, he felt her drifting off, but was woken the following morning by her hand on his cock.

"Sorry about yesterday," she purred. "I felt drugged, but I'm better now."

"No aches and pains?"

"Only my aching need."

"I see. Roll on your side."

Slipping into her hot, wet sex from behind, he moved his hand around her hips and pressed his finger against her clit. Thrusting as he massaged the sensitive nub, he rode her into a tingling climax.

"I'm purring," she murmured as she melted against him. "Can you hear it?"

"I believe I can. What would you like to do once we're up and about?"

"Harrods for some clothes, then lunch at some trendy, expensive place, then—"

"Then I have an errand, and tonight we'll have dinner at a very special restaurant."

"Finally, a life!"

"Yes, finally," he said with a grin, "though I don't want to overdo it."

"Duncan, you don't need to baby me. I'm absolutely fine."

"If I decide you need babying..."

"I'll do my best to humor you, but now I want to go shopping."

A SHORT TIME LATER they were climbing into a taxi on their way to Harrods, Brittany using a gift bag to carry her wallet and other essentials. Though the police had returned most of her belongings, the Ralph Lauren bag had remained with them.

"This will be embarrassing," she mumbled, staring at her paper sack, "though my bag is probably purple. I couldn't have used it even if they had given it back to me."

"Once you're inside Harrods you'll have so many purses to choose from, you'll stand there for an hour just gaping at them."

"You don't know this side of me," she said with a wink.

Though Brittany was from a small town, she was an ace shopper, and it took her just fifteen minutes to select the bag she wanted.

"I'm impressed," Duncan said with a grin, watching her transfer her belongings. "You know what you're doing."

"Yep, now to the jackets and coats."

As she zoomed from department to department, quickly making her choices and whipping out her credit card, Duncan stood back with his arms crossed, a bemused expression on his face.

"I think that's it," she declared, collecting a receipt for two warm jumpers. "I'm glad they deliver."

"Not as glad as I am. I'd be carting around the packages if they didn't. Are you sure you're done? You don't need anything else?"

"I think I've tortured you enough," she said with a laugh, "but I'll definitely be back. I feel as if I've only seen half the store."

"Not even close to half. You'll have to be here a few times for that."

"I'm definitely ready for lunch and a cup of tea. Two cups of tea."

"Excellent. I just have to make sure we leave through the right exit."

Winding his way through the store, he left through a door on to a side street, then walked to the end of the block, turned a corner, and headed towards a restaurant with the words, La Soufflé across the window. Opening the door and gesturing for her to walk in ahead of him, they were greeted by a tall, attractive hostess.

"Hello, Duncan, how delightful to see you again!"

"Thank you, Arielle."

"Please, follow me. Your favorite table is available," she declared, lifting menus from their holder and walking through the dining room. "How's your sister?"

"She's very well. I'll tell her you asked."

"Here you are. Have a wonderful lunch. Michel has some special soufflés on the menu today. The artichoke and cheese is to die for."

"You must be a special customer," Brittany grinned as the hostess left.

"I bring clients here, and it's one of Catherine's favorite places. The food is exquisite, and Michel, that's the chef, is amazing. I helped him out of a jam a few years back. I've been coming here ever since."

"From Michel," Arielle announced, returning to place two small porcelain soufflé cups in front of them. "This is the artichoke and cheese I told you about, and the other, salmon fennel."

As she walked away, Brittany picked up a spoon and tasted them both.

"You have got to be kidding me," she murmured, rolling her eyes. "I want this every day for the rest of my life."

"You said that about crumpets, and scones with cream and raspberry jam," Duncan said with a chuckle. "Keep this up and you'll be eating a few too many things every day for the rest of your life."

"You're right, but I won't be complaining!"

"Brittany there's a very special place I want to share with you," he said, lowering his voice and leaning across the table. "About an hour from here there's a magnificent estate called Andover Abbey. Did you watch Downtown Abbey?"

"Absolutely. I loved that show. I actually cried when it ended."

"Andover Abbey is almost as grand as the castle used in the series. It's been in the family for generations. When they faced the same challenges as many of the landed gentry, their solution was—shall we say—creative. At the time the family was immersed in some infamous sex scandals, so they decided to exploit their sinful reputation and turn it to their advantage. They started an exclusive club."

"A sex club?" Brittany whispered.

"I believe that's how it began, but over time Andover Abbey has become something truly unique. They separated the wings, and now cater to many appetites, including Dominants. Rooms are available for getaways, but they also host parties and themed weekends. What do you think so far?"

"I think it sounds fantastic!"

"I thought you might feel that way," he said with a grin. " I was so sure you'd want to visit Andover Abbey I booked us a room, but you must be appropriately attired. When we leave here I'm taking you to a lingerie shop."

"I am so, so, excited. What a wonderful surprise. When are we going? To Andover Abbey, I mean."

"As long as you're sure you're up to it, tomorrow night."

"Wow, this is incredible! I can't believe it."

"One thing though," he warned. "Andover Abbey is where I plan to punish you for taking off like you did, and not returning my texts. I was frantic with worry. I understand the reasons behind your actions, but you need to be punished. You know that, don't you Brittany?"

"Yes, Sir," she breathed, her butterflies bursting to life. "Um, can you tell me a little more about the Abbey."

"I'll tell you about dinner. A few minutes after the plates have been cleared a gong sounds. The man at the head of the table stands up, raises his glass and says, and over."

"The name!"

"Yes, they've cleverly exploited it. The women must bend across the table. As a general rule, the head of the table gives each of the subs a decent swat to start things off," he said with a grin. "There's something else as well, but I don't want to spoil the surprise, and dinner is just one of the activities available."

"Call me crazy, but I want to participate in everything."

"Be careful what you wish for."

"Have you taken other women there?"

"Once or twice, and I've attended by myself as well. They have resident subs on the weekends."

"Duncan, my head is spinning."

"I know it's a lot to take in, but I'm very happy you're so enthusiastic."

"I am. I truly am."

He could see the sparkle in her eyes, and for a moment he was temped to tell her what he'd learned about the portrait, but decided to wait. He'd save that surprise until later.

CHAPTER FIFTEEN

THE LINGERIE SHOP WAS a ten minute walk. Thinking she'd be trying on skimpy, sexy garments, Brittany had eaten only one small soufflé, and refused dessert and coffee. Standing in front of the window display, she was glad she'd resisted temptation.

"They're so beautiful," she murmured, admiring the lacy outfits in the window.

"Brittany," he said softly, putting his arm around her, "you're about to fulfill one of my long-held fantasies. We're here to buy you a corset."

"We are? You mean you haven't done this before?"

"Only in my dreams—and my books!"

"That makes me so happy."

"Me too. Very happy. Let's go in."

Pushing open the door and walking inside, Brittany stared longingly at the array of elegant outfits.

"Don't let me loose in here," she said softly. "I'll walk out a pauper."

"We're going up those stairs," he said, guiding her past the sales clerks towards a wrought iron staircase.

"How do you know about this place?"

"Andover Abbey. Apparently it's very popular."

"I can see why."

Climbing the stairs and reaching the landing, they turned down a short hallway and found a door with a shining brass plaque.

"Corsetry! This must be the place," he said, knocking lightly.

The door was opened by a tall, stately woman wearing a black skirt and cream silk blouse, and her blond hair swept back into a bun.

"Good afternoon."

"We spoke on the phone. I'm Duncan Rhys-Davies, and this is Brittany Carter."

"Delighted. My name is Mildred. Please come in. May I offer you refreshment? We have a selection of cakes, chilled champagne, fruit juice, coffee, tea, and cognac."

"Perhaps in a few minutes," Duncan replied, glancing around as they entered.

A blue and white sofa sat behind a coffee table, and a counter against a wall offered a variety of drinks and finger food.

"We design and sew all our own garments," Mildred declared proudly. "There's a mistaken belief corsets are much the same, but you can see that is not the case. As I mentioned when we spoke, because your event is tomorrow you'll need to make your selection from our ready-made collection, but please be assured they still offer our exceptional quality. Do you have a particular color in mind?"

"I'd like you to choose the corset, Duncan," Brittany said, speaking for the first time, silently adding, *this is your fantasy, and I want it to be perfect.*

Duncan read the unspoken message in her eyes. His heart swelled, and he had to fight the desire to pull her into his arms and hug her.

"Why don't you take a wander?" Mildred suggested.

"I will. Thank you."

As he began moving through the room, Mildred hovered nearby, while Brittany settled on the couch. He stopped only once, to study a cream corset covered in pearls.

"No, none of these are right," he said, turning to Mildred. "Do you have anything else?"

"There might be something already made in our Primrose collection, I'll check for you, but I need to take Miss Carter's measurements."

As Mildred and Brittany disappeared behind a mirrored door, Duncan wandered towards the refreshments, but as he reached for a glass of water his eye caught sight of a mannequin tucked away in a corner. Intrigued, he moved towards it, but as he neared a sudden shiver pricked his skin. Gold beadwork flamed upwards from the waist, the tapered ends ending halfway around the cups, as though holding them up. Black sequins dancing haphazardly near the beads brought the sparkling pattern to life. The garment took his breath away.

"Excuse me," he said, walking quickly to Mildred and she and Brittany reappeared. "I'm interested in the corset in that corner."

"Isn't it simply divine?" Mildred remarked with a smile. "We found it at an estate sale. It was damaged, but it was too unique to pass up. We just completed its restoration, that's why it's not yet on display."

"May Brittany try it?"

"Certainly."

"You think you found the one?" Brittany asked excitedly as Mildred left to fetch it.

"I believe so. I just hope it fits."

"Here we are" Mildred declared, returning with the corset over her arm. "Miss Carter and I won't be long."

As they moved into the fitting room, Duncan ambled to the refreshment bar and splashed a small amount of brandy into a snifter. The rich liquid glided across his tongue and slid down his throat, He let out a breath. The corset had mesmerized him. It was almost unnerving.

"Sir? We're ready for you," Mildred said, snapping him from the moment. "You'd think it was tailored just for her."

Turning around, Duncan found himself dazzled.

"I think it's absolutely wonderful," Brittany murmured, walking towards him with her eyes sparkling. "More wonderful than I can say. Do you like it?"

"Absolutely," he managed, trying to curb the thrill in his trousers. "Thank you, Mildred."

"Please join us in the dressing room. I'll show you how to lace."

"Thank you, but I must have a private word with Brittany first."

"Of course. I'll wait for you in there."

The moment the door closed, he took her hand and moved her around so he could view her from the back. The sight was even more alluring.

"Duncan, I feel weak at the knees," she said as she faced him again.

"I'm having a similar reaction, in my own way, of course. You look exquisite."

"You're making a fantasy of mine come true as well, except it's a fantasy I didn't know I had."

"Brittany, I asked Mildred to leave us because I have to tell you this," he began, holding both her hands. "When I found that corset I experienced a very odd sensation, and just now, when I saw you come out of the fitting room, I was overcome with a sense of déjà vu."

"Oh, my gosh. Me too. The moment I looked in the mirror I felt almost dizzy. It was the strangest thing."

"I'm a facts and figures man. This is throwing me for a loop."

"What do you think it means?"

"I don't know."

"We shouldn't keep Mildred waiting, but, Duncan, this is one of those special moments we'll never forget."

"Brittany, I believe you're right."

ARRIVING HOME JUST in time to receive the delivery from Harrods, Duncan suggested Brittany take possession of the guest room. While she enjoyed a busy afternoon sorting through her new clothes, Duncan reviewed his many files, making notes and emailing his clerk. When the late afternoon became early evening, they met up in the living room dressed for dinner.

"Duncan, you look so handsome. I missed you."

"I missed you too," he said with a grin, softly kissing her, "but I liked knowing you were pottering around upstairs."

"It was fun getting organized. Thanks for letting me use that bedroom for my things."

"You need your own space, but let me look at you. I love that dress. Come with me."

"Where? The taxi will be arriving any minute."

"This won't take long."

Leading her to the sofa, he sat down and abruptly jerked her across his lap.

"What are you doing?"

"What do you think?" he replied, pulling up her skirt. "What do we have here? A thong and suspenders! Excellent."

"That was supposed to be a surprise for later!"

"It's a surprise now, and something I'll enjoy thinking about during our meal, along with the hot bottom I know you'll be sitting on."

"Why?" she whimpered with a wriggle.

"I don't need a why, but in case you forgot, you followed me through the streets of London."

"I thought you were saving that for Andover Abbey."

"Consider this a deposit," he declared, raising his hand and landing a volley of hot slaps across the center of her backside.

"Ow! Are you done? Can I get up?"

"Of course not," he said sternly, instantly peppering her sit spot.

"Ow, ow, ow, sorry! I shouldn't have asked."

"No, you shouldn't have," he exclaimed, returning to the center of her backside to rain several hard swats, "and you just paid the price."

"Ouch, oh, Sir, those hurt."

"I should hope so, but now you can have your cuddle. You needed that," he remarked as she curled into his lap.

"I know."

"Once a week, I think. You'll be back over my knee next Friday night."

"Even if I'm perfect all week?"

"What do you think?" he retorted, helping her off his lap as the doorbell chimed. "That's our cab."

Hurrying outside, a chilly gust of wind swirled around them, and when the taxi deposited them in front of the restaurant, they were met with light rain, but once inside the inclement weather was forgotten. A rich aroma filled the air, and Brittany fell in love with the intimate dining room.

"This is gorgeous," she murmured as they settled at their table.

"Are you sitting comfortably?"

"Not exactly."

"Excellent," he said with a wicked grin, then becoming more serious he reached for her hand. "This is the perfect place to tell you about the portrait, and after what happened today, it's the perfect time."

"I'm dying to hear."

"While you were busy getting mugged," he said, raising his eyebrows, "I researched the painter. The young woman was the love of his life, and he referred to her as Fille Précieuse. In English, that's precious girl."

"Duncan! That's what you call me."

"I've never used that term before, not with anyone."

"Ooh, I just got goose bumps."

"There's more. He met her on a ship."

"He did not!"

"He did, traveling across the English channel."

"I can't believe this," she breathed, her eyes widening. "My goosebumps just got goosebumps."

"And the last piece of information is even more startling. It's still difficult for me to comprehend."

"Okay, I'm ready."

"Her name was Babetta Babineaux, and she was a direct descendant from a noble family in Brittany."

"My name! How weird is this?"

"I've never been particularly religious or delved into spiritual things," he said, shaking his head, "but this is truly bizarre."

"Duncan, when I saw you walking up that gangplank, I felt something," she said, squeezing his hands. "Every minute I was on that ship, before we met in the dining room, you haunted me."

"I felt the same."

"So...do you think this means we knew each other in another life? Could I have been Babetta, and you the artist who painted her portrait?"

"I find that hard to accept, but I do want to find out where they lived and visit there. There's something else, something you don't know about me. I love to draw. I have illustrated many of my books. I wanted to become a graphic designer, but family encouraged me to take up law."

"Wow! Yes, we have to find where they lived. I'll do the digging," she said excitedly.

"The artist began his career painting scenes of the French countryside. At the very least I fancy a weekend away with you in a Chateau."

"That would be fantastic!"

"Then we'll plan on it."

AFTER A DELICIOUS MEAL and a bottle of Cabernet, they settled into the back of a taxi for the trip home. As it wound through the dark streets, Duncan whispered his fingertips along the inside of her thigh. Deciding to reciprocate, Brittany placed her hand over his crotch.

"Cheeky girl."

"What's good for the goose," she quipped, squeezing his member.

"Move your fingers now, young lady," he warned, his lips at her ear, but it was too late. His cock had surged to full attention. "Sit on your hands, and don't move them until we get home."

He tickled the gusset of her knickers for the remainder of the short trip, sending a flush to her face and a flood between her legs, and weak with need as they entered the house, she leaned against him. Immediately sweeping her off her feet, he carried her up the stairs and into the bedroom.

"You are a naughty girl," he declared, hastily undressing her. "On the bed, hands and knees!"

Striding to his dresser, he opened the bottom drawer to retrieve a length of cord and a blindfold, but as he turned to walk back to her, he discovered she was touching her sex.

"What do you think you're doing?"

"I couldn't help myself," she whimpered, dropping her fingers away. "Don't be mad."

"Naughtier and naughtier," he scolded, placing the blindfold over her eyes. "Head on the pillow, and put your hands behind your back."

Deftly tying her wrists, he landed several hard slaps across her perfectly poised posterior, then deliberately making her wait, he slowly peeled of his clothes.

"Sir...?"

"Yes, naughty girl?" he replied, kneeling on the bed behind her.

"I need you, Sir, I need you so badly."

As he separated her pussy lips, she whimpered and wiggled, and when he placed his cock against her soaked entrance, her body tensed in anticipation. He thrust forward, landing a hard slap on each cheek. She let out a yelp, then groaned as he began to pump.

As he fell into a thrilling pattern of fucking and spanking, she found herself lost in a dark sky of sparkling sensations.

"Please, Sir? May I come? I'm so close."

"Do naughty girls deserve to climax?"

"Yes, Sir, if that naughty girl loves you. Please, Sir, fuck me hard!"

She heard a long, deep groan, then he abruptly pummeled her pussy. A wail rose up from deep within her, and crying out as the spasm hit, his fingers unexpectedly explored between her cheeks. But the lewd attention only served to heighten her moment. The convulsions sent sparkling currents pulsing through her limbs, until the glorious waves began to wane, and she sank into the afterglow.

His flaccid member slipping from her depths, Duncan quickly untied her wrists and removed the blindfold, then dropping beside her, he wrapped himself around her limp body.

"Fille précieuse" he whispered.

"Mmmm, Bonne nuit mon amour," she replied, and drifted into sleep.

CHAPTER SIXTEEN

IT WAS A CLEAR, BRISK afternoon. After cruising the motorway for almost an hour, Duncan exited and drove down a road that led them deep into the countryside. Rolling to a stop in front of imposing wrought iron gates, he leaned out his window and entered a code on the entry pad.

"This is so exciting I can't stand it," Brittany said as the gates swung open.

"You're going to love this," Duncan replied, driving down the curved gravel driveway. "There it is." As the magnificent manor came into view, she caught her breath and clutched his arm. "I told you it was impressive."

"Impressive? That's like saying a lion is a big kitten. You weren't kidding when you said it looked like Downtown Abbey. Good Grief!"

As they neared the front of the house, two nattily dressed young men stepped forward. One opened Brittany's door, while the other greeted Duncan and gave him a ticket for his car.

"Name, Sir?"

"Rhys-Davies."

"Would you care to have your cases delivered to your room?"

"No, thank you. I'll be taking them myself."

"Very good, sir, enjoy your stay."

Popping the trunk, Duncan collected their bags, and as they walked toward the front door, their feet crunching the gravel, Brittany tugged at Duncan's sleeve.

"You didn't tip him."

"The privilege of rewarding and punishing the staff stays with the owners."

Walking through the immense wooden doors held open by a liveried butler, Brittany gazed in wonder at the magnificent reception area. Tapestries and portraits graced the walls, and everywhere she looked was a bronze, an oversized floral display vase, or some other work of fine art.

"Duncan, how delightful to see you again." An elegant middle-aged woman wearing a black and white Chanel suit, sparkling diamonds on her fingers, and a stunning chunk of sculptured gold around her neck, stepped up to meet them. "When Penelope told me you were bringing a guest I made sure you were given a larger room with some very special amenities."

"You're too kind. Please allow me to introduce Brittany Carter. She's visiting all the way from South Carolina. Brittany, this is Lady Edith Collingsworth."

"Welcome," the woman said with a warm smile. "I do hope you enjoy your stay with us. Please don't feel that you need to stand on formality. Call me Edith."

"Thank you, Edith. Your home is magnificent."

"Andover has been very good to us, and we love sharing all it has to offer. Ben will show you to your room."

"This way, Sir, Madame," a young man said, stepping forward and picking up the cases as the countess gracefully glided away.

As Brittany and Duncan followed him up the wide staircase, she glanced back to the foyer. Edith was greeting more guests.

"Don't worry," Duncan said softly. "Everyone is like us. We can be who we are while we're enjoying the history and beauty of this place."

"It's hard not to be intimidated," she whispered as they were led down the hallway.

"I understand, but that will pass."

The young man opened the door to their suite, and stepping inside, she moved to the center of the room and gazed around in wonder.

"If you need anything, sir, the bell cord is by the fireplace," the footman said.

"Is afternoon tea being served in the drawing room?"

"Yes, sir, in twenty minutes."

"Thank you."

"Duncan, I am blown away," Brittany exclaimed the moment the young man left. "This place is amazing."

"Check out the bed."

Turning her eyes to the dark wood, heavily carved, four poster bed, it took her a moment before she saw the thick metal rings on all four posts.

"Oh, my goodness."

"You see this chest of drawers," he continued, standing next to a chunky, antique dresser. "Do you know why the brass plaque says Master's Chest?"

"I can guess," she said, moving across to join him.

Opening the top drawer, she saw an array of riding crops and small whips lying on red velvet. Pulling out the second, Brittany stared down at a variety of implements.

"Every dildo is sterilized and resealed for new guests," Duncan declared, opening the last one.

"I probably shouldn't ask this, but how much does it cost to stay here?"

"About the same as Claridges," he replied with a wink.

"Very funny."

"I thought so, but we should head down to the drawing room for afternoon tea. It's held for the weekend guests. If we meet people we take a liking to we can sit near them at dinner."

"This is all so..."

"So much to take in," he said softly, wrapping her in a hug. "I know."

"I'm thrilled, really, but I'm not sure about involving other people."

"You don't have to do anything you find uncomfortable, and in the clubroom you can watch for a quick five minutes, or an hour, or not at all. You'll find everyone is very respectful. The owners are strict about that. Do you want to freshen up before we go down?"

"Yes, please. Where's the bathroom?"

"I don't know. Let's explore."

There were only two doors. One led into a walk-in wardrobe, the other, a large bathroom with a claw footed tub, two sinks, a built-in vanity, and a wide shower stall with two shower heads.

"Duncan, I love those twin showers."

"I've seen them before. I think they defeat the purpose of showering together, but that doesn't mean we won't!"

"I don't think I'll ever want to leave this place."

"I felt that way the first time I came here. It's another world, and you're right. I'm always sorry when my visit comes to an end."

"I feel it already," she murmured as they returned to the bedroom. "I'll get my things and fix my face."

As she disappeared into the bathroom, he strolled to the bed and ran his fingers over the metal rings. His cock stirred, and a wicked grin curled the edges of his lips.

IN THE DRAWING ROOM a short time later, perched on the edge of a sofa cushion with Duncan sitting next to her, Brittany did her best not to rattle the porcelain cup and saucer. She was holding it in one hand as she tried to reach across the inordinately high arm of the couch and place it on the side table. Finally managing, she selected a bite-sized custard tart from a three-tiered serving dish sitting on the coffee table in front of her. The pastry melted against her tongue, and she gazed at Duncan with wide happy eyes.

"Let me guess. You want one of those every day for the rest of your life."

"Uh-huh. Absolutely! Every single day!"

Several couples began to wander in, and Brittany was relieved most were contemporaries in age, except one man who had salt and pepper hair, an odd mustache, and was with a woman who appeared barely old enough to drink.

"Duncan, everyone seems so normal," she remarked under her breath.

"What did you expect?"

"Um, I'm not sure. The guy in the tan sports coat with the girl in the black slacks, they look like I felt when I first arrived."

"We should say hello. That's one of the reasons for this get together," he said quietly, taking her hand and leading her across the room. "Former guests can meet newcomers and help them feel comfortable. They definitely need rescuing."

The couple introduced themselves as Scott and Theresa, and their nervousness was obvious.

"The first time I came here," Duncan began, "I was a third wheel with another couple. I didn't know what to do with myself, but being in such beautiful surroundings and meeting like-minded people I felt at home fairly quickly. I'm sure you will too."

"Only a minute ago I said to Duncan everyone seems so normal," Brittany piped up.

"That's hilarious," Scott said with a chuckle.

"Don't laugh," Theresa said. "I was thinking the same thing."

The conversation helped ease the tension, and the couple were soon chatting with the other guests.

"Enough afternoon tea," Duncan murmured, taking Brittany aside. "I want to take you on a tour."

"Yes, please. Can we wander wherever we want?"

"As I told you, the house offers separate wings and we're restricted to this one, but there's plenty to look at."

"No kidding. I can barely take in what I've seen already."

Moving down a hall, he took her through a reception room towards wide, double doors, paused, then opened them with a flourish.

"After you, madame."

"My gosh, what is this?"

"The main ballroom," he answered, moving up beside her. "Back in the glory days, this would have hosted some extraordinary parties. The massive crystal chandeliers are still hanging, and look at the murals running along the sides of the ceiling."

"I can hardly believe my eyes. Why is it empty? There's not a stick of furniture in here."

"It's reserved for special events, and they furnish it accordingly. There's a costume ball coming up. I don't know the theme yet, but would you like to attend?"

"I'd absolutely love to."

"About the dinner tonight," he began, taking her hand as they wandered the great room, "if Monty is here, he'll probably be head of the table."

"Monty?"

"Edith's son. The last time I saw him he had Sandy Sullivan on his arm."

"The supermodel?"

"The supermodel, but I've never seen him with the same woman twice. The thing is, if Monty is the head, it's likely he'll have something up his sleeve. He likes to offer surprises."

"I might regret saying this, but I'm up for it," she said with a grin. "Duncan, thank you so much for bringing me here."

"I've wanted to share this place with someone special for a long time," he said softly, bringing her into his arms, "and you, Brittany, are that someone special."

Staring at the tiny blue flecks dotting his warm brown eyes, she felt a delicious rolling in her stomach. His fingers slipped into her hair, and tugging back her head, his lips pressed against hers with a demanding heat. He was gripping her tightly, owning her, kissing her with a passion that made her body weak and sent a surge of moisture through her sex. The kiss was endless, his lips devouring hers, his tongue exploring her mouth, and when he finally released her, she was breathless, weak, and aching for his cock.

"Tonight you will learn more about me," he said huskily, "and more about yourself. You'll feel what it's like to be possessed. Are you ready for that?"

"Yes. At least...I think so."

"Are you wet?" he asked, thrusting his hand under her skirt. "I'm going to make sure." Pushing aside the gusset of her panties, he slipped his fingers into her slit. "Very wet, but you're wearing underwear. Take them off."

"Here?"

In an instant she was bent over, her skirt was up, and his hand was slapping her bottom.

"Sir, ow, ow...!"

"Lesson number one," he said sharply as he continued to redden her behind, "you do as I say, when I say, no questions."

"Yes, Sir. Ow! Ow!"

As quick as he'd yanked her forward, he pulled her up.

"I am your Dominant, and we are in a place where I expect complete obedience at all times. If you're uncomfortable tell me, but when I give you an instruction you must follow it without so much as a blink—unless you want to provoke a profound reaction."

She flashed back to the ship. His stern demeanor and strict discipline had taken her breath away. An unexpected aching wave of need rippled through her body. Reaching under her skirt, she quickly slipped off her knickers.

"Place them in your bag."

Immediately dropping the panties into her purse, she looked up at him expectantly.

He smiled down at her, then kissed her softly. He'd created the short, tantalizing scene to prepare her for the evening ahead.

"Good girl. I trust there will be no further incidents."

"No, Sir. May I say something?"

"The term is, permission to speak, Sir."

"Permission to speak, Sir?"

"Granted."

"You just melted me. I love you so much. I love how you are and what you do. May I have a hug?"

"You certainly may."

As she sank against him, he closed his eyes and engulfed her in his arms.

"I love you too, Brittany. I love everything about you."

CHAPTER SEVENTEEN
Dinner

STANDING IN FRONT OF an antique oval mirror while Duncan stood behind her and laced the corset, Brittany thought she looked like a Princess from an erotic fairy tale.

"All done," he declared, leaning forward to nuzzle her neck. "You look spectacular. Finish dressing. I'm going to put on my ascot."

"Can you hug me for just a second?"

"Of course," he murmured, cradling her softly.

"Duncan, why do I feel so strange?"

"Nervous excitement. It's only natural. Take a deep breath and try to relax. I'll be back in a minute."

Kissing her tenderly, he retrieved his silk scarf from his overnight bag and disappeared into the bathroom. Smiling at his reflection in the large mirror above the marble counter, he began the ritual. He could have completed the task in the bedroom, but he wanted to give Brittany a few minutes to finish dressing, and the ascot was a surprise. Tying the silk around his neck, he imagined her pulling on the fancy lace knickers and silk stockings, then carefully stepping into the shiny black stilettos. Enjoying the imagery as he finished the fancy necktie, he returned to the bedroom, only to find her in a seductive pose by the side of the bed.

"Brittany, what a vision! You're going to take everyone's breath away!"

"As long as I take your breath away," she replied, her soft southern accent sounding like a bird's song. "Duncan!" she suddenly exclaimed, noticing his scarf. "Your ascot, it's black and gold. We match!"

"We do, but I have to complete your outfit," he said, taking her hand and leading her back to the mirror. "Wait here."

Opening the double doors of the armoire and sliding out a drawer, he picked up a black leather collar and leash.

"You must wear this," he said solemnly, moving back to her and buckling the leather band around her neck. "I'll be leading you with a leash, so you need to stay a step or two behind me."

"Yes, Sir," she murmured, her goose bumps popping. "Do you know long I've dreamed of having a collar around my neck? You've made me so happy."

"The feeling's mutual, precious girl. There, now you're perfect," he declared, clipping on the leash. "I do love this rolled leather. I must pick up a leash like this. It's not just a piece of leather with a snap at the end. The finer details matter."

"Like your black and gold scarf?"

"Yes, like that. Shall we go?"

"Absolutely. I'm ready for whatever."

"That's a good thing to be ready for," he said with a chuckle.

Giving the leash a slight tug, he led her out the door, along the hall and down the stairs. As they approached the reception room adjacent to the dining hall, he spied the ginger-haired, handsome Monty in the center of a large gathering with an exotic beauty at his side.

"Brittany, do you see the red-headed chap? That's Monty."

"The woman he's with is gorgeous, but what an outfit! I can't say I find it attractive."

The girl was dressed in a cut-off, aqua, spandex top with a stand up collar. Below her naked midriff she wore satin shorts, fishnet black stockings and thigh-high boots.

"I have to agree," Duncan murmured. "I like my women soft, sexy and feminine—like you."

"Thank you, kind Sir."

"Time to join the fun. Remember, stay a step behind me."

Moving into the fray he saw a few familiar faces, then spied Theresa and Scott standing by the fireplace sipping champagne from crystal flutes. As Theresa spotted him, he noticed relief cross her face, and walked quickly through the guests to join them.

"You look beautiful, Brittany," Theresa exclaimed. "Where did you find such a beautiful corset?"

"At a specialty shop in Knightsbridge. I love your outfit too," Brittany replied, eyeing the strapless, scarlet bustier and short, black pencil skirt.

"I'm embarrassed to say we're still a bit intimidated by all this," Scott said ruefully. "I didn't expect so many guests."

"I promise it gets easier. Did you read the rules? No questions about work, place of residence, politics or religion."

"I did, and I think they're very wise."

Duncan helped the couple socialize, but it was only a few minutes before the dinner gong sounded and the crowd moved into the dining room.

"Wow," Brittany mumbled. "Is it always like this?"

"Yes, but the setting sometimes changes."

Large platters of food in the style of a Tudor feast graced the table, and the champagne flutes were full. In front of the plates sat two small, black paper sacks, alternatively marked with a capital D, and a lower case pink, s. As Duncan led Brittany to their seats, she noticed several of the women had remained standing behind their Dominants.

"I assume those women like to serve," she whispered. "I want to do that sometime, but dressed in a maid's outfit."

"You've mentioned that before. I'll have to buy you one."

"Or maybe I'll pick it up and surprise you one night," she suggested with a cheeky grin as they sat down.

As the guests settled into their chairs, Monty stood at the head of the table and tapped his glass with a spoon.

"Good evening everyone. I'm delighted to see such a large gathering. Perhaps it's because spring is in the air, and we all know that when spring is in the air a young man's heart turns to thoughts of love. Here at Andover Abbey, we say a man's heart, young or not so young, turns to thoughts of decadence."

There was a titter among the group, and waiting until it passed, he raised his champagne.

"Welcome to our new guests and old friends. Here's to a sinfully, naughty night."

The guests lifted their flutes, clinked glasses, and sipped the bubbly wine.

"Gentlemen, when you look inside your gift bag you'll see I have arranged a special dessert to follow the delicious sponge pudding at the end of our meal. Enjoy your dinner."

As the guests reached for their mystery gift, Brittany noticed the women were waiting until their Dominants gave their permission.

"What's in there?" she asked as Duncan peered into his.

"Never you mind. You may look in yours, though I can already guess what's in there."

"A blindfold," she exclaimed, reaching inside and pulling it out. "Why will I need a blindfold?"

"You'll find out, but now it's time to eat, and I'm starving. I'm sure you are too."

"I certainly am. I'm hungry and very happy!"

FINISHING UP A DELICIOUS meal with a brandy soaked pudding served with warm custard, the plates were cleared, and the table fell quiet as Monty rose to his feet.

"If anyone does not wish to participate in the after dinner activity, now is the time to leave."

"Brittany?" Duncan whispered. "Are you sure you want to stay?"

"Yes, definitely."

"Apparently you are all choosing to remain," Monty continued. "I'm delighted. Ladies, blindfolds on, then stand up and over the table."

"Okay, now I'm suddenly nervous," Brittany muttered.

"You had your chance. Do as you're told, or Monty might take it into his head to make an example of you."

"Holy crap," she said under her breath, immediately sliding the blindfold in place and laying across the table.

She heard a humming sound, then Duncan's fingers slipped inside the gusset of her knickers and slid a buzzing dildo inside her. Letting out a cry of surprise, she wriggled her hips, but anticipating her reaction Duncan had kept his thumb pressed against the base.

"Settle," he said firmly. "It's not to fall out. If you think it might, put your hand between your legs and hold it in place."

"Yes, Sir."

She was suddenly grateful for the blindfold. He had slid her lacy panties into the cleft of her cheeks and was fondling her backside. Facing the other guests would have been mortifying. Quiet murmurings floated in the air, and in spite of the circumstances she found herself surrendering to the scintillating sensation of the vibrator, but the distinct sound of a slap broke the spell. It was followed by another, and another. She abruptly realized Monty was walking around the table and spanking the submissives.

The smacks drew closer, and as Duncan's fondling hand dropped away, she assumed she would be next. The sharp swat suddenly landed, the alien palm quickly delivering a second smack on her opposite cheek. She gasped from both embarrassment and the fiery sting, but the moment had barely passed when Duncan's finger massaged her clit. The vibrator's pulsing pleasure, and Duncan's intense erotic massage, sent her back into her blissful, submissive state. Finally withdrawing the dildo, he sat her back down and removed her blindfold. Breathlessly leaning against his shoulder, she slowly opened her eyes. To her surprise, everyone had left.

"How do you feel?" he asked softly, moving his arm around her.

"I have no idea."

"Try."

"I need you. I need to be naked and in bed with you."

"I feel the same," he said huskily, taking her hand and placing it against his bulging cock, "but we're going to the library, though I'm not sure how long we'll stay. I want you in that bed chamber very badly."

"I want to be there too, Sir."

As she molded her hand around his rigid cock, he slipped his fingers inside the top of her corset to fondle a breast, evoking a long, low moan.

"I think we'd better leave before I drag you under this table and ravage you," he muttered, pinching her nipple.

"I wouldn't object. We're supposed to be truly decadent here, aren't we?"

"Always so cheeky," he said with a grin, withdrawing his hand. "What am I going to do with you?"

"If you need to ask, we're both in trouble."

"On your feet, young lady!"

As she slowly pushed back her chair, Duncan dropped the vibrator and her blindfold into his gift sack, then taking her hand he led her from the dining room and down a wide hall.

"Here we are," he announced, stopping at a closed door with a gleaming brass plaque boasting the word Library. "Are you ready?"

"Yes. I'm ready, willing, and hopefully able. Lead the way."

CHAPTER EIGHTEEN

BRITTANY STARED IN wonder. At the end of the cocktail bar, a blindfolded woman stood on a low stage shackled between poles rising from the floor. Her pale pink blouse hung open exposing her ample cleavage, and her short, tight skirt had been shimmed up over her hips. Dominants wandered by, slipping their hand beneath her shirt to fondle her breasts, touch her pussy, or move behind her and land a spicy swat.

"Duncan, what am I looking at?"

"It's called the Display Frame. Would you like to be up there?"

"I, uh, I, don't know."

"I'd like a brandy. Do you see how the drinks are being served?"

But Brittany couldn't bring herself to shift her gaze. A Dominant had stopped in front of the shackled woman and was stroking the inside of her thighs.

"Brittany!" Duncan barked, landing a sharp smack.

Letting out a startled squeal, she darted her head up.

"Ignoring me is not an option."

"Sorry, Sir."

"Look at how the men are being served their cocktails."

Glancing across the room, she noticed women carrying silver trays bearing a drink, then dropping to their knees in front of their Master.

"Yes, Sir. I see. This whole thing is amazing."

"I know it's lot to take in," he said softly, "but I'd like a drink. Go to the bar, ask the bartender politely for a tray and a snifter of brandy, then bring it over to me and kneel like the others."

"Yes, Sir."

Releasing the leash from Brittany's collar, he sent her off with a solid slap, then made his way to a couch in the center of the room. The girl in the frame was being unshackled, and he noticed another ready to take her place. Moving his eyes back to Brittany he had to smile. She had paused to watched the switch.

"Hello, Duncan! How are you, old man?"

"Monty, my goodness, you'd make a good cat burglar," Duncan said with a chuckle as his host sat next to him.

"You were just busy feasting your eyes on the Display Frame."

"Guilty as charged! Where's your lovely lady?"

"My lovely lady is naked but for a G-string, locked in a cage in the gymnasium waiting for me to give her a jolly good flogging."

"What was her crime?"

"I'm just in the mood," Monty said with a sigh. "I wish she had misbehaved. She's very beautiful and makes the most delightful noises when we're shagging, but..."

"But?"

"The but is, she's too—this might sound a bit oxymoronic—too compliant. The woman has no spirit, no challenge. Your new girl is gorgeous, by the way. What's her name again?"

"Brittany."

"Yes, Brittany. She appears to have some fire in her."

"She certainly does."

"Look at that corset sparkle," Monty remarked, watching Brittany walk slowly towards them. "She's beautiful enough to wear it. It would overshadow most women."

"Sir," she said softly, as she approached, "I don't know how to kneel without spilling your drink. My heels are so high."

"She has a point," Monty said with a grin. "We don't want any broken ankles, or brandy snifters for that matter."

"Hand me the tray. I'll hold it while you remove your shoes, then you can kneel," Duncan suggested.

"Thank you, Sir."

Handing him the tray and removing her shoes, she knelt in front of him.

"It appears you have homework when we get home," Duncan declared, giving her back the tray and picking up his drink. "You'll practice, and next time we're here you won't have a problem."

"Yes, Sir. Now what?"

Duncan couldn't suppress his grin, and leaning back, Monty expelled a short, loud chortle.

"When I finish this brandy you'll be spanked for speaking out of turn."

"Oh, right, sorry, Sir."

"Eyes down, knees apart, and wait quietly."

"Yes, Sir."

"She really is delightful," Monty commented as he rose to his feet. "Have an excellent rest of your night, though it's clear I don't have to worry about that. Are you staying through Monday?"

"No, just tonight. I'd like to, but I was told the room was already booked."

"I think we're packed to the gills. Maybe I'll see you at breakfast. Ciao."

Duncan sipped his brandy as he watched Monty stride from the room. Brittany had been noticed, and he couldn't deny his sense of pride. Placing his finger under her chin, he tilted up her head.

"You really are lovely, and I'm immensely proud of you."

"I'm so happy I please you, Sir. I want to, I really do."

Impulsively he leaned down and planted a soft kiss, but when his tongue moved between her teeth, his semi-hard cock surged in his trousers. Sliding his fingers into her hair, he gripped it tightly as he devoured her lips.

"Permission to speak, Sir," she said breathlessly as he pulled back.

"Granted."

"I want to curl into your lap, but I want you to ravage me as well."

"I promised you a spanking for speaking out of turn, and I always keep my promises, but I can assure you, I will definitely plunder your body."

Finishing his drink, he ordered her across his knee, and as he began peppering her bottom with hot slaps, a couple stopped to watch.

"So, Brittany, a public spanking," he murmured, as the couple wandered away. "How did it feel?"

"Embarrassing, but exciting, Sir."

"You can get your cuddle now. I think your bottom is sufficiently red."

"It hurts, Sir," she whimpered, shifting herself to nestle against his chest, "but I want you so much."

"The two go hand-in-hand," he remarked, "if you'll pardon the pun."

"I just feel so good here. It's surreal, but it's not. I can't wait to be naked with you."

"The feeling's mutual, and I think it's time to go," he muttered, his rigid cock aching to slide inside her, "but first I want to show you the gymnasium."

Slipping off his lap and sliding into her shoes, he snapped on the leash, led her from the room and down the hall. Stopping at double doors and pushing them open, he moved inside. As Brittany dutifully followed, she spied Monty's date bent over a vaulting horse. The girl's feet were held apart by a thin bar attached to cuffs around her ankles, and Monty was flying his flogger over her backside.

"Sir, what's that between her ankles?"

"A spreader bar."

"Do you have one of those?"

"Of course, and there's one in our room."

"Really?"

"Really," he said with a wink.

Unlike the Library, though many couples were swept up in their kinky pleasures, there was no chatter, only the sounds of soft moans, spanking hands, and swishing leather.

"Sir, why is it so quiet?"

"It's the rule. This room is for punishment, not socializing and speaking of punishment, young lady, it's that time for you."

"But you already spanked me."

"Now you're just being coy. You know very well why you must be properly disciplined."

"Looking through your drawers, following you around London, and not calling you back after getting your text."

"Correct. Come along. We're going back to our room."

THEY FOUND THEIR BEDSPREAD turned down, and a single lamp burning on a nightstand washed the room in a soft, golden light. Taking her by the elbow, Duncan guided her to the foot of the bed and ordered her to kick off her shoes.

"Now wrap your hands around the post and stand there quietly."

Using the blindfold given to them at dinner, he slipped it over her eyes, then gripped her knickers and moved them swiftly down her legs. As a fresh wave of butterflies abruptly burst to life, she felt him move away, then heard him open a drawer, but he quickly returned. Shackling her wrists, he moved her arms apart, securing them to the metal rings on the bedposts.

"Spread your legs. I'm placing you in a spreader bar."

Her pulse raced as he deftly cuffed her ankles and attached them to the pole. Not being able to close her legs was an odd sensation, but he landed several quick slaps, distracting her from the thought, then slid his fingers into her soaked sex. She moaned as he teased her, but the pleasure was brief. He slowly trailed his fingers up to her rosebud. She instinctively recoiled, and her protest was met with a hard slap.

"Don't fight me," he warned huskily. "Surrender and thrust out your bottom. If you don't, I'll untie you and we'll call it a night."

She did as he asked, but groaned loudly as he applied a large dollop of lube and pressed a dildo against her hidden hole.

"It will be much easier if you relax," he crooned, nuzzling her neck. "Tell me you'll accept this. Do it for me."

"I will, Sir," she murmured, then taking a deep breath, she thrust out her backside.

He pushed it gently forward, then cupping her chin, he lingered his mouth on hers, gliding softly, and lightly biting her lower lip before stepping back to study her. Impaled, spread-eagled, blindfolded and helpless, she was a glorious sight, and to his joy, she let out a heavy breath. Though she'd accepted the small butt plug and moaned through his caring kiss, he wasn't sure if he'd hear her sigh of surrender. They were in sync, and shared the magical connection he'd waited and hoped for throughout his life.

She suddenly wriggled.

He grinned.

She was growing impatient and wanted more.

Moving back to the Master's Chest, he withdrew a flogger. The leather strips were thinner than his. They carried a sting, rather than a burn.

"Do you know what I'm holding?" he whispered, moving his fingertips across her bottom.

"A flogger, Sir?"

He paused, delighted that she'd guessed correctly.

"It's not like mine. This one delivers a sharp sting. This is your punishment, Brittany, for doubting me, doubting us, but most of all, for doubting yourself. Even though you knew I cared for you deeply, you gave into your insecurities. Understand?"

"Yes, Sir."

As he kissed her neck, his lips touching just above her collar, he thought—didn't speak—his last words.

I'll only lash you if you ask me to, but you must ask by showing me.

Stepping back, he raised the flogger. To his great joy, she arched her back and thrust out her backside. Swinging it down and sending the leather straps across her cheeks, though she gasped and threw back her head, she wiggled provocatively. He obliged, landing several in quick succession, but each one at her squirming invitation.

"You're drenched," he muttered, moving up to her and pushing his fingers into her soaked sex. "You're ready, and I'm going to consume you."

He felt her quiver.

Hurriedly stripping off his clothes, he unhooked her stockings, and unlaced the glittering garment, but the process took time. As he pulled the ribbons through their narrow holes, her chest rose and fell with her ragged breathing. Finally removing the exquisite corset, he laid it on a nearby chair, gently withdrew the dildo, unshackled her wrists from the poles, and removed the spreader bar.

"Sir, I need, you," she muttered, falling back against him.

"I need you too, precious girl."

Lifting her into his arms, he laid her on the bed, sheathed his member, and resting his weight on top of her, he removed the blindfold, placed his cock at her entrance and pushed home. Letting out a grateful moan, she gazed up at him with half-lidded eyes.

"You feel unbelievable," she whispered, "like your cock is where it's supposed to be."

"Because it is!"

Relishing the joy of being inside her hot, wet depths, he began to thrust, slowly at first, then swiftly accelerating, pummeling her pussy with fast, powerful strokes, but the salacious night was sending them both into a quick climax. He saw the red blush cross her chest a moment before she wailed her plea.

"Please, Sir, I have to come, I have to."

"Yes, come for me," he commanded, feeling his cock about to burst. "Come for me now!"

Her body grew taut, and with a loud cry her fingers dug into his back, sending him over the edge. As she writhed beneath him, he let out a loud groan, surrendering to the powerful convulsions.

Lost in a sea of swirling sensations, Brittany called his name as sparkles and hot prickles washed through her limbs. Spasm after spasm shuddered through her, until the orgasm finally passed and her body grew limp.

Slipping from her depths, Duncan shifted to her side and wrapped her into his arms.

"Please hold me," she mumbled. "Hold me and never let me go."

"Always," he promised breathlessly, loving the feel of her body molding into his. "You belong exactly where you are."

DUNCAN AND BRITTANY slept until late morning. Finally waking and making leisurely love, they blissfully dozed off, their limbs entwined, until she let out a yawn and stretched her arms above her head.

"I love this room," she said with a heavy sigh. "You were right. I never want to leave this place."

"We'll come back soon, I promise."

"I'll hold you to that, mister," she quipped with a cheeky grin. "Do you think we've missed the breakfast buffet? I'm starving."

"We'll get ourselves cleaned up, then head down for whatever's on offer. It's already eleven o'clock. They may have started serving lunch."

"Before we go down, how long should I plan to stay in London? A few more days, or..."

"Brittany, I keep thinking of that classic Stevie Nicks song, Leather and Lace. There's a lyric, *I carry this feeling, when you walked into my house, that you won't be walking out the door.* That's how I've felt from the moment you stepped into my foyer and started babbling about crumpets. But your life is your life, and you live it in South Carolina. You sell high-end clothes on line, you have family and friends, but I've already told you, I'd love you to hang around a while. A long while."

"Well, good, because I don't want to go anywhere."

"I have a suggestion. Can you commit to staying for a month?"

"Not a problem. Before I left on the cruise I put a notice on my site that I'd be away. I like my little business and I'm good at it, but it's not a passion."

"Great. Then we'll have a month to run around the block together."

"You mean, see how things go."

"Yes, to see how things go. I'm sure we'll hit some speed-bumps, but I'm not worried. If you're difficult—"

"You'll spank me."

"I'll spank you anyway."

"What about when you're difficult?"

"I'll beg your forgiveness and make it up to you."

"What will I do while you're at your office?"

"I have a new top priority. I'm buying you that maid's outfit. My house can use some sprucing up, and you can start with the kitchen."

EPILOGUE
One Month Later

DUNCAN AND BRITTANY settled into a comfortable routine. Convinced her future would be in London, she explored the possibility of starting a business similar to the one she had in South Carolina, but she discovered estate sales often sold collections of vintage jewelry. She would no longer have to store racks of clothes and worry about dry-cleaning, and the items would be easy to ship.

Though Duncan's work kept him busy during the week, every weekend he made it a point to whisk her away to a country hotel, or find some local excitement they could share, and he never neglected her Friday night spanking. Though she didn't tell him, by midweek she looked forward to the trip over his knee. His discipline centered and calmed her, and when it was over she'd melt into his arms.

Catherine and Brittany formed a warm friendship, and one night, when Duncan was working late, the two friends met up for a drink. Brittany sensed Catherine was troubled, and with some gentle prodding, Catherine shared her worry about her fiancé's unpredictable temper.

"He smashed my favorite coffee mug yesterday afternoon," Catherine said woefully, "but then he came home with flowers and a new mug just like it. He was so sweet. I find it impossible to stay mad at him."

"What does Duncan say?" Brittany asked, shocked that his beautiful sister was with a man who displayed such violent tendencies.

"That marriage is a big step and I should postpone the wedding if I'm not sure."

"Sounds like good advice."

"I agree, and I don't know why it's so difficult to come to a decision."

"Let me ask you something," Brittany said solemnly. "Do you feel safe with Robert? That might sound corny, but, do you?"

"Do I feel safe?" Catherine repeated thoughtfully. "My gosh, Brittany, you've just hit the nail on the head. I don't. I've just never thought about it like that, but the truth is, I never know when he's going to blow up. How can I commit to him if I'm always walking on eggshells?"

"I think the answer is pretty obvious."

"Brittany, thank you! I see it so clearly now. I'll tell him it's off tomorrow night, but would you mind if I came and stayed with you two for a little while? I don't fancy being alone, and if he shows up with some grand gesture I might weaken and take him back."

"Of course I wouldn't mind, in fact, I insist you stay, and for as long as you want."

Duncan had been profoundly relieved when he heard the news, and grateful to Brittany for helping his sister see sense.

AS THE END OF THE MONTH drew near, he couldn't imagine his life without Brittany in it. Wanting to celebrate, he called Claridges to reserve a room, but Harry had immediately stepped in to offer a luxurious suite compliments of the hotel.

"That's so kind of him," Brittany exclaimed when Duncan told her.

"I'm sure the hotel is just thanking their lucky stars you're not suing them."

"It's not their fault I stupidly went off with some stranger."

"No, but they have celebrated guests who need privacy and security. If you had taken them to court, it would have harmed their reputation."

"Regardless, I still think it's great, and I'm so excited to be spending our anniversary there."

The night they checked in, Harry personally showed them to their suite, and assured them the hotel had changed their security protocols.

"I'm sure you heard that dreadful man has been arrested for other crimes," he said solemnly. "It looks like he'll be going away for a very long time."

"It couldn't have happened to a nicer chap," Duncan remarked sarcastically, "and I'm glad others will have their justice."

"I'm just pleased he's off the streets," Brittany interjected, "but that's behind us now. Harry, thank you for this wonderful room. It's just perfect."

"It's my pleasure. If there's anything you need, anything at all, don't hesitate to ring down and ask for me."

As he left the room, Duncan took Brittany into his arms and stared down at her with a twinkle in his eye.

"What? Something's up," she declared."Tell me!"

"First, any thoughts about our month?"

"Only one. It's been the best month of my life!"

"For me too. Would you like to stick around a while longer?"

"Of course I would."

"When do you need to go back to South Carolina?"

"There's no rush. Why?"

"Prepare yourself. I've tracked down where Francois Benoit and Babetta lived."

"Oh, my gosh."

"The house is a few miles outside a village in the South of France."

"Duncan, I just got chills! Is there anyone living there?"

"Apparently it's owned by an elderly couple, but it's been empty for a number of years. I've made arrangements for us to visit. We can actually go inside and look around."

"That's fantastic. When?"

"We're flying out on Saturday morning."

Thrilled with the news, it was the only thing Brittany wanted to talk about over dinner, and Duncan was just as excited, but when they returned to the suite he suddenly became reserved.

"What is it?" she asked. "Please don't tell me there's a problem."

"This is crazy. I just remembered something. I meant to ask you at the time and I forgot. I suppose it came to me now because we were talking about Francois and Babetta. Do you speak French?"

"I know merci, and bonjour, but that's it. Why?"

"Brittany," he said solemnly, dropping on the edge of the bed, "Do you remember the night we had dinner at that wonderful restaurant? I told you what I'd learned about the painting, and when we got home I introduced you to my flogger."

"Of course I remember. I'll never forget that night."

"When we were going to sleep, I whispered, fille précieuse, and you replied, bonne nuit mon amour."

"I did? Are you sure?"

"Positive."

"But I don't even know what that means."

"It means, goodnight my love."

"Oh, I just got chills," she whispered, leaning against him, "but I'm suddenly feeling so close to you."

"I feel it too."

"Please will you hold me?"

"I'll do more than hold you, precious girl."

Peeling off her clothes, then stripping quickly, he laid her on her back, and kissing her fervently, he placed himself at her slick entrance. As she moaned his name, he pinned her arms above her head, thrust his cock into her slick pussy, and rode her with slow, strong strokes. Taking his time and building their orgasms, when her cries signaled she'd reached the brink, he had no desire to make her wait. The powerful climaxes shuddered through their bodies, leaving them both breathless and their hearts pounding.

Their lovemaking had been intense, passionate, and spellbinding.

FRANCOIS BENOIT'S FORMER residence sat only a few miles from Moustiers in southeastern France. Duncan had reserved a room at a hotel in the picturesque village, and though it had been highly recommended, the romance of the place swept them up the moment they arrived. The arrangements to see the house had been made with the elderly couple's lawyer. When they checked in, an envelope with the key and directions was waiting. Anxious to see the centuries-old home, they left their bags unpacked in their room and set off, Brittany navigating while Duncan drove. The fifteen minute trip led them up a gentle hill, then a turnoff took them to the house. Stopping in front of a high wall with black metal gates, they stepped from the car, pushed them open, and found a large courtyard flanked on three sides by a two-story dwelling. Walking across the stones, they stopped in the center and stared at each other.

"I feel as if I've just stepped back in time," Brittany said softly, staring at Duncan with wide eyes, "or is my imagination getting the better of me?"

"Then mine is too," he replied, then pointing to a paned window in the middle of the second floor, he said, "That's where the studio is."

"This is so strange. I think I might cry."

"Deep breaths," he said, putting his arm around her. "Shall we go in?"

"Definitely."

Arm-in-arm, both completely unnerved, they unlocked the door and walked inside. Though dusty and run down, the old-world charm of the home shone through. Instinctively following a hall to a flight of stairs, they found the room Duncan had pointed out from the courtyard.

"This is filled with natural light," he remarked. "It would have been the perfect place to have his studio."

"And Duncan, the bedroom, it's at the end of the passage."

"Yeah, I know."

"What are you thinking?"

"I'm thinking this is where we need to be. This is where I need to write, this is where you need to...what? What do you want to do, Brittany?"

"Remember I told you I'd found some great vintage jewelry and I thought I'd like to start an online business?"

"Sure, but you also said you weren't sure, that you had something else in mind."

"I don't want to buy and sell it, I want to design my own jewelry. Being in this room—I'm getting ideas already."

"I believe it. The energy in here is amazing, but God only knows how much work this place needs," he muttered, then staring up at the wide beams across the ceiling, he broke into a grin. "You know what's weird?"

"Seriously? You mean besides knowing I've been here before, and wondering if I was once Babetta and you were Francois?"

"Yeah, besides that. My home in London. The beams. The moment I saw them I wanted the house. Brittany," he said, pulling her into his arms, "the night I flogged you for the first time, it was surreal. It was like you were meant to be there, shackled to the ropes hanging from those beams."

"What are you saying?"

"Seeing the portrait, then meeting you on the ship, that was no accident. Neither was finding that corset tucked away in a corner. I don't know if we're distantly related to Francois and Babetta and we have memory in our genes, or if there's some other explanation, but I do know you and I belong together."

"We do. I feel it in every part of me. Duncan, I love you with my whole heart. I want to be with you wherever you are, but this place," she murmured, moving her eyes around the room, "this place is magic."

"I never thought, when I left on that cruise, I'd meet a girl from South Carolina, invite her to stay with me in London, and end up in a French village holding her my arms and asking her to marry me."

"Oh, my gosh. Is that what you're doing?"

"That's what I'm doing, and if you don't say yes I'll spank you until you do."

"You don't need to spank me, Duncan," she whispered, a tear springing from her eye. "Yes. A thousand times yes."

"Precious girl, I love you to bits," he murmured, lowering his lips to hers.

Kissing her softly, then fervently, devouring her mouth as she pressed against him, he felt almost giddy. When they finally broke apart and he gazed down at her, he thought his heart would burst.

"Duncan, do you really think you can buy this place?"

"I have no doubt. This whole thing is meant to be."

"Then let's get married here," she said breathlessly. "This place has so much room for everyone, and we could have the wedding in the courtyard."

"I was going to make the same suggestion. Brittany, for a logical barrister like me this is all pretty crazy, but as I said to you driving to The Crafty Fox, there are more things in heaven and earth..."

THE END

Dear Reader:

Thank you for buying this book. If you have a moment I would greatly appreciate your review. I constantly strive to offer interesting and enjoyable content and your feedback is valued. Feel free to contact me at any time. I love to hear from readers. My email is: MagCarpenter@yahoo.com, and here are my social media links should you care to check them out.

My very best wishes,

Maggie

http://www.MaggieCarpenter.com

https://www.facebook.com/MaggieCarpenterWriter

https://twitter.com/magcarpenter2

http://pinterest.com/submaggie/

JOIN MY MAILING LIST
AND RECEIVE A FREE BOOK
GO TO
MAGGIECARPENTER.COM/FREE